STEEL CUT STEEL

STEEL CUT STEEL

MAX BRAND

COVER BY
WALTER DE MARIS

POPULAR PUBLICATIONS · 2023

TABLE OF CONTENTS

STEEL CUT STEEL

*His Job Seemed Clear-Cut Enough to Red
Toomey—He Was the Hired Hand of Wrath
and the Big Fellow Was His Quarry*

1

STEEL CUT STEEL

TOOMEY DRESSED HIMSELF with as much care as though he were going to a wedding or a funeral, for he had a feeling that he had come to the last day. He brushed the dust from his blue serge suit; he picked away the lint from it with the patience of a woman or a tailor. He knotted his necktie again, smoothed back the dark red of his hair, and put on the soft gray hat. The storm had brought an early twilight over the city and his room was so dark that he had to narrow his eyes to see the thin, brown face in the mirror before him.

Then he went out to beg.

It would be the first time that he ever had asked for alms, from Zanzibar to Singapore, from Patagonia to the frozen North. Wherever the wanderlust had driven him, like a sea gull on the wind, looping his way with a mighty leisure around and around the world, he had been one to take with the hand and give with the hand, but he had never begged. Forty-eight hours of hunger and a far longer despair had worked in him like an acid, etching new designs on the stern metal of his soul.

From the threshold of his room, he looked back for a moment. Then he closed the door forever upon that dinginess and went rapidly down the stairs. There was a gas

*Red Toomey
tasted danger
in the air.*

leak somewhere. The foul smell of it was in the air like the thoughts that were corrupting his mind.

The instant he was on the street, he purified his lungs with a deep breath or two; he could not purify his mind so easily, but he walked up the street with a step as light as ever it had been when he moved the ships of the South Sea traders. He was more than half assured that the thirty-one years of his life were about to end on this street and on this day, but the soul of Toomey was a flame redder than the red of his hair; it would keep shining to the end.

He took up his place under the shallow eaves of a closed newsstand, a green-painted stand like a sentry box. The traffic paused at that corner obedient to the red light that stopped the traffic or the green lights that let it flow.

Automobiles came sweeping in clusters, or singly, trailing fumes behind them, trailing happy voices, too. For on Friday evening all who can leave the city and set their faces towards the October colors of the countryside. Men came

"We'll Identify you first. George, bring Sally Moore in."

by, in sauntering groups, in pairs; but the single pedestrians were the ones who stepped out most briskly, putting down their heads against the wind.

Toomey picked out a cheerful group of young fellows.

"I beg your pardon," he would say. "I'm sorry to bother you. But I'm so broke that I'm hungry. Will you help me out?"

He stepped out towards them, but suddenly it seemed like publishing a private shame to the ears of the entire world. He shrank back again under the eaves of the newsstand.

A big solitary man came striding, a man with a hearty stomach shaking before him, and a rosy face. Toomey drifted like an eddying leaf towards him, but a keen blast of rain and wind struck him, staggered him. He retreated again. That one volley of rain had been enough to drench him. The edge of the wind had found his old weaknesses, fingering the wounds of body and soul.

He shuddered and told himself that it was only a touch of the old tropical fevers that had set him trembling. But not being a fellow who loved self-deception, he turned his head and looked bravely towards the sweep of the bridge that bore off to the right. He was not at a sufficient angle from it to see the whole length of the structure, but the roadway simply rose before him with its two parapets, its two lines of street lamps like warm little golden moons, vaulting upwards with the end of that step into space unseen.

If he walked out there and climbed the parapet, one step would bridge the distance that lay between him and another world.

An odd fancy struck him that the other world was, in actuality, on the far side of the bridge; that fancy gave him a strange comfort and made him nervous to be gone. Not much of him would be left; perhaps no word would ever go back to the South Seas that even Red Toomey had at last blown out the light. Yet even then he did not regret that he had taken himself away from the blue seas and the white beaches. He had been too long luxuriating in that warm bath. If a man were to die, for instance, it was better to die among one's own kind.

A SINGLE AUTOMOBILE came hurrying to make the crossing before the lights changed, but the red flashed and the car stopped near the curb with a groan and shudder of brakes. There was only the driver inside the machine. He had a pale face without a profile, and he had blond hair, slicked back till it shone.

Toomey looked up and down. The storm had whipped the street clean of all pedestrians, so he took a quick breath and stepped forward.

"I beg your pardon," said Toomey. He raised his hand to tip his hat; disgusted by his own humility, he changed the gesture to a mere salute. The driver eyed him for an instant, then opened the door and half stepped from the car.

He was a bulldog. His shoulders were sleek with strength; his neck was as thick as his head.

"Crawford send you?" he asked. "I thought it was the other side—"

"I simply wanted to ask for a handout," said Toomey. "I'm broke and hungry—"

Then tenseness went out of the fellow. "Out, bum!" he said, and waved Toomey away.

The vocabulary of Toomey was a dangerous wealth. That gesture was enough to tap it.

"Are you calling *me* a bum, you flat-faced mug?" said he.

The other glanced to the side, as though unwilling to waste driving time, but since the red light was still on, he stepped clear of the car and hit Toomey away from him.

"There's your handout for you," he said.

Where the punch had started and how it had landed, Toomey could not say, but he recognized the craft of a master. However, this was the sort of a compliment that Toomey knew how to trade in, so he stepped in with the weight of his body behind a punch. He should have missed, for the man began a sidestep as lightly as a dancing master. But the man slipped on a spot of wet slime and that blunt face jutted forward straight into the path of Toomey's punch. The stranger went down with a bump and a skid.

Certainly his hands were empty when Toomey hit him, but now a bigmouthed automatic was gripped in one of them. Toomey leaped for shelter. He landed in the driver's seat of the car. Slumped far down, he glanced over the rim of the cushion. The man was stumbling to his feet, cursing. He looked as though he had used guns before; he looked as though he had used them on men. Then the flash of the green light told Toomey how to get away.

The car leaped ahead as he meshed the gears. He shot for the long arch of the bridge. A cluster of automobiles charged at him as though they were on a one-way street. As they began swerving to the right he ventured a glance to the rear. The bare-headed fellow was not firing. There was no longer a gun in his hand. He waved his arms as he ran; perhaps he was shouting to have the thief stopped.

Toomey slid the car into high as he reached the crest of the bridge. This was stuff for a policeman to handle—a fellow who pulled a gun as casually as though it were a handkerchief. Furthermore, it would give Toomey a chance to tell his story and policemen know the ropes; they're good fellows and can find a man a job at something.

Relief went smoothly through the taut body of Toomey. Laughter came up in him and made a rapid, silent pulsation in his breast.

Down the slope of the bridge he eased the car. A traffic cop at the next intersection would be the best bet to catch that gunman red-handed, gun and all, as he followed. But there was no officer on duty: only a concrete post with a light that showed green in the top of it at the foot of the bridge. Then out of the mouth of a side street slid another automobile, gray-painted, long, low and powerful in line. Men inside it leaned out and waved to him.

Plainclothes men who knew so instantly that he was in a stolen car. He had forgotten about the danger of that accusation.

"Oh, you be damned," said Toomey through his teeth, and stepped on the gas.

By the way the machine picked up, he knew that he was in a speedster. It did not stagger as it felt the gun, but leaped past the nose of the gray car as deftly as ever a salmon leaped past the teeth of a shark.

The angry shout of voices wailed away behind him, the sound turning flat. They might try to stop him by shooting at the tires. He took the next corner with a skid turn to the right, and jerked the car again to the left down a narrow street with the glimmer of a boulevard at the end of it. It was like sighting down a gun barrel.

When he glanced back, he saw a pair of dimmed head-lights shoot around the corner, stagger and straighten out in pursuit. Toomey gave his roadster the gun again. On the lighted instrument board he saw the name of the makers and it was an instant comfort to him. Those fellows behind, if they wanted him, would have to step out, on this night. Afterwards, it might mean jail, but in a jail there are two important things—food and warmth.

HE TURNED RIGHT onto the boulevard, against a red light. A police whistle screamed. He saw the officer taking out a note book in the rain. Toomey laughed aloud.

The roadway opened before him with a wide invitation. The speedometer marked seventy, seventy-five, eighty, then climbed slowly and paused and wavered between eighty-three and eighty-five. That ought to be enough, if a fellow knew how to shave corners and squirt through the pressure of traffic. Toomey knew how.

He kept the feed full down. The machine began to back-fire like gun shots. He made the mixture a shade richer and the backfiring stopped; the speedometer needle marked eighty-seven.

His right hand window was open. He screwed it up. The gusts of rain struck the glass as with the flat of a hand, obscuring the windshield with puffs of fine dust.

Here arched an intersection suddenly, whipping around a curve. Headlights glared at him; a red light levelled a long spear at him; automobiles were in movement from two sides. He picked a spot and went through. Brakes screamed. He saw a car skidding sidewise, staggering. Horns roared. Voices pitched needle-fine by fear jabbed into his brain.

But he was through. Electricity prickled in his forehead and shot down in tingling waves through the tips of his fingers. But now there was only the rain-polished blackness of the road ahead of him. Houses disappeared. The open country yawned on either side, a wide gloom of greenness.

As a matter of fact, it was not quite sunset time. He remembered that, and smiled; the stiffness of his face made it hard to smile.

Suddenly he relaxed. The motor was growing warm. There was a sweet smell of oil from the engine.

The pockets on the front doors bulged. He reached into them. On the left hand he found an automatic and a box of cartridges. On the right hand he found a flask of whisky and a paper bag of sandwiches.

He held the silver flask between his knees, unscrewed the top, and took a sip. The stuff was smooth in the throat. It reached a pain that had been in his stomach for many hours and paralyzed the ache of it; it threw up aromatic fumes into his brain.

"Hell, I'm lucky," said Toomey.

He began to eat the sandwiches. They were ham and Swiss cheese, buttered thick with English mustard. He took another sip of whisky. The mustard and the whisky flavors went together like two notes of music. Suddenly the sandwiches were finished. He loosened his belt a little, and settled deeper into the cushions.

There was another intersection. Two state policemen stood in the center of the road. He went straight on. One of them blew a whistle; the other drew a gun. He went straight through between them. The gun chattered. Bullets bumped the car here and there.

"Forty-five calibre, those babies, or they wouldn't sock the car like that," said Toomey.

He looked back. Two headlights shot out around a curve and steadied to the straightaway. That car was travelling! Anyway, the big state road was getting pretty thick. He ducked the car onto a gravel by-way. The bumps began to throw him up into the air; it would have been better to be tied to the seat, for such going as this.

He cut down to eighty, to seventy. The road twisted. Wet branches from the hedges flashed silver in the head-lights and whipped the car. He reached a straightaway. The towering hood of a truck pulled by slow inches out of a side pass. He made the horn scream in a staccato. The truck hesitated, lurched ahead, and stopped squarely across the road.

Toomey put on the brakes with expert softness. The head of his car began to bounce. Then it hugged the ground and sloughed off to the side in a tail skid. He corrected the skid, stopping twenty feet from the truck.

A big man in overalls came out of the driver's seat and put his foot down on the wheel.

"What the hell kind of a fire might you be going to?" he shouted.

Toomey picked up the automatic and switched off the safety catch. He was feeling very careless. Then he laid the gun back on the seat and laughed. The truck driver disappeared into the dark cavern of the hood again, but up the road behind Toomey came the whine of a high-speed motor.

Toomey took up the gun, opened the door of the roadster, and looked out. He could break through the hedge and get away, but he would get drenched, and afterwards he would have to run through mud. He closed the door and settled back on the seat. Sooner or later they'd get him. It didn't make any difference.

Headlights blazed on him from behind. He picked up the silver flask, took a good swallow, and appraised the stuff as pre-war as it slid down his throat.

Brakes ground. The long gray car slid to a halt beside him as the truck, straightening clumsily, roared off down the narrow lane. Two men jumped out of the gray car and ran at him, shaking their fists, shouting. The other two in the machine leaned out, also, brandishing their hands, roaring. Their faces looked foolishly distorted.

A big man with a red face jerked open the door of the roadster and bellowed: "You've got the whole damn state police force on our trail, now! I never saw such a fool play. Crusty, you're a fool! You're a damn fool! We knew you could drive a car, but you had to show off. Crawford is going to raise hell!"

Two words of that speech came sweetly home upon the ear of Toomey. "Our trail"—not "his trail," but "our trail." Somehow he was one of them.

He held out the silver flask.

"Have a drink, Fatty," said he.

2

YELLOW EYES

ALL FOUR OF them were clustered about him, regardless of the rain. He took the automatic under the flat of his hand and passed it out of sight among his clothes. He knew how to do that.

Suddenly the blustering stopped. They were left merely panting. The fat man began to laugh.

"Crawford wanted something extra, and he's got it. Crusty's just a fool. He's just a crazy damn fool. Slip, you get in and show him the way."

Slip prepared to get in.

"You don't like my driving. You drive," said Toomey.

He hunched over into the other front seat. Slip was a little man with a starved chest. He ducked into the car and sighed as he settled himself under the wheel. He took off his hat and threw it onto the back of the seat.

"Great jumping—good Lord—that was a little drive, all right," said he. "Those intersections—that pair of cops— one of those guys was dying of apoplexy. You airplaning bum!"

He laughed, weakly, felt out the gears, and started the car. Toomey took another drink. He said nothing. Never whip a winning horse. Sit still and hand-ride the leader.

"You big, airplaning bum!" said Slip. He slid down in the seat a little. The padded shoulders of his coat hunched up. He had a meagre, beautiful face, except that the upper lip was stiff and hard.

"What made you do it?" he said.

The car seemed to be standing still, bouncing on soft springs. But the speedometer marked forty-five.

"Oh, I don't know," said Toomey. "Have a drink?"

Slip glanced at him, up and down.

"You know you're going to see Crawford in a few minutes," said Slip. "Why the hooch?"

"That's all right, too," said Toomey.

He took another drink, a very small one.

"All right," said Slip. "You may be hard, but a lot of hard guys crack."

"That's all right," said Toomey.

"Yeah, you seem to know," murmured Slip, with a reserve of wisdom. "Did you know Crawford was out this way? Was that why you bolted in this direction? How could you know that?"

Toomey said nothing.

"Oh, go to hell, then," exploded Slip, suddenly. "You can't high-hat me, and I don't care who you are."

Toomey said nothing. The food he had eaten made him sleepy. When a man is riding his luck, he relaxes, and Toomey was relaxed.

Crusty had spoken about Crawford. Now the others spoke of him. Whatever the game was, it was probably outside the law. That was a comfort to Toomey, also. He had food in his stomach, and he yawned, which made Slip snarl: "That's a bluff, too."

"Oh, shut up," said Toomey.

They drove on in silence. The darkness fell. A wavering cornucopia of light extended far before them. They reached a town, slid through it, turned into a lane, and stopped in front of a big house, under great, ancient trees.

There they got out. The rain had diminished to a mist. From the trees big drops were falling, singly, or in noisy showers. The fat man with the rosy face took charge. Slip was his lieutenant.

The fat man said: "You boys take care of this car. After Crusty's little tricks, it needs a new face on it. You fix it."

"That ticket's been punched," said Toomey. "You'd better plug the holes."

Slip went around behind the car. He began to swear, but the fat man only laughed.

"This is Crawford's racket," he said. "We don't have to worry. We're delivering the bird, is all, and Crawford can cook it any style he wants. Come on, Crusty."

Toomey followed to the front porch, and through the front door, which was opened by a tall butler in a tail-coat. He showed them into a little front room with a low ceiling and small windows, like a cabin on a ship.

"I'll see him first," said the fat man.

TOOMEY SAT DOWN on a couch, fitted a pillow under his head, closed his eyes, and relaxed. There was a fire glimmering on the hearth. The pungency of wood smoke made the air seem pure. The fat man talked for a moment. Toomey paid no heed. He saw his room in the rooming house, the street corner near the bridge, the upward sweep of the lights like little golden moons. He tasted the whisky under the bridge of his nose. His thoughts blurred.

The door opened; footfalls padded over the rug. He opened his eyes, and found himself alone. This was the time to leave, to step quietly out of the picture.

He got up and went to the window. Outside, on the porch, sat a man with the collar of his overcoat turned up. He was not there to enjoy the evening and the weather.

Toomey went back to the couch, found his former position, and relaxed again. Why look a gift horse in the mouth?

One floor lamp glowed in a corner. It showed the lower half of a picture of autumn woods and a winding road. He closed his eyes. The whisky settled in his throat to a thirst that was worth saving. The muscles twitched along the back of his legs as though he were still bracing himself against the lurches of the speeding car. Then thoughts and pictures blurred in his brain, and went out.

"Wake up," said the voice of the fat man.

He opened his eyes.

"Crawford wants you now," said the fat man.

He was about to say something else, but he pinched his lips over the words, and held his mouth cruelly firm. Something was about to happen to Toomey, and the fat man hoped that it would happen.

Then they went down the hall. The fat man opened the door.

"Here he is, sir," he said.

Toomey stepped into a big room. The door closed behind him. He saw a great hearth with a fire flaring up from logs that kept hissing and sputtering. The rugs made colored patches on the sheen of the floor. Big chairs leaned back, waiting to give comfort. Over in a corner was a desk, and

behind it was a man with a face like a lion's. That was Crawford, Toomey knew. Behind him stood a Negro, a hulk of
a man with a head that mattered no more, on the great
shoulders, than a bubble on top of a wave.

But the Negro, the room, nothing mattered, except
Crawford and his lion's face. Three divergent wrinkles laid
deep in his brow gave him wisdom. The jaw thrust forward
aggressively, and was locked in place. His whole head was
like that of a lion, massive and shaggy.

Toomey went up to him. He stopped at a little distance
and put his hands in the pockets of his coat. He saw nothing but Crawford. The room vanished. Perhaps it was the
dark face of the Negro that suggested the South Seas,
bright teeth in swarthy faces, spear-heads glimmering,
the taste of square-face gin in the mouth and a danger in
the air.

Crawford spoke in a voice that mated his throat and face.

"We'll identify you first. Sally Moore is here, Crusty.
She'll know you. George, bring her in."

THE GREAT NEGRO walked out of the room with a cush-
ioned step; he closed the door soundlessly, and Crawford
looked at Toomey. He had yellow-hazel eyes. They seemed
to Toomey like the yellow eyes of a lion, not as one sees
them where there are bars between the beast and the world,
but where they come out of the African brush.

The door opened at the side of the room and a girl with
sunny hair came in. Even in the shadow it had a glow, but
it was not golden or red.

"Here's Crusty, on time," said Crawford.

She made no pause, but her eyes narrowed, and she went
straight up to Toomey.

He told himself that he was sitting in the electric chair. He looked straight back at her, feeling that it might be the last pleasant sight he saw in this world.

She opened her eyes, suddenly, just before she reached him; she had green eyes. She smiled; and she had a crooked smile. She came close up to him and paused and waited a moment.

"Hello, Crusty," she said.

He was more amazed than pleased. Why had she saved him?

He saw that she was the right height and the right everything. She was a perfect fit. The more he looked into her, the more doors in her kept opening. She was brown. There was no powder on her nose and it was a trifle pink at the tip. He didn't mind that. He liked it.

"Hello, Sally," he said.

He swayed towards her a little. The terrible picture of Crawford grew dim. All the women he had ever known fled through his mind and out, like a flight of lovely birds across a bright room and into darkness.

"I'm glad you're up in the big time, at last," said Sally.

"You're all brown," said Toomey.

"Indoor sunshine," she said. "Sally has to be a fashionable girl."

"All right," said Crawford.

The booming note of that voice sent a tremor through Toomey, as though he were the gong that had been struck to produce the sound. The girl turned to go. Toomey went with her, holding her arm lightly. It was round. Her throat was round, too. When they passed near a tall floor lamp, the flash of her hair was right under his eyes. He opened the door for her.

"I'll see you later," said Toomey.

She kept turning back, as she stepped into the dimness of another room She kept smiling too.

He closed the door, leaning his hand on the knob for half a second. Her lie had saved him. But she knew Crusty, and Crusty had a pale face without any profile. Toomey shuddered; then he went back to Crawford.

3

THE AGENCY OF WRATH

CRAWFORD BECKONED. THE Negro came up to him with a step that made no sound except that of air being expressed from a cushion.

"I'll sit over by the fire," said Crawford.

The Negro pulled back the chair from the desk. The legs and hips of Crawford were wrapped in a plaid steamer rug. George lifted him with horrible ease, and carried him across to a big chair that angled towards the fire. Toomey grew a little sick, for he saw that Crawford was a lion only to the waist. The legs were withered to nothing.

"Sit there," said Crawford.

Toomey sat facing him. In ten seconds he had forgotten that Crawford was only half a man. He seemed more like a lion than ever.

"How did Flannigan happen to pick you out?" said Crawford.

Toomey shrugged his shoulders.

"Go on, talk," said Crawford. "You don't look to me like Flannigan's Crusty."

"I'm here to listen," ventured Toomey. "You do the talking and I'll do the listening."

Crawford shook his head.

"What have you done with yourself?" he insisted.

Toomey wanted another drink. He said so. "I want a drink, if I'm going to tell pretty stories."

"You can't drink in this room," said Crawford.

"Then you don't get any pretty stories," said Toomey.

Crawford made a gesture with the back of his hand. "Move on!" he said, like a traffic cop. Toomey stood up.

"Wait a minute," said Crawford. "D'you mean to say that Flannigan didn't tell you—"

"I'm no repeater," said Toomey.

He watched the yellow eyes until he thought again of a great lion charging out of brush that was sooty with the evening shadows.

"Well," said Crawford, "bring him a drink, George."

Toomey sat down again. He took out a cigarette and lighted, it, and flicked the match towards the fire. He settled himself into the chair and hoped that a drink, in this house, would mean whisky. So it did. It came in a tall, silver carafe with a silver lid, and a silver girdle around its throat. It stood on a silver tray, spilling a deep amber shadow into the polish. George poured one of two glasses three-quarters full. He made a small gesture with the carafe towards Crawford, but Crawford shook his head.

Toomey lifted the glass and breathed of it.

"Here's in your eye," said Toomey. "May it be yellower, day by day."

But he only rolled a few drops over his tongue and looked at the ceiling till he was sure of the taste. Then he finished the glass.

"How did Flannigan come to know you?" said Crawford, with a slight stress on the last word.

"I'm not a repeater," said Toomey.

He waited through ten seconds, while his heart seemed to strike a hundred times.

"Start in, then," said Crawford, at last.

"Ten years ago I started out," said Toomey.

"Where did you start from?" said Crawford.

"Ten years ago, when I was twenty-one, I started out," said Toomey.

"All right. Go on, then," said Crawford.

"I spent ten years doing Africa, India, the East Indies, Malaysia, the South Seas. I began to get soggy, so I came home."

He stopped.

"Is that the story?" said Crawford.

"That's all. No value?"

"There's no dollar sign in front of all the figures," said Crawford.

"I'll put that in now," said Toomey.

He rose, pulled up his sleeve, and showed a long scar that wavered like a silver snake over the smooth ridges of his forearm.

"A kris, eh?" said Crawford.

Toomey pulled down his sleeve and returned to his chair. He poured out another glass of whisky.

"Do you have to have that stuff?" asked Crawford.

"No. But I enjoy it. This is a party for me. Sitting with Mr. Crawford and telling stories of my experiences by land and sea. Here's in your eye."

He swallowed the drink.

"YOU WANT ME to take a chance on you," said Crawford. "Perhaps I shall. But Flannigan was a fool to send you up without warning me about your stage manners. I've been on the verge—"

He paused.

"George, bring me five thousand dollars," he said.

George opened a drawer in the desk and came out of the shadow with a little green sheaf in his hand. Crawford took it.

"I think I'm going to try to use you, Crusty," he said. "Mallow. That's your last name, isn't it?"

Toomey inhaled a deep breath of cigarette smoke and made the gesture of his head that goes with such an inhalation.

"I've had a pack of names," he said. "They're as useful as a pack of cards, if you know how to shuffle them."

Crawford tapped the sheaf of bills on his thumb. It gave out a soft, crisp rustling.

"You know the point of the business," said Crawford.

"Flannigan's point may not be your point," said Toomey.

Very slowly a smile began on the face of Crawford, reached his eyes for an instant, and then went out. The thought he had digested was pleasant to his taste, no doubt.

But those yellow eyes fixed upon Toomey again, dwelt on him, pondered his problem. A shadow came over the brightness.

"Mallow," he said, "I was going to give you marching orders and put you to work. I see that it will be better to take you into the council of war. I am going to put my cards on the table, face up."

The Negro, in his corner of the room, smiled. His teeth flashed through the shadows, but Toomey did not see. That one glint of mirth would have been enough to warn him, but it was unheeded.

Toomey merely waited, and Crawford went on: "I'm a hard man, am I not?"

"You seem hard enough," said Toomey.

"What makes a metal hard?"

"A hot fire and plenty of hammering," said Toomey.

"I've been in the fire and I've had the hammering," said Crawford. "I've had my back against the wall for a long time, and I suppose Flannigan told you who put it there?"

"Flannigan," said Toomey, "told me to come here and pick up some big money. That's all he told me."

The yellow glimmered back into the eyes of Crawford, but gradually receded again among shadows.

"You know of Lawrence Elliott Oliver?" asked Crawford.

Lawrence Elliott Oliver—of course he knew about him. He had seen pictures of that handsome, full-fleshed face. Newspaper reporters loved to refer to him as the Big Fellow. Everything about him was big—his person, his voice, his racing luck, his business acumen, his fortune. Toomey nodded. "The Big Fellow," he said.

"We were the closest friends in the world, at one time," said Crawford, his voice growing suddenly gentle as he peered into the past. "In those days I was as tall as the Big Fellow—and stronger." He made a gesture with both hands, slowly, as though filling out in his mind's eye the picture of what he had once been. "We lived together, played together. And once we were shooting in Switzerland. We were high up. The day was ending; the evening was filling up the valleys like blue water; and there was an accident. The Big Fellow's rifle exploded and the bullet hit me. It went—through." He passed his hand across his body, hip-high.

"We tied up the wound. The Big Fellow went to get help. No help came. It was cold, up there. It was a clear night, with wind. The wind and the starlight seemed to go through me. My legs began to grow numb. And no help came."

He paused. He linked his mighty hands together and regarded the fire. Toomey said nothing, but he was leaning forward in his chair, staring. Again the Negro, in the corner shadows, grinned—a white flash that might have hinted many things to Toomey.

But he saw nothing except the picture of the wounded giant lying in the cold of the mountain night, waiting for help that did not come.

"The Big Fellow is fond of wine," said Crawford, calmly. "And when he reached a tavern, he was only able to think how tired he was, and about the wine. He forgot—till the next morning. They came and got me, finally. The Big Fellow wasn't with them, to show the way. He had a wine headache. They got me to a doctor, finally. He did what he could, but it was a few hours too late. Since that day, I've been like this."

He pointed to the rug that covered his legs.

"PEOPLE THAT HAVE injured you will always hate you," said Crawford. "The Big Fellow hated me, after that. He went on to make a fortune, to win a host of friends. He became an international figure. And—"

A pause came after this, and when it had endured for a long moment, Crawford turned his head, and his yellow eyes looked straight into the face of Toomey, straight into his mind and soul.

"There is one sacred thing in this world," he said. "That is friendship. In the old days, the Big Fellow was my friend, and when I saw that he was something else, I buried him, and tried to keep the memory of what he had once been before my eyes. No, I never talked for publication, and I'm not talking for publication now. But by degrees the enmity of the Big Fellow increased. I won't go into every detail. I'll only point out that he lives not many miles from this house, for the reason that he can still stretch out his hands and trouble me."

"Damn him!" said Toomey, softly.

And again, among the shadows, the Negro smiled, unheeded.

The voice of Crawford lowered to a murmur. "I have a fortune of my own, Mallow," he said. "And no matter how rich the Big Fellow is, he has determined to take from me what I own. Even my life—this half-existence which I now can lead—is endangered. I have had to fill my house with armed men, with gunmen, with low, criminal animals whose sure hands can be bought. But all these years I have endured without striking back. Only now that the Big Fellow has transgressed the last boundary, I am ready to try to reach the source of the fire. Mallow, I have a son."

The booming voice went out, like a light. It began on a new note, curiously musical, and the heart of Toomey swelled in him. "I have a son," the cripple was saying, "a big, strong, carefree fellow who had no more evil in him than there is in any other free and noble creature. Then the Big Fellow put his hands on my lad, my Jack."

"How?" asked Toomey, his voice abrupt.

"By surrounding him with bad companions; by pouring money into their hands so that they could appear to Jack as bon vivants. He considered them 'good fellows,' and young men are easily led; young men are easily persuaded that the pleasant way is the best way.

"Jack was like a fine tree, growing straight and strong; now they are corrupting him at the roots. And finally I have decided that the time has come when I must strike back.

"I already had savage men around me, but I wanted someone still more formidable, someone whose face would be strange in this part of the world, and who would be capable of anything. That was why I sent for you, when I had inquired. To tell you the truth, I thought that you would appear as a mere savage, but I see that you're something more. I thought that I would simply give you orders, but instead, I've given you reasons. Do those reasons seem sound to you?"

"Sound enough to make me cut out his heart!" said Toomey suddenly.

He reflected after speaking. He was here under false pretenses. The true Crusty Mallow must even now be fumbling to find the way to Crawford. He was tempted to burst out with his true name, and all that had happened to bring him to this place. But on the other hand, he had to keep in mind that Crawford was a desperate and a dangerous man. Perhaps it was the long torment of pain from his crippled body; perhaps it was the constant persecutions which he had endured from the Big Fellow; but at any rate, Crawford was now as much lion as man.

He had poured out his confidences, he had poured

out his heart. It seemed to Toomey that all of Crawford's cards had been placed before him, face up. And if, now, he admitted that he was an impostor, what would happen? He remembered the yellow light that could burn in the eyes of Crawford, and knew that he dared not speak.

"The thing that I've determined to do," said Crawford, "is to cause the Big Fellow to disappear from his house; I am going to kidnap him and isolate him in another place. And there I'll bring pressure to bear on him until he has bound himself to take his hands from my life, and from my son. I want you to take him. I want you to guard him for me. Will you undertake it?"

Toomey paused. How long would it take Crusty Mallow to find this place? Perhaps a day, or more. He did not know the way, or otherwise men would not have been sent to guide him. In the meantime, Toomey himself could become the instrument of Crawford's just vengeance.

Just? Yes, if there were justice on earth! A life of wrongs was now to be righted, and the stern heart of Toomey burned in him. That fire came up in his face, came up in his eyes. If it were only for twenty-four hours, he would undertake the cause. Afterwards, when the true Mallow appeared, he could slide out of the picture. But in the meantime his hands would be the agency of wrath.

"I'll undertake it," he said. "I'll take care of him."

"UNTIL I SEND you a flash, and then you step out," said Crawford. "I see that you're a man such as never has worked for me before, Mallow. If I need you for other things, I'll send you a flash. Then leave the Big Fellow, by night or day, and come straight to me."

"What will the flash be?" said Toomey.

"Bring me a pen and paper, George."

When it was brought, Crawford scrawled on it, and tore off the sheet, which he handed to Toomey. It was a big, loose-flowing monogram, that looked a "W," an "F," and a "C," all worked intricately together.

"If you get another slip of paper with those letters scrawled on it," said Crawford, "you know that you've had the flash, and you slip out."

"I step away from the Big Fellow, and let him drop, eh?"

"You step away from Lawrence Elliott Oliver and come to me. I may need you. When he disappears, there'll be a commotion that may destroy us all. And in the pinch I may have to send for you."

"I understand," said Toomey.

"But you probably won't get the flash," said Crawford. "If you don't, you watch him like an egg that lacks an outer shell. You watch him day and night. You spread your nervous system all over that house. His friends will be angry, Crusty."

"I know," said Toomey.

"Mallow," said Crawford, "I've trusted you with my confidence, and after that, it's a small thing to trust you with hard cash. Here's the advance payment that Flannigan promised you. You can guess that if this thing goes through, there'll hardly be a limit to your fee. I'm putting the honor of my son and my own hope and happiness in your hands."

He extended the money. There were five one thousand dollar bills. Toomey took them, folded them across, and slid them into a vest pocket.

"Slip and Bushmill can tell you what arrangements I have in mind for the Big Fellow," said Crawford. "But if you want to use your own ideas, you're free. I give you the right to think for yourself. We can't have a written agreement, but I'd like to shake hands with you, Mallow."

The hand of Toomey started, with an impulsive gesture. But he stood there in the midst of a lie. The very name he wore was false. He had wanted to aid this man. But he could not pledge him his hand while there was a shadow of deception between them.

He drew back his hand.

"I don't kiss the Bible, either," said Toomey.

Crawford leaned forward, with the yellow danger gathering in his eyes. But gradually he relaxed.

"Very well, then," he said. "George will take you to Slip or to Bushmill, and you can talk with them. The devil seems to be in you, and you'll probably need his help before this business is finished."

He held Toomey with the pondering consideration of his eyes.

"But unless you're willing to be a blindly disciplined soldier for ten days, you'll be of no use to me. Can you march in the dark as long as that?"

He could see Toomey straighten a little.

"Why in the dark?" asked Toomey.

"Because," said Crawford, "from the moment that the Big Fellow and his crew know that you're working for me, they'll be at you. Not with guns only, but with lies, persuasions, flatteries, briberies with which they'll try to swerve you. You understand me? Unless you have a soldier's blind faith and obedience, you'll be useless to me. You'll have to hear every possible persuasion, and close your ears tight against it."

"I'll close my ears against it," said Toomey. He made half a step forward. "Words are cheap as dirt. Do you think that they can handle me by talking? No, I'll walk in the dark! You can trust me to do that!"

"I can," said Crawford, his voice full of solemn pauses. "I know that I can trust you, and I do trust you. And the day will come when you'll understand how completely you can trust me, also. But remember, that you'll live in danger. If they can't buy you, they'll deceive you, and if they can't deceive you, they'll murder you! The Big Fellow is chiefly a rich investor, but he's part lawyer, too. His partner is Henry Sewell, and Sewell handles the dirty work that they wish to do. He has employed a professional handler of crooks, a bloodless, cruel devil they call the Doctor. The Doctor is the man who will cross your way.

"But I'll tell you no more. You must fight it out in your own way, and God help us both. George, show him the way!"

The Negro took Toomey from the room, but returned again almost at once.

He found his master lying back in the chair, with closed eyes.

"Hard work, George," said Crawford. "Very hard work, with a hard man."

"Yes, sir," said George.

THE WEARY VOICE of Crawford went on: "An honest man. That's why he was worth working for.

Flannigan was a fool not to warn me. But an honest man is a treasure, George. A fellow who has fought his way around the world, too! When you took him out, just now, you warned the boys not to talk to him?"

"Yes, sir," said George. "I gave them the sign. They won't talk to him about you."

"Then he's mine—for a few days," said Crawford. "He's a dangerous devil, George, but I'll use him. Did you see his eyes turn green when I told him those fairy tales about the Big Fellow?"

"Yes, sir," said George. "I didn't watch nothin' but his face."

"A red coal out of the fire—but I'll handle him," murmured Crawford. "Did you notice that he wouldn't shake hands? Because when a man like that gives you his hand, solemnly, he pledges the faith of his honor, at the same time. But that will come later. You see that the Crawford brain still functions, my boy. A red coal from the fire, I say, but I'll use him!"

"Yes, sir," said George, "if you got thick enough gloves."

"What?" said Crawford, opening his eyes suddenly.

"He won't burn your hands if you got thick enough gloves, sir," repeated George.

"What do you mean by that, nigger?" asked Crawford, frowning.

George scratched his head.

"I been livin' with you kind of a long time, sir," said he.

"Go on," said Crawford. "And you've been paid for it. What are you driving at?"

"Well, sir, I've seen some mighty hard faces, but never none as hard as this gentleman, sir."

"He *has* a hard face," said Crawford. "He's made out of iron. But that's what I want. The tough ones. That's what I want."

"But his eyes is clean, sir," said George. "And I thought

maybe that would make a lot of difference. There ain't no smoke in his eyes, Mr. Crawford."

Crawford pondered a moment.

Then he chuckled: "There is smoke in his eyes, now. And I've put it there. A bright fellow—a regular keen blade—but I've enlisted his heart on my side, George. But you're right—I'll have to handle him with very thick gloves!"

He added: "But I never did better work than this of today. I've found the proper tool; and I'll use it to carve out the heart of Lawrence Elliott Oliver."

"You hate the Big Fellow a lot," said George. "Did he ever hurt you?"

"Hurt me? There was a day," said Crawford, "when I stood taller and broader than he. I was his master in body and in mind. I was the leader, he followed. And now I'm blasted. I sit like a statue in a chair—and he walks through the world—and laughs and drinks and carouses his way through the world—damn him!—smiles his way through the years—curse his rotten heart!"

He groaned out the last words in the depths of his bitter emotion.

"Yes, sir," said George. "I was only asking you, has the Big Fellow ever hurt you, in any way?"

"There's no need for him to do anything," said Crawford. "For every time I think of him, it's a bullet through my heart. He has out of life what I should have had. But I'll get my own from him! For every ounce of happy blood that runs in him, I'll have two—his own and mine. I'll press the juice of life out of him!"

George blinked. And then he gasped: "But how are you going to set about that, sir?"

Crawford jerked open his coat and pulled from an inside pocket two picture postcards, and a poker chip.

"This is what will make him yell for help and run to cover. Two postcards and a poker chip will be enough. Blackmail, George! That's the poison that I inject into him with these little devices. I'll turn that hulk into a flabby, shuddering mass."

George moved slowly back into a deeper and deeper shadow, out of which his eyes gleamed like the eyes of a beast.

"He's got plenty of money," said George. "He could make a lot of trouble."

"And what he has, I'll have," said Crawford. "I've got him in my hand. He belongs to me. He's mine. I'll have the blood out of him, I tell you! I'll have every ounce of the blood out of him, and I'll melt the gold out of him at the same time. He has millions, but the millions will become mine. Blackmail is the greatest of the arts, George, and I am its greatest master!"

4

THE SPY

TOOMEY HAD BEEN brought into a small room where Slip and the fat-faced man, whose name was Bushmill, were sitting with tall glasses of Scotch and soda. As Toomey came in with the Negro behind him, he noticed that the eyes of both men turned to George and dwelt on him for an instant.

Obviously, some sort of a sign or a signal had been given to them. What its purpose might have been, Toomey could not guess. He became as wary as a hunting cat.

"Sit down and have a drink," said Bushmill. "That was a ride you gave us tonight. Feeling your oats, eh?"

Toomey took a chair with his back to the window, and smiled at them. He shook his head when they pushed the whisky bottle toward him.

"I've had my rations," he said. "What's the Big Fellow's game? I'm to ask you how the furniture's to be moved."

Bushmill and Slip looked at one another. Finally Slip shrugged his shoulders.

"Aw, hell, go ahead and talk to him," said Slip. "He's on the inside, now. I thought he'd get—but my thought didn't work out. You tell him."

"They're having a party at the house of the Big Fellow,

across country, tonight," said Bushmill. "After it's over, we could slide into the place and try our luck. It's only a general plan. You're the Big Shot that ought have the smart ideas about it."

"The Big Fellow's salted down with gunmen of his own. You know that," said Slip. "But what's a few guns to a hard guy like you, Crusty?"

He grinned sourly as he spoke.

"That sounds like a bright plan," said Toomey. "You just wait till the party's over and the gunmen are on the job, and then you step in—and take your chance, eh?"

"He don't like our ideas," said Slip, sneering. And his eyes glittered vindictively at Toomey. But Toomey overlooked him.

"Why does the Big Fellow keep all the bulldogs around?" he asked.

"You *wouldn't*," said Slip. "Not after a couple of your pals and bodyguards had been shot to hell or blown to hell with bombs. That wouldn't make any difference to you, of course. Not a bit!"

"You like me a lot, Slip, don't you?" said Toomey.

"Yeah, I took to you at once," said Slip.

"Don't be jealous," urged Toomey, gently. "When you grow up you'll have man's work to do, yourself, perhaps."

Slip trembled like a bull terrier struck by a cold wind; but he said nothing.

"Who's with me on the Big Fellow lay?" asked Toomey. "Both of you, or do I work alone?"

"We both go along," said Bushmill. "And plenty more, too, if you want 'em. You can have all the men you want.

Tonight's more of a look-around than the main chance, though."

"Well, get out a car," answered Toomey, "and the pair of you hop in. That's enough. I don't want an army. Where's Sally Moore?"

"She's back in the library, likely," said Bushmill. "Down at the end of the hall, last door on the left."

Toomey left them and went down the hall. With every moment he wondered more and more that he remained in the place. The real Crusty Mallow might turn up at any moment. But still he thought of that cold, starry night when half the body of Crawford had died; and with all his heart Toomey yearned to be the thunderbolt of vengeance that might strike down Lawrence Elliott Oliver, traitor and hypocrite. He had to see the girl first, and know if he could trust her to maintain in secrecy her knowledge that he was not the real Crusty Mallow.

How had she ever known that pale-faced brute?

He pushed open the door and entered the library, a big room with soft leather chairs grouped here and there, and the sheen of bound volumes rippling down the walls. All of these things were dimly revealed, for there was only one floor lamp lighted, that stood near the fireplace where the girl was curled up in a chair with her hands behind her head. When she glanced at him, there was no expression in her face. She looked back at the fire and kept on looking at it. He went and stood behind her chair.

"All right," she said. "Start in explaining."

"WHERE SHALL I start?" said Toomey.

"At the beginning."

Toomey said nothing.

"What's your name?" she asked. She had been smiling when he last saw her. There was no smiling about her now.

"My name is Al Toomey," he told her.

"Come around here where I can see you."

He went in front of her and dropped on one knee.

"I can see you better if you'll sit over there," said she. "I can think better, too."

"I don't want you to think," said Toomey.

"How do you figure in this?" she asked.

"I was broke and hungry. I went out and stood on a street corner. A fellow drove up and waited for the green light. I asked him for a hand-out. He thought Crawford had sent me, and stepped out of the car. When he found out I was simply a bum, he slipped me one. I knocked him down. He pulled a gun. I jumped into the car for cover. I ran the car across the bridge. A gray car slid out and the men in it waved to me. I thought they were plainclothes birds, picking me up for stealing a car. I gave her the gas, and she started jumping. She kept jumping a long ways, till a truck pulled across the road. The gray car pulled up beside me. They turned out to be friends, not enemies. They brought me here, and call me Crusty. That's how I happened to meet you."

"That sounds too crooked to be crooked," said the girl. "I'm willing to believe part of that."

He took one of her hands.

"Don't do that," said the girl.

He kept her hand.

"I thought you were going to spoil things for me," said Toomey. "When you first saw me, you looked ready to spoil things."

"I'm a silly fool," she answered him. "You were in a bad spot, but you looked at me instead of at your own trouble. That was why I played simple. You're laughing at me now, I suppose."

"About Crusty," said Toomey. "Why did you pick up Crusty?"

"I didn't," said she. "He's tried to squeeze himself into my hand. That's all. I've barely seen him often enough to know him."

"That's a lot better," said Toomey. "What's your place in this house?"

"I'm secretary and spot of sunshine," she answered dryly. "What's your job?"

"I'm to hang around with a gun," said Toomey.

She shook her head.

"Come clean," she demanded.

"That's the fact. I'm to do the strong-arm."

"They sent for you for a special job. What is it?"

Toomey said nothing.

"You mean that you're going to hold out on me?" said Sally. She sat up straight in her anger. "You're in my hands, here, and you're trying to hold out?"

Sitting up had brought her closer. He swayed toward her.

"Don't do it," said the girl. "When I say 'don't,' I mean it with a lot of meaning. I can't let you hold out."

"I'm not holding out," said Toomey.

He took the five thousand out of his pocket and dropped it into her lap.

"What's that for?"

"To make your eyes greener, Sally."

"Who gave you this coin?" she asked. "Crawford?"

"I'm giving it to you," said Toomey.

"You can't hold out," said the girl.

"I don't want the money. I want the news."

SHE THREW THE greenbacks on the floor. He let them lie there. He stood back in front of the fire and watched the firelight like sun in her hair. She was up, also. Anger made her pale. Her eyes glinted at him, green and suddenly small.

"You may not know, Toomey, if that's your name, but I beat a typewriter for a year, for the Big Fellow."

He lighted a cigarette and said to her, through the smoke: "You like him, eh?"

"He saw my father through the last stretch of hell and made him die happy. Now I'm afraid that Crawford is after Lawrence Oliver. I'm afraid that you're the special agent. And you're going to tell me."

Toomey went on smoking, looking down at the ash as it slowly formed.

Crawford had said that Lawrence Oliver was reaching out his hands to ruin him. This girl, whose beauty worked with poisonous sweetness in his blood, was a spy for the Big Fellow. He looked at her and loathed her, but even then the mysterious alchemy was working in him.

"I've told you that I'm for the Big Fellow," she said. "And now you're going to talk. Will you?"

He shrugged his shoulders.

Then she burst out at him: "You don't believe what Crawford told you, do you? You saw that he was a liar from the start? Toomey, you've never met the Big Fellow. If you did, you'd love him. And Crawford—"

"Is a cripple," said Toomey.

"He's a devil! He's a fiend!" said the girl.

Toomey watched her with cold eyes. Crawford had prepared him for just this sort of thing, but it was sickening to hear the attack under Crawford's own roof.

"Half of Crawford is dead," said Toomey. "But I'll tell you what I'd do. I'll tell you what I feel like, after talking to this 'devil,' this 'fiend': if they could be grafted into him, I'd like to give him my own legs. He needs 'em more, and he could use 'em better than I can!"

"That's it, is it?" said the girl. "I'll give you a sporting chance. Open that window and hop out. As soon as you're through it, I'm going to yell for help and say you're not Crusty, after all. You'll get the run of your life."

Toomey knocked off the ash on the hearth.

"Do you think I don't mean it?" she asked.

"I think you mean it," said Toomey.

"Are you crazy?" said the girl. "Do you know who Crawford is?"

"I know. I'm a little crazy," he told her.

She came up so close to him that she had to put her head back to watch his face. She smiled at him. He smiled back.

"I like you a lot, Al," she said. "I could like you a lot more, too. I like the stuff that mean face of yours is hammered out of. I could let go of everything. But you don't know about the Big Fellow. I'd see you dead before I'd let anything happen to him. You tell me the inside, Al. We'll work it out together. We'll be partners. I'll be the best partner you ever had."

Toomey kept on smiling at her. She drew back. She kept on going backwards towards the door.

"You murdering rat!" she said.

She reached the door and put her hand on the knob of it.

She opened the door a little and then closed it and put her arms against it, and her face against her arms. The highlight on the back of her neck began to tremble.

Toomey went up to her.

"Keep your hands off me. Don't touch me!" she whispered.

HE TOOK A handkerchief from his breast pocket, shook it out, and reaching around her, pressed it softly over her eyes.

"Oh, God, oh, God!" said the girl. "Tell me what to do?"

He said nothing.

"Are you a lying, shifty rat?" whispered the girl.

"Perhaps," said Toomey.

"If I call them, they'll kill you," she said.

"They will," said Toomey, and thought of Slip.

She turned suddenly, and caught him by the lapels of the coat. She shook him, swallowing hard, trying to speak. At last she said: "Look, Toomey. I'm not threatening you now, I'm giving up. I'm just saying for God's sake, is all. Don't laugh at me. I'm not a fool about men. You're the only one that ever put the sick shudders in me. I'm not bad, Toomey, and I could be good to you. But tell me what they're going to do to the Big Fellow!"

He dabbed the tears from her face, softly, carefully. There was a straight chair against the wall. She slipped into it. He picked her up and put her in the big chair before the fire.

"I'll be all right," she said. "Pretty soon I'll be all right when I stop feeling so sick."

He kept on his knees beside the chair. He took her hand and kissed the palm of it.

"I don't know what to do," she said at last. "Is it only

meanness that keeps you from talking, or are you after the Big Fellow?"

"Are you all right?" asked Toomey.

"Yes," she said, and stood up. "Do I look a lot as though I've been crying?"

"Your nose looks a little pink," said Toomey.

"That damn nose!" said the girl.

"I like it that way," said Toomey.

She smiled at him, crookedly, sadly, wistfully.

"Are you really—" she began. Then she broke off, and shook her head as though realizing that she could draw nothing out of him.

"I think I'm real," said Toomey. "Whatever's inside me, I hope it's real."

She took his handkerchief and dried her face with it. Then she slipped it into her breast and smiled at him again, in a different way.

"Pick up the money," she said.

"It's yours. I gave it to you," said Toomey.

"Are you just a crazy man?" she asked. "But listen, Toomey—suppose that anything should happen to him, and I had the money. That would kill *me,* too. You take it. I don't want it. I don't want the dirty stuff."

"Burn it, then," said Toomey.

She picked up the greenbacks, shuddered, crunched them into the palm of her hand.

"I don't see the whole of your game, here," said Toomey. "You're working for the Big Fellow? That's clear. But how did Crawford happen to employ you?"

"He thought that he could buy me out," answered the girl. "He thought he could pay me a high enough price, and bring me over to his side, along with everything that I know about the Big Fellow."

"And so you're here, spying on him, eating your way into the heart of his affairs? I'll tell you this, Sally: I'm in your hand, today, but tomorrow you'll be in mine, and if you're still hanging around this house, I'll tell Crawford. I'll let you hang!"

As he finished, he was at the door; he slammed it behind him on the last words.

5

SALLY REPORTS TO THE BIG FELLOW

NOW THAT SALLY was alone, an impulse of fear made her run to a closet. She snatched a coat and hat and started to huddle into them; but after a moment, she overmastered that strong impulse, and dragged off the coat again with a slow reluctance. She hung up the overcoat in the closet, fumbled inside of it, and took out from an inner pocket a flat little automatic revolver, and a set of keys that glittered with newness.

The thoughts that went with the gun and the keys, pinched her face and opened her eyes. She had to sit down by the fire for a moment with a hand pressed against her throat, where the cold fear was gathering. After a while, she stood up, suddenly, crossed the room with a quick step, jerked the door open, and passed into the hall.

It was empty, but her eyes, bright as glass, sent darting glances into every corner. She climbed the stairs, turned down the upper hall, and paused at a door. Again she swept the hallway with her glance; but no footfall was brushing over the thick carpet.

She fitted one of the keys into the lock. It turned softly.

She entered a room filled with thick darkness, closed the door behind her, and pulled an electric switch.

It lighted a chamber which contained little besides a desk in the center, and in one corner a tall, massive, old-fashioned safe. The window shutters were closed; the air in the room was stale and still. The silence was to the girl like the hush of a funeral, or the pause before a battle. She had to set her teeth hard before she could move again.

With careful fingers, she turned back a corner of the rug, exposing an electric fixture, countersunk in the floor, with a network of fine copper wires extending from it in all directions across the floor. She pulled out the plug and thereby killed that electric detective for the moment.

A moment later she was leaning in front of the safe, fitting the largest of the keys into the lock. When she tried to turn it, there was a rigid resistance. The strength went out of her with a gasp. She had to lean her forehead against the painted steel surface for a moment. Then she tried the key again; it turned, and the heavy door sagged gradually open by the force of its own weight, pulling against a suction that made a whispering sound.

Inside, there were rows of compartments, each locked, and into those locks she fitted her keys, one after another. When the drawers were free she went through them, one after another. Bundles of cash, valuables in chamois bags, she touched without interest. She came to some big ledgers and continued to search. Time went by her slowly, and every second pulled more and more strongly at her. The fear grew up like a gigantic ghost beside her, and the face of Crawford with his yellow eyes wavering constantly across her mind.

She paused. What she wanted she had not found. She started up, gritted her teeth, and sank again on her knees to resume the search. There was only one possibility. She took out the ledgers, opened them, let the pages whip rapidly across her fingers; and at the second try out from the larger book fell a little gray notebook with a stained canvas cover.

Joy and relief brought a moan from her throat. She replaced everything with flying hands, closed the drawers, heard the locks click in swift succession, and shut and locked the massive outer door.

She left the room, stepped into the hall—and confronted Bushmill. He started at the sight of her.

"Hey!" said Bushmill. "What's the idea? *You* been in there?"

"I had to get something for the chief," she answered.

"The devil you did," said Bushmill. "What?"

"This."

She showed the gray-bound notebook.

"It don't seem possible," said Bushmill. "Lemme have a look."

"What sort of a fool do you think I am?" she asked him, angrily. "The chief sent me to get it, and gave me the keys."

She showed them. To Bushmill, they appeared as a crushing argument and she, calmly turning, locked the door of the safe room.

"That's the way," said Bushmill, bitterly. "You take a man, and he can work all his life, and he never gets nowhere, but you take a girl with a face and a smile and—what the hell?—she walks right into the best spot on the job, and stays there!"

She merely smiled at Bushmill, then hurried down the

hall, down the stairway, and into the small room where she had left her things. She was in them in a moment. The window that she had pointed out to Toomey was the one she opened now. She slipped over the sill with the easy activity of a boy, dropped to the ground, ran straight forward into the darkness of the night.

Straight across country, among dripping trees, through wet brush, she kept on, headlong. She was soaked to the skin. Sharp ends of branches caught at her clothes like teeth, and tore them, but she went on, sometimes walking, sometimes running, until at last she came out on an open road, and crossed it to a large entrance gate. She rang a bell vigorously; a light flashed over the gate.

"What the Sam Hill!" cried the gatekeeper. "Miss Moore?"

"HURRY! HURRY!" SHE commanded, and looked up and down the road, expecting every instant that great headlights would swing into view and bear down upon her.

The gate yawned wide, she went scurrying past the astonished face of the gatekeeper and so, still running, to the back of the big Tudor house. She ran in through a small door that she instantly locked behind her. To the left was a small study with the dull flicker of a fire offering warmth to her. She entered that room, rang the service bell, and stood on the hearth, dripping, ragged, triumphant. Music was throbbing in the front of the house. She heard more of the pulse than of the sound until a door opened and let in the singing of the violins; a maid appeared on the threshold. She held up her hands and gaped at Sally Moore.

"Go get Mr. Oliver," said the girl. "Tell him that I'm here. Tell him to come at once. Hurry! Then rattle upstairs and get me a blanket or something to wrap up in. Telephone to the cottage that I'm coming over in a short time, and tell them to have some hot tea ready. Scoot!"

The maid vanished. After a moment, a heavy stride passed down the hall. A tall man with ponderous shoulders, and with a florid, handsome face, came lurching in at her.

"Sally, what deviltry—" he had begun to say, as he entered, but his voice jerked to a halt as he saw the wreck of her clothes, and the rain-darkened streak of hair that clung against her face.

She merely laughed at him, and held out the canvas book.

"You got it?" exclaimed Lawrence Oliver. "Sally, you witch—you got it?"

He opened it, incredulously staring. "Cipher!" he exclaimed. "It's all in cipher!"

"Of course it is—but I'll work it out. I have some clews to the key, already," she answered him.

The maid came, trailing a blanket, aghast. The Big Fellow took the blanket and wrapped Sally Moore in the soft gray down.

"Get a hot bath ready," he ordered the maid. "You're soaked, Sally! You'll get pneumonia out of this!"

"I don't want a bath here," said the girl. "I'll take one at the cottage. And I won't get pneumonia, either. There's a fire in me, Big Fellow; I could laugh and shout; because we've got him, now! That's his pay book, all right. Before long, I'll have that cipher worked out, and I'll be able to tell you every penny that he's spent for bribery and crime, and who he gave it to. Think of Crawford being such a fool as to keep accounts on that sort of thing? We've got him,

Big Fellow! Oh, he has murder in his mind, I know, but he won't dare to move. You're safe."

She slipped into a chair by the fire and leaned back her head against the cushion and laughed at him with rejoicing. The Big Fellow kept the notebook in a tight clutch.

"Maybe you're right," he said, "and if you are, it's the greatest day in my life. Sally, my dear, I've been walking in the fear of death for years; and now Ranny Moore's daughter sets me free from it. I can't believe it! Sit closer to the fire. Sally, if you're ill after this—"

"Hush!" broke in the girl. "My skin is tough. Water won't hurt me."

"I'll get you brandy—"

"I don't want it. Go back to the party, Big Fellow; I just wanted you to know!"

"The devil take the party. Sally, how did you do it?"

"I told you how I got the impression of the keys in wax. But the keys were not ready till today, and it's been a hard fight, lately. Every day, Crawford has been pumping me, about you. I've told him some truth. I had to; but I mixed it all in with a set of lies. I was scared to death, too. But it was fun. It was the most marvelous fun that I've ever had in my life. Every minute of it was a horse race—my life bet on the chance. It was glorious. Big Fellow, I'm the happiest person in the world—and you're safe!"

"If you've tied Crawford's hands," said the Big Fellow, "you've done a miracle. But it's better to have you safely back here than to be safe myself. I've been burning in hell-fire, ever since you went to Crawford. I haven't slept. It's been a torment, Sally."

"You couldn't keep me from going," answered the girl.

"It was my own fault if anything happened to me. Oh, Big Fellow, to think that we're about to tie the hands of that fiend!"

He pulled a chair close to her and got hold of her hands.

"It's the end of the long trail, then," said he. "I suppose it's fitting and proper that I should owe my life to you, Sally, because I've owed most of my happiness to you, since you came to stay here. Sally, I've asked you before, now I'm begging you again; let me adopt you. You can keep right on being Ranny Moore's daughter; but you can be mine, too. You'll have to be my heir, anyway, and I want you to be legally sure of getting whatever I have in the world."

She shook her head at him, cheerfully. "You're young, still," she told him. "You'll be marrying one of these days. You'll have a dozen youngsters of your own. It's better to have real ones than a mere amateur daughter like me. Besides, I don't want to let anyone have a claim on me; not even you, Big Fellow. I want to be free. It's life and blood, to me, to go my own way and get out of leading strings."

"I WON'T ARGUE," said Lawrence Oliver. "I never could convince you of anything. But if you throw yourself away in some crazy adventure, one of these days, you'll be leaving me a hollow life, my dear. Tell me one thing—will Crawford find out about the missing book, soon?"

"Not soon, I hope—unless he happens to want to make an entry in it. I hope he may go days without knowing. And by that time, I'll have the cipher worked out—and then it's a mere matter of letting the police do the rest of the work! Big Fellow, why does Crawford hate you so?"

"Because he used to be my friend," said Lawrence Oliver, rather sadly. "Because we were always together, and he was the leader in everything. I was a shadow for him, that was all. He was the master in every situation. He had a stronger body, and a better brain. And then there was that accident in the mountains in Switzerland, and I managed to carry him down to safety—but you know what happened, and how the doctors were unable to save half of him from whatever they call it—that paralysis which has withered up his legs. He began to hate me when they told him that he couldn't be cured. He hated me for still being healthy and strong. I tried for years to be close to him, still. Then I saw that he was trying to stab me one day, and cursed me to the bottom of hell and back. I've never seen him since. But I've seen his handiwork, often enough."

"That's ended," said the girl. "There's only one stumbling block that may snag you."

"What's that?"

"He has a new man working for him. A fellow called Toomey."

"He's had men before, plenty of 'em."

"Never one like this," answered the girl.

She began to brood on the fire.

And the Big Fellow, watching her, moving his eyes with joy over her face, like a father, grew suddenly sober and concerned.

"Tell me about him," he demanded.

She shook her head. "I have to think him over. I don't know how to place him. He's all steel, and yet he's all human. He's the kind that could walk through fire. And he's convinced that you're a devil and that Crawford is a saint. I tried to tell him the truth. But it was no good. I couldn't make any impression on him. Nobody could make an impression on him, once he's made up his mind."

"He's only one," said the Big Fellow. "Why should he trouble you so much?"

"Because I never met a man like him before. He's all new."

"Look here," said the Big Fellow, "you're not worrying about what he may do to me?"

"I am, though. Watch yourself, Big Fellow. Watch like a hawk. Put a guard in your room. Keep your men on the watch. Anything might happen—because he's a devil—this Toomey."

"He's something more than a devil," said Lawrence Oliver. "Or else why should you smile, that way, when you think of him?"

"Yes, he's something more," she agreed.

"Are you a little dizzy about him, Sally?"

"I'm a little dizzy about him," she agreed.

"Confound him," said Oliver, "I'll have his neck twisted for him! An infernal hired thug—and you're interested in him?"

"He's not a thug, and he's not hired," said she.

"What is he then?" asked the Big Fellow.

"He's different," she said.

"In what way?"

"I don't know," she answered. "I want a chance to think him over. I'm going over to the cottage now, and muddle at the cipher, and I'm coming over later on to tell you about him—as well as I can. After the people have left the house. May I come over then?"

"Come then," agreed the Big Fellow. "Come any time."

"I'll come up to your room, and we can chat a little in front of the fire before I go back to bed," she told him.

"We'll go back to the cottage together," said the Big Fellow. "This Toomey—damn him—I hope he's not on your mind. But he won't be a danger to me. No man can be a danger, Sally. Come on, and we'll step across to your cottage."

He added, with a groaning sigh of relief: "The worst is over. The worst is ended. Oh, Sally, I've had to get Sewell to hire a scoundrel of a thug from the underworld, that devil they call the Doctor—I've had to have him to hire yeggs and murderers to protect me from the devices of Crawford. But now that you have the book, I'm free. I can get rid of the Doctor. I'm able to stand up and be an honest man."

6

THE MAN FROM CRAWFORD

WHEN TOOMEY CLOSED the door of the room behind him, his strong impulse was to go straight to Crawford and tell him that there was a traitor in the house, but his hands were tied. She had foreborne to use her advantage over him; he could not in turn betray her. Besides, though she might be in the pay of the Big Fellow, she was apparently bound to Lawrence Elliott Oliver by a real affection.

And a man cannot know where to have a woman. Her instincts are different. To attempt to judge her is folly.

Toomey's conclusion was that he would wait until his own position with Crawford was consolidated. Then he could quietly urge Sally to withdraw. He felt that there would be time. She would hardly suspect that he might begin action on this very night.

In the hall, he got his hat and left the house. A heavy closed car was waiting, with one man in the front seat. It was raining a succession of heavy gusts with a fine drizzle in between. One of those gusts struck Toomey before he could slip through the rear door of the sedan. Bushmill had to be waited for. Until he came down, Toomey's questions went unanswered, for Slip stared sullenly straight ahead, and refused to speak.

Bushmill appeared in the depths of the gloom.

"Even Crawford," he said, "is a fool about girls," and then he slumped into a seat, growling.

"Can this car step?" asked Toomey.

"Around eighty," said Bushmill.

"Anything inside?"

"Two machine guns; two pairs of automatics. Two flasks of whiskey. Want some?"

"No. You know the way to the hangout where the Big Fellow is to be lodged?"

"I know the way."

"Let's go, then," said Toomey.

"We'll call on the Big Fellow. Put the car somewhere near his house. Wait a minute. Got a plan of the house?"

"Yes, in my pocket."

"Come back here, show a light, and we'll study it on the way."

Bushmill came back. The car started. Under the pale light of the electric bulb in the ceiling, Bushmill unfolded several sheets of paper. Toomey studied them. They were all marked in neatly, but Toomey's eye dwelt mostly on the bedroom of the Big Fellow. He studied all the approaches with care, then turned out the light and visualized the plans in his mind's eye.

The wheels began to dash through shallow puddles of water that sent roaring spray against the fenders and the bottom of the car; then they slowed and entered slowly among trees. The machine stopped.

"Where are we?" asked Toomey.

"You can see the lights of the house through the trees," answered Bushmill. "What's the plan?"

"Leave Slip with the car," said Toomey. "Slip, back her around, and get ready for a fast start."

There was no answer. Toomey climbed out. A volley of rain struck him and beat through his clothes to the skin. The force of the whiskey had burned out. He felt a little dizzy and weak in the elbows and the knees, but he turned and walked slowly among the trees until, from the verge of them, he could look across the top of a stone wall, over broad lawns that gleamed with a silver brightness where the cones of light streamed from the windows of the house. It was a three story building with a green spray of ivy washing half way to the top, and two sets of bow windows bulging out of the facade. Strains of dance music came dimly through the rush of the storm. Off to the side of the house, a parking circle was nearly filled with automobiles.

"Hot stuff, tonight," said Bushmill, at Toomey's ear.

"Come on with me," said Toomey.

HE CLIMBED THE wall and led the way through the darkness of trees and shrubs below the lawns until he had circled the house and come close in under the side of it. The ball room was before them, with shadows of dancers swinging grotesquely across the drawn, luminous shades, and the curtains. It paid to be a treacherous, cowardly thug, thought Toomey, as he shivered in the rain. He looked up to the bedroom of Lawrence Elliott Oliver and shook his head as he saw that the windows were faintly lighted.

Then he took off his hat, coat, necktie, shirt, shoes and socks. He rolled them into a bundle and gave them to Bushmill, who crouched in the shrubbery beside him.

"What's the game?" said Bushmill. "What crazy business?"

"A little South Seas," said Toomey. "Keep this junk. Wait here. Keep your gun dry, and wait here. I don't care if you freeze—wait here until daylight—or until you see them take me out in an ambulance."

"Wait a minute," said Bushmill. "What's in your head?"

"I'm going to bring out Lawrence Elliott Oliver," said Toomey.

"Don't be a nut. Don't be funny," grunted Bushmill.

Toomey rose. The rain soaked his clothes flat against his skin. The drops seemed to be stinging his naked flesh.

"You wait," he said, and ran out of the brush and swiftly into the shadow of the house, crossing the gravel driveway. The small stones bit at his feet; the lawn beyond it was wet and cold, but as he paused in the shadow, fumbling with his hands down the wall, he was smiling a little.

Far south, far south, where the autumn never nips the foliage to turn it crimson, where the palm trees spring like green fountains, where the beaches burn white in the sun and the blue sea rises like a wall against the horizon, he had gone in clothes like these, or far more nakedly, with his bare toes gripping the deck-boards of a schooner that reeled in the wind. He felt himself again; clothes were a stifling mask to him.

He found what he wanted, as his hands moved along the wall. It was the big round of a drainage pipe, and he went up it like a monkey, or a sailor. It passed between two of the second-story windows. He reached out, caught a window-sill ledge, and swung himself across. It was dangerous business, gripping that slick stonework, but Toomey smiled.

The curtains that draped the window sloped off to the sides in multiple folds of fine red velvet.

Red velvet for the bedroom windows of a man's room! Toomey's lip lifted from his teeth. He could see the foot of a great canopied four-poster bed. Firelight flickered on the ceiling, though his view of the fire itself was blocked by a davenport drawn in front of it. He saw the lustre of the rug, the intricacies of color and design in the Persian pattern. He saw a big portrait of a warrior of the seventeenth century, in breast plate and lace glimmering above the mantel.

It paid to be a Big Fellow; his treacheries were readily forgotten and forgiven by the world.

Last of all, he saw a big young man seated at the side of the fire, a fellow almost without forehead or nose—a face that seemed made to bite. As Toomey peered in, the young fellow got up, came to the window, looked out. He was gripping a pistol. Toomey held himself out of sight, and the man went back to the fire. So, an armed guard was kept in the bed chamber of the Big Fellow, day and night.

To swing from the drain pipe to the window ledge had been hard enough. To swing back to the pipe and get a safe hold was ten times harder. But he had both hands and feet, and knew how to use them.

So down he went, sliding, to the ground.

He edged about to the front of the house. It was not nearly so safe, from this angle, for there were infinitely more lights; on his nervous eye it seemed to pour like sunlight, but he saw above him a balcony, whose supporting corbels looped far down above the windows of the ball room. If the outside of the house were guarded like the inside, he would be lost, if he tried this adventure.

But Toomey was still smiling, and smiling men are the

most dangerous. They were playing a waltz inside. And in rhythm with the music he climbed to the lower windowsill, caught hold of the corbelling, and presently was crouched on the balcony.

He took a breath, waited for the beating of blood in his temples to subside, and then went to a window of the room adjoining that of the Big Fellow. It was not locked, so he had no difficulty in working it up.

THE WIND ENTERED with him, a strong blast that set drapery flapping. He pulled the sash down and closed his eyes through a long moment. After that, the night light was sufficient to help him across the bedroom by the dim glimmers that came from glass or from varnished surfaces until he found the door. It opened upon the hall only a step from the door that led to the Big Fellow's chamber.

Toomey retraced his steps, re-opened the window, and let the wind come hurling through. He went again to the door, set it wide, and stepped into the hall. His feet had been dried, crossing the thick pile of the rug in the bedroom; he would leave no traces now.

Even the runner down that hallway was beautiful enough in fabric and color to be cut into short lengths for museum pieces, it seemed to Toomey. He looked at the diminishing double row of glimmering doors that receded to a distance. One of those doors might open at any moment.

But he was filled with recklessness by the music that throbbed in the air more clearly, now, and that seemed to come with a trembling vibration through the floor, through his flesh and blood. They were laughing and talking, down there, and he could hear the whispering feet of the dancers.

Still the wind blew strongly behind him through the door that he had left open. He stepped to the door of the Big Fellow's room and turned the handle so slowly that even had an eye been fixed upon it from the inside, the motion would hardly have been marked.

When the latch was cleared, he pushed the door in, gently. The draft took hold and swung it wide, inside, an oath exploded, and Toomey leaped back behind one of the heavy pilasters that projected between this doorway and the next. It was not thick enough to shield his body perfectly, so he exhaled his breath, and held it.

A muttering voice came closer. That fellow with the lost forehead and nose strode into the hallway with a naked automatic in his hand, held hip high. His body crouched a little over the gun, as he looked from side to side. If with the very corner of his eye he should flick the partially exposed body of Toomey—

But the eye will usually only see what it expects. The guard stepped on towards the door of the vacant bedroom, cursing.

"French maids!" he said. "A French damn for French maids. Floodin' the damn room out—on a night like this!"

He disappeared into the darkness, while Toomey slipped from his place and entered the bedroom of the Big Fellow. His rapid eye wavered from place to place—the closet doors, the curtains. Then he took the oldest and least expected of hiding places by sliding like a snake under the bed.

There he lay on his stomach, and heard the throb of the music come to his ears as over an electric wire.

The guard came back. He still had the gun in his hand.

He had slammed down the window in the next room and crashed the door of it shut. Now he remained for a moment peering about.

Toomey could see him clearly from beneath the bed. His own gun was crunching into his belly, but he dared not move, for the moment.

"French maids—a French hell for 'em," said the guard, muttering.

He closed the door, and put up his gun.

"French maids," he said. "The hell with 'em!"

And he resumed his place by the fire, settling well back in the big chair. He took a folded magazine out of his coat pocket and began to read, leaning his head forward, gnawing at his fingernails. The shadow of his moving head was on the floor near Toomey.

And Toomey, making himself comfortable, felt the cold of the floor enter his damp body. The instant he noticed it, an almost irresistible desire to sneeze convulsed him, but even the writhing, the convulsions, had to be slow and stifled.

Yet it was enough to rouse the guard.

He got up, suddenly, kneeled, and looked into the darkness under the bed. His face was not three feet from the face of Toomey. He stared for a moment, then rose to his feet.

"Funny," said the guard, and went back to his chair. "Like I'd heard something, pretty near."

The ice of death melted slowly away from the soul of Toomey. He knew, then, that no inferior cold would be apt to move him again, on this evening.

Then an hour passed. Then endless hours. No matter

how he turned, the floor bit through the thinness of his meager flesh and made his bones ache. But still he waited and endured. He told himself that it was a pleasure to endure, in this fashion. Yonder, across a night of rain and wind, was the ruined body of Crawford, enduring as he had endured for years, never whining. And in this house, under the floor, the traitor Lawrence Oliver moved serenely among his guests, laughing, drinking with them.

A lot of good liquor had been sponged up, long before this.

Then automobiles began to start with a dull roar that faded away. Horns honked near by, more distantly. Doors closed. Voices came up the stairs, with laughter, and retreated again. He heard the faint, faint tinkling of the voices of women, speaking, laughing, in front of the house.

At last there was stillness; then a heavy step came down the hall. The door opened, and Toomey, from beneath the bed, saw the Big Fellow framed in the doorway.

HE FITTED HIS name. His body was big. He was as large as Crawford about the head and shoulders, and he did not stop at the waist. He had not been left until one half of him died in the Alpine night! He was huge, thick, solid. He was one of those men who put on fat all over but never develop a heavy stomach. Except for his bald head, he might have been a prizefighter a year or so out of training. He had a swarthy face, a handsome face except for the thickness of the lips. There, it seemed to Toomey, the beast showed forth; and in the rosy brightness of his skin, and of his flushed, bald head. Across this picture arose the fumes of the cigar that he held in his hand.

"Well, Jerry," he said.

The guard finished reading a sentence, rose, stuffed the magazine into his pocket, and yawned.

"Listen," he said.

The Big Fellow closed the door behind him and went to stand in front of the fire.

"Listen," said Jerry. "Those birds next door—the whoo-zeits—"

"Mr. and Mrs. Graham, eh?" said the Big Fellow.

"They got a French maid?" said the guard.

"They have," said the Big Fellow.

"A French hell for French maids, is what I says," said Jerry. "She goes and airs the room, she does, and she opens the window, with the rain and the wind blowin' through it, like tonight. And the door blows open so hard that this here door of this here room, blows open, too. Now what'n hell you think of that, chief, anyway? I mean, for a fool, would you pick a French fool, first."

"All right, Jerry," said the Big Fellow. "Things like that happen. You can run along, now."

"What I mean," said Jerry, "is a damn fool like that to leave a window open, is what I mean. A French hell for a French maid, is what I says to myself. It kind of give me a start, is what I mean, the door blowin' open, like that."

"Sorry," said the Big Fellow. "How're the kids?"

"Fine!" said Jerry, heartily. He grinned, and Toomey saw the upper half of the face disappear altogether, beneath waves of wrinkles. "This here kid of mine, this Mike, you oughta see. I mean, what he learns. Poetry. He learns a thing that begins: 'The stag at eve had had a drink'—and it runs on, a lot of tripe like that. The stag at eve! Ha, ha, ha! A lot of stags have had their drinks at eve, yeah, and at midnight, too, and a little eye-wash in the mornin'. But the way the kid says it, you oughta hear. Like nothin' at all, he says it. The stag at eve—and all that tripe. You know."

"I know," said the Big Fellow. "He's a fine kid."

"He's gotta head, is what he's got," said Jerry, going to the door. "Well, so long. Good night, chief."

"Good night, Jerry."

The door closed. The Big Fellow teetered back and forth in front of the fire, puffing at his cigar, his eyes seeing before him visions that were not too distant. He began to laugh, and still laughing turned towards the fire.

Toomey came snakelike, softly, from beneath the bed, and held the automatic to cover his man. He bent forward, a stealthy step at a time, and saw the body of Lawrence Elliott Oliver stiffen, suddenly.

"No yelling," said Toomey.

He heard a breath exhaled with a gargling sound. "Oh, God!" said the Big Fellow.

"No yelling, no funny moves," said Toomey. "I'm a man that'd like to give you what's coming to you. I'd like to saw you in two with a machine gun. You sneaking crook! You fat, yellow dog! Put your hands over your head!"

The whole body of the Big Fellow was shuddering; so were the arms that he raised above his head.

"Crawford!" he gasped. "Crawford sent you?"

Toomey said nothing. He stepped up behind Lawrence Oliver and sank the muzzle of his gun into the soft of the fat. With his other hand he patted the clothes rapidly and found what he wanted. He brought out a chunky little automatic that fitted well into the hollow of his hand, and then stepped back.

"Turn around," said Toomey.

The Big Fellow turned. His face was yellow dough. His lips were parted by his breathing.

"Sit down, you welcher," said Toomey. "You can't even take it. You're such a dog that you can't even take it."

The Big Fellow sank on the overstuffed arm of a chair.

"Crawford!" whispered the Big Fellow.

"How soon will there be a clear way out of the house?" asked Toomey.

"I don't know."

"We'll try," said Toomey. "Pretty soon, we'll try. We'll walk right along together, and if there's a peep out of you, you get a lead fist shoved through the middle of you. Understand?"

The head of Lawrence Oliver jerked back, as he swallowed. And it was then that Toomey heard rapid footfalls pattering down the hall. A hand rattled at the door, and opened it a little.

"Big Fellow! Big Fellow!" called the voice of Sally Moore.

She waited hardly half a second before she ran in, the door slamming behind her. Then she saw Toomey, the gun and the captive.

7

AT THE WHITE HOUSE

THAT DOUGH-FACED HULK, the Big Fellow, was of no importance. Toomey had the girl by the arm before she could move. She turned to water under his grip and slipped to her knees.

The Big Fellow stood like a yellow stone, a Buddha immovably carved. He still had the stub of the cigar in his fist, and now and then his hand made a small, futile movement, and the smoke rose wavering past his face.

"It's the end," he said thickly.

"Get up," said Toomey, to the girl. He pulled at her arm, and she stood up. The wall was near. He pushed her back so that she could lean against it, and he studied her face. Fear makes people hideous, but she was not hideous, to Toomey. It was merely that a whiter light had fallen upon her, and that he could look farther into her eyes as she stared at him.

She talked, but not to him—to Lawrence Elliott Oliver.

"I could have smashed him by lifting my voice and saying three words," she said. "I didn't do it. Oh, Big Fellow, God forgive me! Something went wrong in me, when I saw him. I couldn't think straight. I went to pieces. But all the while, I guessed."

Her voice had lifted.

"Stop talking. Stop making that damned noise," said Toomey.

The Big Fellow had not moved, only his hand was still making futile gestures before the gun that vaguely pointed towards him.

"Don't make any noise, Sally—don't!" said the Big Fellow. His voice sounded as though he had just finished eating something greasy. There was a bubbling in his throat.

"Are you going to kill him?" whispered the girl.

Toomey looked away from her eyes to the shuddering of her lips, though it was hardly any better to watch them.

"Don't be a fool," said Toomey. "If I were going to kill him, would I have waited?"

She shook her head, violently. She seemed desperately eager to agree with him, to placate him, perhaps, by agreeing with him, as one would agree with a madman.

"No," she said, in that same whisper, a ghastly thing. "No, you wouldn't kill him. You wouldn't kill him, Toomey, you wouldn't murder the Big Fellow."

"Quit it," said Toomey. "Quit it, will you?"

"Yes," she whispered. "I'll quit it. I won't make any noise. Toomey, you won't hurt him. He's the best man in the world."

"I like to hear you say that," said Toomey, "because it shows me what you are. It shows me that I'm right. You went to Crawford's house to spy. You went there like a rat to eat a hole in a sinking ship. You wanted to sink Crawford. I'll tell you what you are—you're nothing. You're a traitor. You're like Oliver. You're a traitor."

But all the while there was a weakness under his strength. He knew, suddenly, what he wanted, and it was this girl, with the white fear leprous on her face. If she were ten thousand times a traitor, still there was something in her that he could love. But he put down that emotion, crushing his heart out against the iron fist of his will.

"Come along with me," said Toomey.

He made her go back along the wall until he reached a door that he hoped would open on a closet. It did. A deep closet, half filled with clothes that hung in close order.

"Get in there, and stay there, and be still," said Toomey.

IT SEEMED TO him seconds of agony while he thrust her in, and took his reluctant hand from her, and shut the door in her face. He heard her hands beat against the door. Then her voice went up in a scream that mounted higher and higher, like a climbing flame.

Toomey turned the key in the lock and faced Lawrence Elliott Oliver.

"All right," he said. And he listened. He did not think that that sound would penetrate through the house—not for a few moments.

"There's a back way," said Toomey. "Show me the back way, and show it fast! Walk straight ahead of me. If anybody shows up, send them away. Send them away with a loud voice. Listen, Oliver, I don't want to take you away alive. I hate to. I only want a good excuse for ripping the heart out of you."

The Big Fellow went before him with short, fumbling steps, like a man just risen from a sick-bed. And Toomey followed from the room, down the hall.

A door opened just before them, the back of it swinging wide. Lawrence Oliver threw out his arms and stood with his head bent stiffly back, as though he expected the bullets

Behind them every light in the house was suddenly illuminated.

to tear through him. From the doorway, a woman spoke, laughingly, to someone who was still in the room. Then she closed the door without coming into the hall.

They went on; they descended stairs at the end of the hall, stairs that turned rapidly, many times, and so they came to a small hall, and an outer door. The Big Fellow opened it. They walked out into the open breath of the night. Something went back and forth across the mind of Toomey like a shutter before a bright light. A miracle had happened, was behind him in the presence of that great looming house.

"To the right," he said, and Lawrence Oliver went like a soldier to the right.

All was blackness to the rear of the house, as they started around it, but voices began, and footfalls, and running and the slamming of doors; then lights snapped on here and there. Toomey knew what had happened. He knew that the shrieking of the girl had soaked through the thick walls, at last, to give the alarm.

But that would be too late, unless there were outer guards posted.

"Run!" he commanded, coming up beside the Big Fellow.

There was a groan for answer, but the Big Fellow ran, stepping out with amazing strength and lightness, until they rounded the corner of the house.

"Bushmill!" called Toomey.

A form arose from the shrubbery, staggered, lurched towards them. They ran on in a trio, crossed the lawn, climbed the wall, and found the car. Behind them, every light in the house seemed to be suddenly illumined, and an uproar of human voices contended against the storm.

The Big Fellow made one effort, his hand on the door of the machine.

"Boys," he said, "if you'll listen, I can make you all rich. I've got more money than Crawford. I can—"

"Damn you!" said Toomey. "If you waste time. I'll—I'll smash in your face with the heel of my gun!"

THE BIG FELLOW slunk into the car. Toomey sat beside him. The automobile started; the trees began to slip past them, while Toomey eased his cold back against the depth of the cushions and retasted some of those moments that had just gone by. He gave only one glance to Lawrence Oliver; the man was a loosely filled sack, a collapsed, dead thing, with the cigar butt still crushed between his fingers.

On the front seat, Toomey could hear broken phrases, as Bushmill related what had happened: "A crazy man—all by himself—God, I froze and froze—all by himself—then I heard them running—all by himself, in there—"

"I want a drink," said Toomey.

"Here!" said Bushmill.

He reached around with a sudden eagerness and Toomey's hand found the icy cold of the flask. "I'll bet you need a drink, all right," said Bushmill. "And so do I."

Toomey unscrewed the top of the flask, and drank. He passed it to the Big Fellow.

"No," said a faint, deep, husky voice.

"Drink, damn you," said Toomey.

The Big Fellow drank.

Bushmill was still twisted around in his seat.

"How'd you do it?" he asked.

"I had a couple or breaks," said Toomey. "That was all. I don't want to drink. Let's get there, because I'm cold."

"What'll Crawford say?" said Bushmill to Slip. "My God, what a night's work! The Big Fellow! How'd he do it, I wonder?"

"Aw, shut up," said Slip. "Maybe it wasn't so much. Shut up, will you? I hate his nerve!"

He said it loudly, drawling the words out, but Toomey hardly heard him, for he was thinking of far other things— the thick blackness of the closet, and the white fear in the face of the girl. Like velvet, he thought, with a jewel laid against it. Not like that, either, but a light shining out of the darkness.

They went rapidly over rough roads, the car swaying often as it took corners. Once the weight of the Big Fellow jounced against the shoulder of Toomey.

They whisked among the weak, scattered lights of a

small town. The darkness of woods covered them. Then they slowed, twisted on a narrow gravel road, and the lights flashed over a little white house that was perched on the side of a hill.

"Here!" said Bushmill. And the car stopped.

8

THE PARTNERSHIP OF "MOM"

THE HOUSE HAD two stories and an attic; Toomey could see that; and a shed or two at the rear. Nearby, there were no trees—only shrubs. The woods began at a greater distance up the hill or to either side.

They went in, a solid body, herding Lawrence Oliver.

"Where's the electricity?" said Slip, as he opened the front door.

Bushmill seemed to know more about the place.

"Nothing but oil lamps," he said. "Electricity is no good in a pinch. A snip with a wire-cutter, and you're sunk in darkness, like in a grave. But you can trust oil lamps. There's an oil lamp on the hall table."

The flashlights picked out a narrow hall with a bit of worn red carpet stretched over the boards. A stairway with a graceful white banister climbed towards the shadows above, at the farther end of the entrance.

Suddenly the Big Fellow laughed, and the sound set all the nerves of Toomey jangling.

"That's right," said Lawrence Elliott Oliver. "It's like home. Nice soft light you get out of oil lamps."

Slip turned around and looked at the big man. "Aw, shut up, will you?" he commanded.

But the Big Fellow, chuckling again, set to work lighting the hall lamp. He scratched a match, touched it to the wick, and when he fitted the chimney down into the wire brackets, a soft cone of light spilled out from under the shade.

Toomey went ahead into a small parlor that opened back through a double sliding door into a sitting room. The place was filled with fragile old furniture; faded faces looked at them from the walls, enlarged photographs that preserved dead fashions more than dead people; weather stains dripped down the wall paper; and yet the Big Fellow seemed contented. He strode through the two rooms, his steps growing longer, every moment. A fire was laid on the open hearth. He lighted it. Billows of white smoke rose. Then the flames plunged through and took command.

"You fellows are all right," said the Big Fellow. He took out a cigar, fitted it into a corner of his mouth, and lighted it. "You take the luggage in, will you? I'm all right here. I feel better here than I have for months. You can't murder me in a place like this."

Bushmill and Slip made several trips with the contents that were piled in the car. There was a large, gold "M" stamped into the leather of two suitcases. The other baggage he put in the big front room. What was marked "M" was the possession of Crusty Mallow, and they were placed in the room next to that which the Big Fellow would occupy. There were only four bedrooms on the second floor.

Toomey went into the attic and the flashlight showed him the rafters, the dusty silk of cobwebs, a few great boxes with clothes thrown over the heaps that had been packed in them.

He went down through a house made cheerful by two

lamps in the hallways, and more lamps in the bedrooms. The autumn chill had soaked through the flimsy old building, but the light relieved it for the eye, at least. He went into the cellar. It was almost larger and deeper than the house above it. There were two floors to it.

When the kitchen lamp was lighted, they found provisions in every cupboard. Even the fire in the stove was laid.

The whole kitchen table was heaped with baskets or paper bags of fruit, vegetables, and other things crowded together. The mouth of Toomey watered. Even the Big Fellow seemed to forget his fear and enjoy this sight of plenty.

"This is pretty good. This is what the women and the servants have a chance to live with. They have the better half of things, my friends," said Lawrence Oliver.

He rubbed his cheeks; the color was slowly returning to them, and for a moment there was a silence as Toomey delighted his starved body with the promise of what was to come.

"We'll eat," said Toomey.

"We'll eat!" exclaimed the Big Fellow, his cheerfulness returning to him in an amazing manner.

"Shut up, punk, or I'll shut you up!" said Slip, turning suddenly on the big man.

LAWRENCE OLIVER SHRANK and blinked at the threat. Toomey turned sick when he saw that bulk of a man show yellow before such a wasp as Slip.

Said Toomey: "Boys, get this. While I'm here, I'm boss. And while I'm boss, I'll hand out the rough stuff to Oliver. The rest of you are not asked to horn in. He'll get plenty from me."

"Who put you on top?" said Slip eagerly. All the flame of that burning, malevolent soul of his was in his eyes. "Who gave you the right to kick us around?"

"Nobody," said Toomey.

"Nobody?" snarled Slip, anger making him waver a little from side to side.

"Nobody," said Toomey. "But I'm taking the right. I only work for one man at a time. So I'm taking the right."

"Steady, Slip. Quit it," said Bushmill, hastily.

Slip turned on his heel and left the room. Bushmill sighed, and added: "He's a great guy, Slip is. But he's queer. He's kind of quick and queer. You know how it is. Go easy with him, Mallow. That's all. Go easy, and he'll be all right I have to go back, now. Slip will stay with you here. So long. A great job, boy. A wonderful job. It'll keep the chief awake. So long, Big Fellow. Sorry to see you down. But get some ham and eggs under your belt, and you'll feel a lot better."

He went to the door, waved his hand, and was gone. Toomey already was working at the stove. Upstairs, he could hear Slip getting into a bed. The Big Fellow had found a case of whisky and was helping himself liberally. He opened a bottle of Perrier and made a cocktail.

"No ice, damn it," said the Big Fellow, "but when we're in the country, we've got to make out with what's at hand. Mallow—if that's your name—put in plenty of eggs and plenty of bacon. I'm going to eat. Crawford may gnaw my bones, but I'm going to eat while I can. Now tell me something, will you?"

Toomey stepped back from the fumes that arose from the pan. It seemed to him almost miraculous, the change that had come over this great hulk of a fellow.

"I'll tell you what I can," he said, wondering.

"It's about Crawford," said the Big Fellow.

"I don't talk about him," answered Toomey.

"You're not really a thug," insisted the Big Fellow, "and I want to know how you ever fell under the thumb of Crawford. You don't mean that you actually believe that he's all right?"

"Listen to me," said Toomey. "I have a job to do here with you, and I'm going to try to do it. But if you open up on me, Big Fellow, with your pack of lies—well, I'll simply shut you up in a way you'll remember. Keep that idea in your head, because remembering it will save you a lot of blood."

"There's something between you and Sally Moore," said Oliver. "What is it?"

Toomey shook his head.

"Today's the first time I ever saw her," he said.

The Big Fellow was studying him keenly, and after a long moment he said: "I want to tell you something. There's a lot of spirit in Sally, but she's a good girl. That's where a good many people make a mistake. They don't understand what a good girl she is."

Toomey felt like remarking that the man who hired the spy was very apt to approve of her. Instead, he asked suddenly: "What happened to you, Oliver? You've been a big shot. But what slaked all the lime in you? What drew off all the bubbles?"

"I'll be all right again," said the Big Fellow, passing a hand over his face. He swayed forward and rested his elbows on his knees. "A couple of years ago there were three of us. That's all. There were Sally's father, and me, and

Dave Mooney. 'Mom,' the boys used to call the three of us. Moore and Oliver and Mooney, see? We worked everything together. I was the office man, the head squeeze. It was big—big real estate, big politics. They were two right hands for me. Then they got Ranny Moore. That was only a couple of years ago."

He stared straight before him.

TOOMEY SPILLED EGGS and bacon into a platter, but he was left to eat them alone. Lawrence Oliver had lost all appetite. He could only talk.

"My God, but Ranny was a card," he said, softly. "They shot him through the body. He seemed to get well, but his insides were all crocked up. It took him months to die. Five months. He never stopped smiling. When he was passing out, he says to me in a whisper: 'Listen to this one I heard yesterday—it's a peach—' He died like that."

"Which left Sally," said Toomey.

"I couldn't do anything for Sally," said the Big Fellow. "She doesn't want charity. She doesn't even want advice. She thinks every day is the first of the year. She's always starting something. I hope to God that Crawford is not taking her into his shop."

He waited for an answer and got none.

"That was Moore gone," said the Big Fellow. "But I still had Dave Mooney. And Dave doubled himself. He was everywhere at once. He was where they thought I'd be, when they threw the bomb. They thought it was me. I heard the crash and saw the door of the next room sag in the middle. I ran in. Everything was pulp. The ceiling was gone. The table and chairs were gone. Dave was gone, too. I had a crazy idea, for a minute. I thought he might have got away. I thought he might have—I don't know what. And I hollered for him: 'Dave! Hey, Dave!' It seemed to me as though I heard an answer. Echo, you know. Then I looked around me and I saw the walls—I saw them all over—"

He clutched his face with both hands, shuddering. Afterwards he tried to pour himself a drink, but only spilled whisky on the floor. Toomey took the bottle and filled the glass. The Big Fellow grasped his right wrist with his left hand, took the glass, and managed to get most of the whisky past his lips.

"Afterwards," whispered the Big Fellow, "there was a funeral. There was a coffin. That was about all. Nobody knew except the priest and me. Nobody else really knew it was hardly more than a coffin. Everybody else followed along. A lot of the boys were crying when we put that coffin underground. They loved Dave. I loved him, too, but I couldn't cry on account of a damned coffin, could I?"

He jumped up.

Toomey took him by both wrists.

"Quit it, you damned baby!" he said.

There was no strength in the arms of the Big Fellow. He was mastered in a moment. Sobs began to shake his body and his fat face. He cried like a child, and every indrawn breath was a groan.

Toomey struck him across the mouth.

"You're going to bed," he said. "Follow me!"

9

WITH CARDS UP HIS SLEEVE

TOOMEY DRAGGED A mattress off the bed in his room and laid it across the door in the Big Fellow's room. He opened the baggage of Crusty Mallow and found a pair of purple-striped pyjamas. The Big Fellow sat on the edge of the bed wiping his mouth and looking down at his hand. There was blood on the hand.

After a time, he began to undress, silently. His back was turned, and he said nothing, but a quavering ran through his body. Toomey twisted himself in the bedclothes and lay on the mattress with an automatic under his hand.

After a while, the Big Fellow was in bed, too. He left the light on. Toomey got up and went to the lamp. The despairing eyes of the Big Fellow followed his movements, but he did not beg; he merely threw his arm suddenly, across his face. Under the arm, Toomey saw that there was a smear of blood across the chin.

He put out the light and went back to his mattress. The pure, icy air of the night entered the bed with him, and he lay shuddering, thinking.

It was a problem of human disintegration. Perhaps in the days of his youth Lawrence Oliver had been a Big Fellow, indeed, and a fit companion for that yellow-eyed lion of a man, Crawford. Perhaps the first sign of failure had been that night and day when he failed to do his duty by the wounded man who was his friend, and doubtless since that time the knowledge of his failure had weakened him constantly. Yet he had endured for many years, building himself a great name. Somewhere inside him there must have been a mighty reservoir of power which had only been drained away by the terrible deaths of Mooney and Moore. Now, softened by whisky and rightly haunted by terror because he was in the hands of Crawford, he was a mere pulp. Even so, he had rallied for a moment when he first entered the small white house that was to be his prison. Yes, there were still elements of manhood in him, and deep in his heart Toomey wondered if those elements could be rallied and reenforced.

A plan began to form in his mind, growing clearer with every instant, exciting him.

He heard a whispering sound, from the bed across the room. He made out two words. The Big Fellow was praying.

It was cold in the bed; Toomey started trembling. "It will be colder in the grave," he said to himself. "It will be colder in the grave. That's a fool idea. I'm letting myself go. I'll be up Cold Creek with the Big Fellow, damn him. I'm going up it now. Damn him!"

He grew warmer. The whispering stopped, and Toomey went to sleep.

He dropped whole leagues at a time towards unconsciousness. Finally he reached it. Sleep began to finger his body. It slacked all his muscles. It reached his brain. With exquisite delicacy it unravelled knots, and smoothed the cunning fabric.

Then he wakened, and found the Big Fellow getting up. The sun, slanting through a window, printed a pattern of the mullions on the opposite wall, but gave no heat.

"Good morning," he said.

The Big Fellow stood in a nightgown. There was still a dark smear across his chin.

"We'll speak when we have to," he said. "Now we don't have to."

Toomey leaped up.

"You'll speak every time you're spoken to," he said. He waited. The breast of the Big Fellow was heaving.

"Understand?" said Toomey.

"Yes," said the Big Fellow.

Toomey dressed, ran down to the cellar, started the fire in the water heater, came up to the kitchen, and cooked breakfast. They ate in the kitchen, silently.

SLIP APPEARED BEFORE they had finished. He greeted them with a nod. Toomey offered him some of the food that had been prepared but he refused with a mere gesture. He boiled his own coffee, strong as lye, and made some dry toast to nibble with it. Then he sat in front of the window and took his poisonous breakfast slowly, never speaking, sometimes running the tips of his fingers delicately over his forehead and temple. He seemed to need little food. His hatred of Toomey nourished him well enough.

"Wash the dishes," said Toomey, finally, to the Big Fellow, and went upstairs again. He stripped, took a bath, shaved, and then tried on some of the clothes of Crusty Mallow. The trousers were short, but they would do. The shoulders of the coats were too wide, but they would do, also. He dressed in a pair of gray tweed trousers and a soft gray sweater. The October sun was giving out more heat, so that a coat would not be necessary.

Then he hung up all the clothes from the two suitcases, or stowed them in the dresser. Downstairs he could hear the pans rattling, and the whistling of a song. It made Toomey shake his head with wonder.

He cleaned the scraps out of the bottom of the suitcases and found one bit of yellow thread, a waxed, hard-twisted thread, such as might be used to tie up a package. But this was full of corrugation; it was not a mere bit of string. Neither could it have been woven into clothes.

Then he saw that the same sort of yellow thread was used to fasten the cloth lining of the lid of the suitcase. Four inches of that thread was missing. The bit had been snipped out with a scissors or cut with a knife, to judge by the clean ends.

He touched the lining here and there, but could feel nothing that might have been inserted. Finally, he tore the lining completely out, but all that he found was a torn-off letter-head. The name on it read: "Sewell and Oliver, Councillors at Law." It was a big, clumsy letter-head printed on good paper. He turned it over. On the back was written: "Call at this address. Ask for Henry Sewell. Say: 'I want to see the Doctor.'"

He looked at the other side to see the address, "17 Flint Street."

He memorized the address, scratched a match, looked again to make sure that he remembered every word of the message, and the name, and then touched the flame to the paper. He waited until a wisp of gray ash floated from his finger tips, with one point of yellow flame pendent from it. That flame went out. The ash dissolved against the wall it touched.

He went downstairs and saw Slip in the front room.

The beautiful face of Slip was composed to stone, and like a stone he sat with his hands relaxed on the arms of the chair, staring at the wall.

"I've got to ask you something," said Toomey.

The mouth of Slip twisted; he turned his eyes askance, but kept his hatred silent.

"Who's Sewell?" said Toomey. "Sewell of 'Sewell and Oliver'?"

"Oldest partner in Big Fellow's law office," said Slip, and looked away towards the wall, again.

"Who's the Doctor?" asked Toomey.

Slip showed a sudden interest that even overmastered his loathing.

"What trail are you on now?" he asked. "The Doctor handles the regiment of thugs that the Big Fellow uses."

"Ah?" said Toomey.

"Yeah, and ah, again," said Slip, sneering. "What's up?"

"I've got to see Crawford," said Toomey.

"Bushmill will be here, before long," said Slip. "And then maybe you can go over—and maybe I can stop seeing you, for an hour or two."

As a matter of fact, it was hardly ten minutes before Bushmill drove up a car to the door of the house. He came in breathing cheer for Slip, but he fixed a cold eye, misted over with thought, upon Toomey.

"The Big Fellow wants you," he told Toomey. "Slip takes you over."

"You take him over," said Slip. "It'll turn my stomach if I have to sit with him all the way across."

Bushmill shrugged his shoulders and hooked a thumb toward the door.

"Orders," he said. "Come here a minute."

TOOMEY GOT HIS hat. The other pair murmured together in the hall and now Slip looked towards him with a smile that he tried to put out by pinching his lips together. If ever a danger signal had flown high before Toomey's eyes, it was the eager malice of that smile.

He was to be taken back to Crawford—for what?

"The chief wants me, eh?" he said to Bushmill. "And for what?"

"Even if I were a mind reader," said Bushmill, "I couldn't tell that. Slip goes over with you."

He walked back into the kitchen. Toomey heard him say: "I'm on the job today, Big Fellow. This is where you get a break."

"I'm glad to see you, Bushmill," said the voice of Lawrence Oliver.

Then Toomey went out of the house, with Slip. He had a feeling that even the smallest part of common sense should tell him to tap Slip on the head and take that automobile and depart on his own way; but he found himself getting into the front seat, pulled forward by a mechanical instinct of movement, as it were. Besides, he knew that he had given Crawford good service. That should be enough to rely on.

Once or twice—it was when they paused at intersections—he was on the point of stepping out of the car. Or perhaps it would be better to lay out Slip, first. But he could not make up his mind to action. He was like a gambler who knows the other fellow has cards up his sleeve, but who has palmed a few honors himself and therefore raises every bet, but with a dreadful uncertainty. This bet, Toomey could guess, would be the matter of life or of death.

But he found himself still in the car when it pulled up in front of the house of Crawford. The rain fell harder than ever. It beat them with many hands into the house, brushing them through the front door. It shook the door behind them, after the butler had closed it.

"This way, gentlemen," said the butler. "Mr. Crawford is expecting you."

So Toomey went down the hall with Slip moving softly behind him. He could feel laughter out of Slip; the quaver of that silent laughter ran up and down his spinal marrow. The door was opened. They stepped into the space and the soft shining of the room of Crawford. He sat as before, behind his desk, with the great Negro in the shadow of the corner.

"That's all," said the voice of Crawford, which found its place with unforgettable magic in the mind of Toomey. "That's all, Slip."

Slip disappeared. Toomey could see the malevolent flash of those bright eyes as the handsome fellow turned.

"Come here, Crusty," said Crawford, pointing to a chair at a little distance from his desk. "Now sit down. All right, George."

George, as Toomey settled into the chair, crossed the room and opened that door through which Sally had entered, on another day. It was not Sally who entered now, but the face which Toomey half expected—Crusty Mallow, with a broad smile stretching his mouth. Behind him walked a taller man, with a very long face, and very long legs, a stooping, gaunt, evil spider of a man. He was smiling also.

10

THE ONE WHO SAW THE DOCTOR

"TWO OF YOU have met before," said Crawford. "And this is Mr. Flannigan."

He waved towards Toomey, who stood up. Flannigan said nothing; his grin was enough. He pursed his lips, and then licked them clean.

"I'll take your guns, my friends," said Crawford.

Toomey walked to the desk and laid down his automatic. He laid it down with a lingering touch; but his mind had not yet been able to work out anything—and there were those cards up his sleeve, if only they might win a trick or two!

Flannigan gave up a gun, also, but Crusty Mallow said: "Say what the hell's the idea, anyway?"

"You damn fool," said Flannigan, gently, and Mallow put another automatic on the desk.

"Now sit down," said Crawford.

They sat down in a triangle, each angle of it facing the other two; Crawford presided from beyond that inner bit of tenseness.

"You have something to say," said. Crawford. "Speak up, Flannigan."

"Why, I sort of hate to talk," said Flannigan. "Damn me if I don't. The poor sucker!"

A short laugh jerked his head back. He bowed it forward again, and looked up at Toomey from beneath his brows.

"Why'd you come back, brother?" he asked. "Why didn't you step out on Slip? The poor dummy," he concluded, looking towards Crusty.

Crusty Mallow examined the clothes of Toomey with an exact eye. He said nothing, but stirred uneasily in his chair, as though he wanted to be up, and in action.

"Well," said Flannigan, "you dished Mallow out of his car, back there in town, and you rode right along into trouble. You didn't know it was trouble. You thought Crusty was out of the game. He was only through the ropes. He had to go back and get me. That's all. And now you're going to take it—and God help you. A poor dummy, Crawford, is all he is!" finished Flannigan.

"Is this the straight of it?" asked Crawford.

"Yes," said Toomey.

"Who's behind you?"

"I was hungry, asked for a handout, and got a clip on the chin from Crusty," said Toomey. "All the rest is a story you ought to know."

"That's well enough," said Crawford, "but who's behind you?"

"I'm behind myself."

Crawford raised one finger.

"Perhaps you don't understand'," he said.

"I suppose I understand," said Toomey.

"But you're not talking?"

"What's the use of that?"

"Shall we take charge of him, chief?" asked Flannigan, in a voice both whining and eager.

"He's interesting," said Crawford, with his chin on his hand, and his yellow eyes burning at Toomey. "He's so interesting—that perhaps I'll take him in hand myself."

The breath went out of Toomey; it came back slowly.

"What other name do you wear?" asked Crawford.

"Toomey is my name," he said.

"That's a fake. That sounds like a fake," said Flannigan. "You can always tell when one of these dumb birds picks an alias to—"

Crawford glanced at Flannigan, and Flannigan was silent.

"You're not a fool," said Crawford, "but still you came back here today with Slip."

"Yes," said Toomey. "I came back."

"Why did you do it? Can you tell me that? Simply playing in the dark?"

"I never play in the dark," said Toomey. "I came to get the pair of them."

"He has another gun," gasped Flannigan. "Look out, chief—"

"I don't need a gun to get you, Flannigan," said Toomey. "I can bag the pair of you without a gun."

"Go right on," said Crawford. "I know I'd be interested."

"You're going to be more interested," said Toomey. "You have a pair of double-crossing stool pigeons here, Crawford. Or did you know that?"

CRUSTY MALLOW GOT to his feet with an effortless ease, like a prize fighter rising from his stool.

"Sit down, Mallow," said Crawford.

"I'm gunna sock him on the jaw, is all I'm gunna do," said Mallow.

"Sit down—damn you—sit down!" said Flannigan.

"You ought to look at Crawford, not at me," said Toomey. "You ought to look at Crawford, Flannigan, because he's looking at you."

Flannigan, his attention thus suddenly called, twisted his head violently around towards Crawford but the leonine face of Crawford showed no change.

"You don't think the dummy has anything on me, chief, do you?" asked Flannigan.

"I'd like to sock him, once. How I'd like to sock him," said Mallow, softly.

"You could report that to Henry Sewell," said Toomey. "He and the Big Fellow would be glad to have me out of the way, I'm sure."

It seemed that a blow had struck Flannigan in the body, for both his head and his feet moved, convulsively. His small eyes flashed suddenly towards Crusty Mallow. Crusty himself had stepped back a little and laid a hand on the back of his chair. Then he came suddenly forward and stood on the edge of a long, narrow Turkish rug, that slanted across the floor towards Toomey.

"I dunno what you want a punk like that to talk for, Crawford," he exclaimed.

"I could talk to the Big Fellow myself, Mallow," said Toomey. "I could ask for Sewell and say that I wanted to see the Doctor."

The reaction of Mallow was like that of a good fighter, a gesture rather than a word.

"Ah? The Doctor?" said the booming voice of Crawford.

And there was Crusty Mallow, bent forward a little, a big automatic in his grip, while he moved the muzzle a bit from side to side, as though it were a garden hose and he were sprinkling a flower bed. It was Crawford and the Negro that he covered.

"Stick your hands up, Nigger," said Mallow. "It's the show-down, Flannigan. You sucker—you got me into this dive! Don't budge, Crawford!"

"I won't budge, young man," said Crawford, with a little more vibrancy in the gong-like sound of his voice. "You know Sewell, and you see the Doctor, do you?"

"It's another kind of a doctor that's gunna see you, Crawford," said Mallow. "Sneak up and get them guns off the desk, Flannigan. I don't feel good with only a port-side rod. It's another kind of a doctor for you, Crawford. It's the last doctor that you're gunna see. Understand? You been a big shot, but you're gunna be dead in a minute."

"Watch Toomey," said Flannigan, gliding towards the desk.

"That punk don't need watching. He'll stay put," said Crusty Mallow. "He'll stay till I'm ready for him; and I got my ideas in order about *him*, too!"

There was a wrinkle in the rug that slanted towards the chair of Toomey. He had been sitting forward, his elbows on his knees. Now he reached down to the fold of the rug, gripped it, and jerked back with all his might. With the footing snatched from beneath him, Crusty Mallow staggered, leaning far back, striving vainly to right himself. He was firing as he fell. Splinters flew from the wall behind Crawford's head. They were unregarded. Crawford, picking up one of the guns before him, pointed it calmly towards Flannigan; he left Mallow to George.

The big Negro, with a bound, struck Mallow with knees and hands. The automatic skidded across the floor. Mallow, twisting like a good wrestler, got to his hands and knees; then George took him by the hair and jerked his head to the side, and back. There was a sharp little sound like the breaking of a match. Mallow lay down on his face.

"The crazy fool!" said Flannigan, keeping his hands as high as his head. "I hope his neck's broke. My God, chief, look at the mess he wanted to get me into, will you? Nothing but a pair of hands. He didn't have no brains."

"George," said Crawford, "take Flannigan away."

A bell jangled musically in the distance, as the Negro came at the tall man.

Flannigan made no attempt to resist. He fell on his knees and tried to crawl to the desk of Crawford. Toomey bent his head so that he would not see. But he could hear the voice screeching. He heard a blow, after that. The voice stopped. George went off, trailing the limp body of Flannigan after him. The door opened before he reached it. Slip and another man came crowding in, with guns in their hands.

"Take this, please," said George, offering them Flannigan. "Then come back."

The hungry eyes of Slip went past the Negro, found Toomey, dwelt on him an instant; then he took his share of the burden.

George returned to Mallow and picked him up by the arm-pits. The head swung over on the shoulder, with a grating sound. The eyes were half open. A little red froth kept bubbling at the dips.

"Is he dead, George?" said Crawford.

"He oughta be, boss," said George. He looked at Crawford; his little face disappeared behind an enormous smile.

"See if he's dead, Toomey," said Crawford.

Toomey went to him and listened to the heart.

"He's not dead. Maybe he'll even keep on living," said Toomey.

"Maybe," said Crawford. "Give him to them, George."

So George carried the body to the door, and gave it to Slip and the other fellow. And again the eyes of Slip found Toomey, dwelt on him, hungered after him. The door was closed again by George as they withdrew.

11

TOOMEY BELIEVES

"THIS IS YOURS," said Crawford, picking up one of the automatics from the top of the desk. Toomey crossed the room and took it, the same one that he had had since he found it in Mallow's car. He held it in the flat of his hand and put it away in his clothes with one gesture. Crawford smiled.

"Why does Slip hate you?" asked Crawford.

"He's the goose in the barnyard too fat to fly, and he saw me scooting overhead. That's all," said Toomey.

"He's not fat," said Crawford.

"All your men are fat," said Toomey.

"So?"

Yes. All fat. Bushmill, too. They're all fat."

"*You* are not fat, Toomey," said Crawford. "Your body's in condition, and so is your brain. I knew that when I first laid eyes on you. And now I'm trying with all my might to believe that there's nobody behind you—that you haven't stumbled into this affair."

Toomey, waiting, lighted a cigarette, and inhaled a long breath of it. He was beginning to relax, little by little. The smoking helped him, but he felt that even relaxation might be dangerous.

"There should be no such thing as coincidence to interfere with my affairs, now," said Crawford. "But you seem to be a sheer coincidence—or a gift from God. I don't flatter people, Toomey."

"No," agreed Toomey, "I don't think you'd do much flattering."

"Then you'll believe me when I say that I can't think of a man who would have managed what you did last night."

Toomey looked straight back through the cloud of tobacco smoke.

"When Crusty and Flannigan came," said Crawford, "I wasn't convinced that you were in the wrong. But I still had a shadow of fear that in some way it all might have been a plant fixed by you and the Big Fellow. I couldn't see the reason for it, but you know that I have to be suspicious."

"I see that," said Toomey. "I see that clearly enough. They've put a net clear around you. Everybody you trust tries to double-cross you. This Flannigan and Crusty Mallow, for instance."

Crawford dropped his chin on his fist.

"You haven't shaken hands with me, Toomey, to bind the bargain," he said. "But I think that I can trust you. And with one honest man to help me, by the eternal God, I'll win in spite of them all!"

Toomey was not a girl; and yet he blushed a deep, sudden crimson. He turned towards the fire to cover the expression of his pleasure. It seemed to him that this bit of praise rewarded the dangers he had run with more than gold.

"Get some of the oldest whisky," said Crawford, "and put it on the table by the fire."

"Yes, sir," said George.

He opened a closet whose interior was full of frosty twinklings; it gave out a sweet breath like lemon blossoms.

"Nothing there is old enough," said Crawford. "Get the best in the cellar."

George left the room.

"Carry me over to that chair," ordered Crawford.

"You're heavy, and I may hurt you," said Toomey.

"Carry me over to the chair," said Crawford.

Toomey went to him and picked up the burden, inching the weight into his hands and arms. It had been light for George, but it was massive to him. He straightened. He knew he was hurting Crawford terribly, but the only sign was that of quickened breathing. So he crossed the floor with short, straining steps and eased Crawford into the chair.

Crawford looked up at the ceiling. Pain could not change his eyes, except to make them a little more yellow. Toomey arranged the rug. His hands shrank from the feel of the limbs that were under it. He heard Crawford take a deep breath, by which he judged that the pain was relaxing.

George came into the room. When he saw that Crawford had been moved, he crossed the room with great strides.

"It's all right, George," said Crawford. "He managed it pretty well. You wouldn't think that to look at him, would you? But he managed me very well."

The Negro was on his knees, rearranging the rug in careful folds. Now he turned savage eyes upon Toomey; he continued to glare while he stroked the rug.

"Fill his glass and get out of sight," said Crawford.

The Negro opened the bottle he had brought. It shimmered with the tremor of his hand. Then he retired to his corner of shadows.

"YOU WERE USEFUL tonight," said Crawford, as Toomey took the opposite chair and picked up the drink. "But you were a fool to come. What you knew was not enough to scare the truth out of 'em. It only happened to work."

"It was worth a bet," said Toomey.

"So you took the chance, faced the music, and incidentally showed me where a leak has been in my affairs. I hate leaks, Toomey. I don't mind bullets between wind and water; I'd rather sink that way than by a sneaking leak. I tell you that instead of telling you that I'm grateful."

Toomey tasted the liquor. It was very good. It seemed older and truer and more mellow than what he had drunk on the first evening.

"Want soda with it?" asked Crawford.

"I wouldn't spoil it," he said.

"And Sally wouldn't betray you," said Crawford. "A good many people find her a weakness, but she's never given a hang for any of the others. What nerve in her brain did you touch? Never mind. Don't answer. I'm not so sure that you touched a nerve."

"Sally's gone back to the Big Fellow's house," added Crawford.

"I know it," said Toomey. "She was there last night. She came to warn him."

"Ah," murmured Crawford. "What happened?"

"She came in after I had Oliver covered, in his room. I put her in a closet. Then I got Oliver out of the place before her screaming had a chance to soak through the walls and stir up the servants."

He felt the glowing eyes of Crawford on him.

"Some men would have stopped her yelling before leaving the house, Toomey," said Crawford.

"I know," agreed Toomey. "Some fellows would have tapped her over the head."

"As a matter of fact," said Crawford, "you did all of these things without telling a word to Bushmill or Slip. They had no details to give me—except what Bushmill saw from the outside of the house. He said that you were like a hunting cat, as you worked up the side of that house—up and down like a cat."

Toomey sipped his liquor and watched the fire.

"As a matter of fact," said Crawford, "if she had been another woman, would you have manhandled her?"

Toomey brushed off the backs of his hands and his mouth twisted.

"I'm not a woman tamer," he said.

"Ah," murmured Crawford. He leaned back in his chair. "I'm glad of that, my friend! I should have known. But God has put me in such a way of life that I have to think the worst of every man until the best is proven. But I'm glad. Now that she's left me, Toomey, I can tell you that I was beginning to put all my trust in that girl! She has ways about her that go to the heart of a man—but she's left me. I thought at first that I had won her over to my side. It was not that I wanted to have her as one taken from the enemy's camp, to talk against them. But this is a dreary house, Toomey. There could be my son, but he—"

His teeth clicked over an unspoken part of that last sentence. Toomey took in a breath, forcing it down, swallowing the pity that choked him. He looked straight down at his feet, unwilling to have his eyes read at that moment. And so, again, he failed to see the grin that flashed and disappeared on the face of George, as the great black man stood impassive among the shadows.

"Well," said Crawford, "I dare say that she touched your heart, also, Toomey?"

"Yes," said Toomey. "But I know her, now."

"KNOWING A WOMAN won't keep us from her. Don't hate the girl, my lad. She's beautiful, brave, and clever. Only— there's a devil in her."

"I know," said Toomey.

"This time," said Crawford, "they almost defeated me. Their hands, as you see, reach everywhere. And if the Big Fellow had succeeded in placing Flannigan and Crusty Mallow in my house, ostensibly my hired men, but really the hirelings of Lawrence Oliver—it would have been ruin. You see what I have to fight against. But ah, young man, to fight fire with fire, and to fight dirt with dirt, is a tragic business. The hands are soiled first. The soul is soiled, afterwards."

Toomey nodded.

"You have the Big Fellow, now," he said. "Can't you put on pressure and end the thing?"

"What would you have me do? Murder him?" said Crawford, apparent horror ringing out in his voice.

"No," said Toomey. "No, no!"

"But I *shall* put on pressure, as I can," said Crawford. "If I were in *their* hands, they would make short work of the business. But my way cannot be their way. You can understand that."

"Yes," said Toomey. "Yes. But by God, if you put him into my hands, I'd wring his heart out with my fingers!"

"Because there is faith in you," said Crawford, "and a belief in honesty and the ways of daylight; because you hate detestable hypocrisy and treachery. But out of a life of pain, Toomey, I have learned some trifling things about patience and forbearance. You must follow my way in this, if you will."

Toomey made a sudden gesture. They fell into a silence.

"Sally, too!" breathed Crawford.

He put back his head, and his eyes were closed, as though by pain. "Well," he said, "it's true that the Big Fellow has more money. It's better for her to be the protégée of such a fortune. She lives over there in the lodge very happily. She could live in the big house itself, of course, if she chose to. Her will is law."

The body of Toomey jerked forward. "You mean that she's his mistress?" he demanded.

Crawford's answer was a look of surprise, and then: "Why, my dear lad—I thought of course you understood that—"

Toomey started up.

"I'll get out in the air," he said.

"I'm sorry," said Crawford. "I understand, Toomey. And I'm sorry."

"It's all right," said Toomey.

"Wait one moment," said the cripple. "Once before, I asked for your hand—"

"You can have it, now," said Toomey.

He gripped the big hand of Crawford and added: "And all the blood in my body, with it!"

Then he went striding out of the room, with no other farewell.

In the hallway he caught up his hat. But before he opened the front door, he put a hand against the wall and leaned his head against it, while waves of pain ran up through his body, and seemed to issue forth into the coolness of the wall.

After a time, he was able to go out where Slip waited in the car.

"You've won a few more tricks, eh?" said Slip.

Toomey looked at him with a cold, careful regard. The bright eyes blazed hatred back at him for an instant, then suddenly widened, and turned away. So Toomey got in, and rode in silence back to the white house on the hill.

12

THE PICTURE POSTCARDS

THERE WAS ONE pause in that ride, when Slip paused in the first small town and bought a newspaper, which he tossed onto the lap of Toomey. Across the whole front page walked huge black letters and subheads more closely compacted, telling of the kidnaping of Lawrence Elliott Oliver. There was his picture on the front page, pictures of his town and country houses and his yacht on an inner page. There were articles describing the course of his life, the rise of his fortunes, the list of his benefactions.

With a sneering eye, Toomey read them over. But upon one point his eye stuck, and there his mind remained.

It appeared that Sally Moore, the former secretary of the great man, hurrying to his house with an important message, had been admitted at once, and allowed to go up to his room, but that when she tapped on the door and had no response, entering, she had found Lawrence Elliott Oliver covered by the gun of a masked bandit, a single man! The fellow had seized her and flung her into a closet, locking the door. And it was only after some moments that her screams had raised the house.

But that was where the mind of Toomey remained. It

was a *masked* man of whom the girl had told, not of Al Toomey.

He could imagine why that might be. The friends of the Big Fellow would feel that if the full information were broadcast to the public, if the toils that were thrown about the kidnapers were too numerous, Crawford might be forced to put Lawrence Oliver abruptly out of the way. That was undoubtedly the meaning, and while the agents of the Big Fellow worked on the trail, the public was to be kept in the dark.

When they got to the house on the hill, Bushmill told them that the Big Fellow was up in his room, asleep, or resting.

"And what did Crawford have to say?" asked Bushmill, curiously, his eyes travelling over the body of Toomey like an anatomist.

"We had a little chat about things in general," said Toomey.

"Crusty Mallow and Flannigan are in the soup," said Slip, "for a doublecross. Crusty's about done for. This bird's name is Al Toomey. I dunno where he comes from. He showed up Crusty and Flannigan, and he's on velvet, O.K."

"Good work," said Bushmill, to Toomey, nodding as he continued to stare. "You work fast and you work right, and nobody couldn't say any more than that."

He added: "What hell is up about the job?"

"The papers are full," said Slip. "But that don't mean nothin'."

"Not a thing," agreed Bushmill. "They gotta do their yammerin'."

"They talk about a masked man. You didn't wear a mask, Toomey, did you?" asked Slip.

"No," said Toomey.

"That's a funny break," said Bushmill. "What's biting Sally?"

"The Big Fellow's crowd wanta keep things dark for a while. That's all," suggested Slip.

Bushmill nodded, and went on: "The Big Fellow took a hard sock on the chin. I seen the punch, but I couldn't make it out. Can you?"

He took a postcard out of his pocket.

"I was given that in an envelope to bring over to him today," explained Bushmill. "He took it and stared at it, for a while. Then he went groggy. He gave a woof and a groan and went upstairs."

It was merely a postcard picture of the steamer "Carmantic," with smoke streaming out of her two funnels, and the sea knifing up sharply on her bows. The back of it was blank. It was apparently an old picture.

"I don't make anything out of it," said Slip. "Did Crawford give you this?"

"Yes," said Bushmill.

Toomey handled the card for a moment. He could remember the name of that ship, now. She had been one of the greyhounds of the ocean, twenty or thirty years before; now she was outclassed. She was a cabin steamer, perhaps.

He remembered what Crawford had said about putting pressure on the Big Fellow in his own way. And there was dangerous subtlety in Crawford. They had forced him by a lifetime of badgering to become a fox. Perhaps in some crafty manner he was putting the pressure on the Big

Fellow through this sending of the picture of the "Carman-tic."

HE WENT UPSTAIRS, knocked at the door of Lawrence Oliver, and stepped inside. The Big Fellow lay on his face, which was hugged into a pillow. That was the man to whom Sally Moore belonged, then?

"Get up," said Toomey.

"I'm resting," said the Big Fellow, his voice stifled. "Let me be alone with my thoughts. God knows I have enough to think about."

"Get up," said Toomey.

The Big Fellow turned, with a groan, and sat up on the edge of the bed. Half his face was white and half red, from the pressure of the pillow. His hair was tousled; wrinkles from the pillow were pressed into his face.

And again Toomey said to himself: "This is the man she chose—or his money!"

"It's you again, eh?" said the Big Fellow. "The rest of 'em leave me alone. What's the matter with you?"

"I wanted to look you over and see for sure what sort of a piece of beef you are," said Toomey.

The Big Fellow put out both hands in a sad gesture.

"What have I ever done to you?" he asked.

"Here's a sweater," said Toomey.

"Thanks very much. I'm not cold."

"Put that sweater on. Then come downstairs."

He heard the teeth of the Big Fellow grit, but a few moments later he came trundling down the stairs, bundled big above the hips in soft wool.

"What's the big idea?" asked Bushmill, looking on.

"I'm going to see what's under the fat—if there's anything at all," said Toomey.

Then he took the Big Fellow outside. Bushmill protested: "You ought not to show him around!"

"I'll be responsible," said Toomey, and then he ran Lawrence Elliott Oliver across country till the heavy man staggered.

He let him walk for a second wind, then ran him again until the sweat worked in rivulets down his face.

They met nothing but a few grazing cattle, for Toomey kept to the brush, or to fields secluded by high hedges.

Clambering walls, struggling through shrubbery, digging across soft places, at last they came back.

"Go upstairs, take a bath, shave and dress," said Toomey.

"I'll have a drink, first," said the Big Fellow.

"Afterwards," said Toomey.

The Big Fellow leaned a hand against the door jamb.

"You've got me now," he said. "But you don't understand. You don't know—me!"

Then he went up and took his bath, and shaved. Toomey took all the whisky into the back yard. He broke the bottles and spilled the liquor, except for one quart which he took back into the house, on second thought.

Slip had seen the last of that sad destruction from a window. He came rushing to meet Toomey at the door, and yelled; "What the devil do you think you're about, you fool?"

"Back up," said Toomey.

He put his breast against Slip and thrust him reeling into the room.

Slip stopped himself by putting a hand against the wall.

His face was colorless; his rage made him tremble and started him gasping for breath.

"If you ever put a hand on me again—if you ever touch me again—" said Slip.

"Listen," said Toomey. "You and I will have a chance to attend to one another, some day. But in the meantime, we're working on a job for Crawford. You ought to know Crawford better than I do. You ought to understand how he'll re-act if you start a civil war. But if I have much more lip out of you, I'm not going to wait for Crawford. I'm going to break you in two like a cracker."

Slip moistened his lips, started to answer, then left the room.

When the Big Fellow came down, Toomey said: "How many drinks have you had today?"

The Big Fellow had come in pale with exhaustion, now he was red. His eyes fought Toomey, but at last he said: "One."

"It was a beauty, too," said Toomey. "There's only one bottle of whisky left, now. I've smashed the others. You get a drink when I feel like pouring it for you. Come in here."

He led the way into the sitting room. There were three boxes of cigars. He put two of them under his arm. The other he opened, and counted the contents. One cigar he offered to Lawrence Oliver. "That's all you get today," he said. "You'd better smoke it an inch at a time. Don't steal another. I've counted 'em."

THEN THE DAYS of still October followed. The crimson deepened in the woods, the yellows flamed and took on orange tints, purples darkened, the browns faded. There was no noise of wind outside the house. There was silence within. Every morning, and every afternoon, Lawrence Oliver ran across country under two sweaters, with a remorseless figure at his heels. Pounds of fat melted and poured from his great body. And every day he had one cigar, every day he had two drinks of whisky—small drinks. He had to pace the floor, his hands gripped hard behind him. Two deep furrows were ploughed between his eyes. And they never spoke. The routine was established. There was no need for words.

Against this whiskyless régime, Slip and Bushmill protested with snarls, but not with words. Their relief came when, on alternate days, one of them returned to report to Crawford. They could fill themselves and their flasks, on such occasions, but neither of them dared to interfere with Toomey.

Once Toomey heard Bushmill say to Slip, when the pair were in an adjoining room; "I told the chief. He says it's funny, but let a good man have his own way. You'd think the sun rose and set on the seat of Toomey's pants, the way the chief talks!"

Other reports, and daily papers, showed that the furor over the disappearance of the Big Fellow was dying down, little by little. The news began to slide off the front page.

The second night, Toomey took his mattress back into his own room and slept on his own bed. Twice in that night, the Big Fellow screamed out, and Toomey went in and stood silently beside him, watching his gaspings and shudderings. Each night Toomey left the house for a walk. Twice, on those excursions, an owl stooped low over his head. He told himself that they would have stranger visitors than this, before the wind-up.

It was on the fourth day that another postcard was brought, this time by Slip, returning from the Crawford place. It was fresh and new enough, and it showed a perfectly harmless facade of a hotel in old Bayeux, in Normandy. It had no meaning except quaintness, to Toomey, but when the Big Fellow saw it, his eyes gradually widened until the ghosts of his mind were almost visible through those windows. He fell back in his chair, and lay limp.

Then, rousing himself, he started up and began to pace the floor until the flimsy old house quivered. He kept shaking his head, muttering to himself that "it couldn't be!"

But that night Toomey heard him constantly turning from side to side in his bed. The fear of being alone was not on the Big Fellow so much, now. He no longer seemed to think that murder was rising at him out of every shadowy corner; but after the arrival of the second postcard, he was never at ease. It was the pressure that Crawford was putting on, and Toomey wondered deeply over it. A picture of a ship, and then a picture of a quiet little hotel had been enough to eat like acid into the soul of the victim. What would the third picture be, and what its results?

It was on the eighth day that the weather turned foul. A wind came out of the northwest, a black wind that stifled the day at a stroke and began to beat the little house with its fist. In the midst of that unnatural darkness, they had to light lamps, and in the false twilight, there was a knock at the door.

Slip and Bushmill, gun in hands, went cautiously to answer that summons, while the Big Fellow sat up, his eyes suddenly bright with eager hope.

That hope darkened, when they heard Bushmill's voice call out a cheerful greeting to "Steve."

"It's you, Toomey," sang out Bushmill. "The chief wants you again."

Toomey went to the door and found a man with sandy hair and a cadaverous face, who chewed his words when he spoke them.

"I dunno what's happened, but hell's loose, and Crawford wants his ace in the pack again. Come on fast. Speed's the word!"

13

DEATH DOESN'T MATTER

THEY WENT ACROSS the country like a jag of lightning, for Toomey sat at the wheel. After two of his skid turns, Steve slid far down in his seat and half closed his eyes, and was silent. He still remained in that position when Toomey came to the house of Crawford and got out.

A light flashed on before the door, as he hurried up the path. The door opened for him; the butler bowing, standing aside, calling him: "Mr. Toomey, sir!" and then hurrying before him down the hall. When Toomey went into the big room it was to find Crawford with a gray, drawn face, and sunken eyes. His jaws were locked, and his cheeks were shadowy hollows. He sat at his desk, leaning forward on his elbows. He looked more like a lion than ever, a very old lion in the act of making a last charge.

Toomey instinctively lightened his step and moved slowly across the room. Crawford gave him no greeting in words, but held out his hand, which Toomey grasped; and Crawford, clinging with a powerful grasp, continued to stare at his mental visions, speechless.

At length he released his hold and waved Toomey to a chair by the fire. George was already swiftly setting out the chosen liquor of this favored guest, murmuring a soft greeting to Toomey as he did so.

"I've lost," said Crawford at length.

Toomey lighted a cigarette. He parted his lips to inhale the smoke more deeply, kept them parted as he blew it out again.

"I took the Big Fellow. So his friends have taken—my son!" said Crawford.

He kept on staring. He must have been there for hours, looking at his thoughts.

"I'm in the hollow of their hand," said Crawford, softly. He gave no sign of breaking down. They might grind him to nothingness, but they would never be able to snap him like a stick. "I have nothing with which I can strike back at them. I have a word from them, and the word is brief. I have till midnight, tomorrow. That's the last moment. Then they'll strike."

"Murder?" said Toomey.

"Murder? Of course not! A drunken young man will fall out of a fifth story window—or in front of a subway train—or off a bridge—or perhaps commit suicide in a fit of despondency, leaving a note blaming me for not paying his debts."

"Does he owe a lot?" asked Toomey.

"A spendthrift," said Crawford. "God gave him brains, a magnificent body, a glorious face—and no desire to use his gifts. Not yet. He's growing up, slowly. If he lives through this, perhaps *this* will bring him to his senses. But they've trapped him. And they'll kill him unless I surrender unconditionally."

*He saw Sally Moore
throwing off a coat.*

"Bluff," said Toomey. "If they kill the boy, they know that you'll finish off the Big Fellow."

"Sewell would hardly care. He'd almost as soon have the whole power and business in his own hands. He won't sacrifice too much for the sake of his partner. And he's as remorseless as a snake."

There was nothing for Toomey to say, and he said nothing.

"There is only one sword with which I can strike a blow," said Crawford. "I have nothing else, for such a case. I have only you!"

Toomey looked up, with a flash, and quickly down again.

"But I don't know how I can use you," said Crawford. "I've been thinking. Nobody else around me is of the right temper—the temper of steel that cuts steel. And how I can use you, I don't know. I've sent for you to have you here, Toomey. If a thought comes to me, whether by night or day, I want you here, to execute it. And if the thought comes,

I'll hurl you at them like a thunderbolt. I'll not regard your safety, Toomey. I have two things in the world—my son—and you. And I'll spend one for the other as, so help me God, I'd spend my son Jack for you."

Toomey stood up, staring. He picked up his drink, and immediately sat down again.

"I'm going to believe you," he said.

There was no answer.

"Lie down on that davenport and go to sleep," said Crawford. "If I have an idea, I'll waken you. George, put something over him. Turn out all the lights. The fire will be enough for me."

"Mr. Crawford," said George, in the softest of voices, "you gotta sleep, sir."

"Do as I tell you!" commanded Crawford, his voice booming.

Toomey lay down, without a word; the lights were turned out; a soft woolen throw was drawn over him. For a time he watched the firelight throw out shimmering beaches across the ceiling, or pool in golden coils, while he thought of a dead father, and of this living man. Then he went to sleep.

WHEN HE AWAKENED, he was shivering a little. The room was cold. The fire had eaten away the logs, one by one.

He sat up, and saw the dazzle of the sunlit autumn beyond the windows. Crawford had not moved at the desk, apparently, and in the corner stood George, wavering with an agony of fatigue, his face dusted over with the gray of exhaustion.

So they must have remained through the night, while

the brain of Crawford grappled with the problem, and found no answer to it.

Again he received no greeting.

The voice of Crawford, deep, throbbing, gong-like as ever, merely said: "Take him upstairs, George. Give him some decent clothes instead of those misfits. Show him a bathroom, and give him my razors to choose from. Give him breakfast, and bring him back here."

It was done.

The breakfast lived in the memory of Toomey, the butler attempting to serve him, but brushed away by the black majesty of the weary George. Next to the master, it was plain that the Negro was the voice of authority in this house.

Afterwards, he went back into the room of Crawford. It was hard for him to look at a face now ghastly; he refreshed the fire and sat facing it for hours. The middle of the day came before Crawford spoke again.

"Toomey," he said, "I've built a fairy tale that will need a wizard to make it come true. It's not a plan, but it's a dream. I'm going to tell it to you."

Toomey faced him.

"It will probably be the death of you," said Crawford. "But death doesn't matter. Not when steel cuts steel. Death doesn't matter. You're going to go in and see if you can find the man who caught my boy. Whoever did the work, the Doctor is behind the trick. You're going to go in and see him, and work yourself into his confidence, and make him employ you. You're going to win his confidence so completely that you will be assigned to the most important job he has on hand. That will be the job of guarding

Jack—till midnight. You'll do all of this in one afternoon and evening."

He smiled, faintly.

Toomey stood up and put his back to the fire—as though that heat could defend him from the chill that was invading his soul.

"Sally's described me to them," he said.

"Beginning with red hair," said Crawford. "George knows how to fit on a black wig, and he can make your eyebrows dark, too, so that none of the darkness will be on the skin."

Steel cut steel, thought Toomey. Well, he would try to prove that he was that sort of steel, but he knew that it was death that lay before him. And life was sweet—there was Sally in it—even if she belonged to another man.

"All right," said Toomey. "I'll go"

"I knew you would," answered Crawford, without the slightest note of enthusiasm. "George!"

But George was already disappearing from the room.

He came back with an assortment of wigs. It took him an hour—and every minute was beyond price—before he had finished Toomey to satisfaction. And then, in a mirror, Toomey saw his own life-battered face made over by the darkness of that hair and the strange accents of the eyebrows.

"Let me have a fast car," said Toomey. "I need to make time."

"Give him the gray car, George," said Crawford. "Here's a picture of Jack. You'll need to know the likeness, perhaps."

The photograph showed a man who might be in his early

twenties, but dissipation had pouched the eyes and loosened the mouth. He was handsome, in a dark way.

Toomey pushed back the picture.

"How's Crusty?" he asked.

"Alive," said Crawford.

"And Flannigan?"

"Eating three meals a day—but perhaps he's fatally ill!"

"I don't give a damn about Flannigan," said Toomey, "but I'd like to see Crusty live."

"You would?" asked Crawford, in surprise.

"Yes. He introduced me—to a lot of things."

"Then he's as good as cured, this moment. We'll save him, Toomey."

"That's all," said Toomey. "I'll be getting along."

He went like that, carelessly, waving his hand. He had no need of addresses. He could remember 17 Flint Street from the letter-head. There was no voice from Crawford following him, calling him back to give a last word of advice. They parted casually, and Toomey went out to the front of the house to find that Steve already was running out the machine.

14

A MAN TO SEE THE DOCTOR

IT WAS A car painted battleship gray, all neck and nose and no hind end. It growled on low and it screamed on high, and it had no springs that were perceptible; but it jumped from a standing start like a frightened dog, and the more it was let out, the closer it put its belly to the ground. Toomey was smiling before he had driven half a mile. He was almost laughing when the tall towers of the city began to lift and lift until they swarmed all around him in the sky. He twisted through the traffic jams of the center of the town like a hungry snake, and went on down to Flint Street, where big trucks were always lumbering and thundering up and down by night or by day.

There he found Number Seventeen, twelve dingy stories of it, with "Sewell and Oliver" in gilt lettering on the windows of the tenth story. On the tenth floor, in an anteroom, a stenographer wanted his name.

"John Jones," said Toomey. "I've got an appointment."

The stenographer disappeared. She came back with a well bred looking young man who frowned with concern. "I'm Mr. Sewell's secretary," he said. "I don't seem to find your name on the list of Mr. Sewell's appointments for today."

"Write it down, then," said Toomey. "It's two fifteen. Write it down for two twenty. I'm a busy man.

"Mr. Sewell is closely engaged," said the secretary, with wistful eyes. "The name again?"

"John Jones," said Toomey.

"John *Paul* Jones, perhaps?" said the secretary, venturing a smile.

"Maybe to you, punk," said Toomey.

The secretary flushed. He was a big young man, and now his coat swelled until the seams creaked.

"Go in and grab Sewell, and tell him I'm here," said Toomey sternly. "You dummy, how long d'you think I can spend in town? How long am I safe?"

It seemed that the secretary had handled people of more than one type, in this office. He hesitated for only a moment, and then disappeared. When he returned, his face was cautiously inquisitive.

"Mr. Jones, Mr. Sewell will see you," he said.

Toomey followed him through three doors, and then into a corner room with plenty of windows about it. It was crowded with tables, and the tables were crowded with papers of affairs. It was a working man's room, and plainly Sewell was the man who worked. He had on a black office coat, loose at the shoulders and big in the sleeves. A stenographer arose, pad in hand, and went out, putting down the last trail of words.

Sewell laid both his hands on the desk in front of him. He looked at Toomey with eyes too wise to be impatient. There was no color in his hair or his eyebrows or his eyes. Time had weathered his face as a glacier weathers a rock, in long, deeply cut striations. He was alert, lean as a tennis player, with a healthy color in his cheeks.

"Mr. John Jones?" he said.

"Sure," said Toomey. "Why not?"

"I've never seen you before," said Sewell.

"You've crowded by that mistake," answered Toomey. "Send this out."

He swayed his head towards the secretary.

"Who sent you to me, my friend?" said Sewell.

"Yeah, maybe I'll be your friend," said Toomey. "That depends. I haven't made promises, yet. Send out the punk."

He nodded towards the secretary again.

Henry Sewell hesitated. He looked down at his hands on the desk, considered the way the blue veins were traced on the back of them, and then said: "All right, Tom."

The secretary was crimson. He withdrew in haste.

Toomey pulled up a chair, sat down, and took out a package of cigarettes.

"Smoking, brother?" he asked. Sewell shook his head.

"You can breathe better," said Toomey, "when mugs like that are out of the way. Looks like a collar ad, don't he? Looks like a damn soap or collar ad. I'll bet he ain't got halitosis."

He laughed, loudly, lighted a cigarette, and snapped the match against the wall.

"Now the reason for your call, Mr. Jones?" said Sewell.

Toomey leaned forward through a cloud of smoke, saying: "You don't get me brother. Flannigan told me to drop in. That mean anything?"

He leaned back again, triumphantly.

"FLANNIGAN?" SAID SEWELL, narrowing his eyes to concentrate his memory. "Flannigan? What Flannigan?"

"Aw, hell, I forgot," said Toomey. "I was to see you and ask for the Doctor. Is that the gag? Show me to the Doctor, unless you're him."

Still Sewell hesitated, looking at the face of Toomey, struggling to read him. At last he shrugged his shoulders and pressed a button. The secretary appeared.

"Show Mr. Jones into Room 1019," said he.

Toomey stood up.

"Kind of cramped for space, eh?" he said, looking around. "Being a president must be a hell of a job."

He went out through the door that the secretary had opened. They went down the hall to a room without glass on the door, and the number "1019" in neat brass letters. The secretary knocked twice, paused, and knocked three times in rapid succession.

"High-headed, ain't you?" said Toomey.

The secretary grew white in the hollow of each cheek. He doubled his fists and forced them open again. He said nothing.

"You know what you look like to me?" said Toomey. "You look like a lousy usher in a lousy movie palace, is what you look like to me. You need a uniform, is all."

The door was opened a little.

"Who's there?" said a voice.

"Partridge—with a client for the Doctor."

"Well, bring him in."

The door opened wide.

Toomey went into a small room past a heavy chunk of a man with cauliflower ears.

"Who is this?" asked the ex-pugilist.

"Jerry, his name is John Jones—and damn him!" said the secretary, and closed the door.

Jerry looked at Toomey, and grinned. Toomey made a motion of throwing something away over his shoulder, and grinned back.

"What's the racket, kid?" said Jerry.

"Are you the Doctor?"

"No."

"Then can the 'kid' stuff," said Toomey, frowning. "Tell the Doctor I'm here, and I'm not waiting. I'm in a hurry."

He sat down, and looked gloomily at the end of his cigarette.

"What pen did *you* get famous in?" said Jerry, sourly.

Toomey continued to look at the end of his cigarette.

"Maybe you're the mayor's doorman, or something," said Jerry, thoughtfully.

Toomey stood up.

"Flannigan was a fool. I'm gonna tell him so," said Toomey. "And you tell the Doctor that a guy like me dropped in and said that your whole crowd could go to hell."

"Wait a minute, mug," said Jerry. "I dunno—but wait a minute, will you?"

He tapped on an inner door, then entered, returned almost at once.

"Go on," said Jerry.

Toomey went inside. Except for the one small window, the room looked like the inside of a vault. It was full of shelves to the ceiling. A strong gust of wind could have blown a million sheets of paper into a white snowstorm.

There was a desk heaped with papers, also, and at the desk a starved little man pinched at the temples and behind the mouth. He had weary eyes and seemed always to be smiling.

"You're John Jones?" he said.

Toomey waited till the door had closed behind him. He put a fist on the edge of the desk and leaned over it a little. He looked straight into the weary eyes of the Doctor.

"You're the Doctor, are you?" he said.

"That's what I'm called."

"You know Flannigan?"

"Yes."

"What's his real first name?"

"Mackay," said the Doctor.

Toomey heaved a breath, as of relief.

"All right," he said. "I just wanted to know."

He took a chair and settled down low in it.

"KIND OF CRAMPED in here, ain't you?" he said.

"Well, Jones, what's the name for a starter?" said the Doctor.

Toomey scowled.

"Didn't Flannigan tip you off?" he said.

"No."

"He didn't send you a word?"

"No. Not a word."

"To hell with Flannigan, then," said Toomey. "Maybe he thinks that I'm a sucker to be kicked around. Is that what he thinks?"

He sat up on the edge of his chair.

"Maybe it wouldn't be safe to write about you—send it through the mails," said the Doctor.

Toomey sighed again.

"That's right. I didn't think of that," he said. "All right, brother. Wiston. That's the name."

The Doctor glanced askance. "Wiston?" he said.

"You know. Casey Wiston," whispered Toomey. He sat back again, smiling, waiting for recognition.

"Or maybe you don't know me? Maybe you never heard the name? Maybe I never crossed your mind?"

"You've been in, somewhere?" said the Doctor.

"Yeah, a little while."

"In what?"

Toomey looked out the window.

"What was ahead of you?" asked the Doctor.

Toomey framed his mouth with one hand and said: "Salt Creek."

"Ah?" said the Doctor. He seemed to grow young. He smiled in reality, instead of in mere appearance. "That was it, eh? And had you done time before?"

"Nine years and seven months. Good behavior," said Toomey and shrugged his shoulders.

"For what?"

Toomey held out his hand and pulled in the forefinger, slowly.

"In the death house for what?"

Toomey held up three fingers. "They came piling in on me," he said.

The Doctor smiled again. "So Flannigan sent you? How does Flannigan look to you, these days?"

"More like a two-legged spider. That's all. He's the same."

"When did you talk with him?"

"Three days ago."

"Where?"

"This side of heaven," said Toomey.

"That's the only place you'll see him again," said the Doctor.

Toomey slid forward, again, to the edge of his chair, and made a quick movement with his hand. The gun came out in the flat of it.

"You double-crossing punk, if I go, you go with me," he said.

The Doctor actually leaned back and laughed, though his laughter made no sound.

"I meant Flannigan," said the Doctor. "He's disappeared. And when a Flannigan disappears, he generally stays sunk the rest of time."

"Oh, Flannigan? Oh, I don't give a damn about him," said Toomey. "I thought you meant—well, it's all right. Who tied Flannigan?"

"I don't know. Perhaps it was a fellow named Crawford."

"Crawford?" said Toomey. "I knew a bird, called Crawford. Crawley, the boys used to call him. He was a snowbird, and he had the prison shakes. How did he get Flannigan?"

The Doctor shrugged his shoulders.

"We must be meaning different people. Wiston, what do you want?"

"Money," said Toomey, "and a job."

"What kind of money?"

"Big. I ain't got long. I'm no sucker, and I know that I ain't got long. While I last, I wanta take it big. That's all."

"Maybe you'll have quite a while, if you use your head," said the Doctor. "Where did you learn that gun trick?"

"Not in jail," said Toomey, grinning.

"How big will you go?" said the Doctor.

"How big is there?" asked Toomey.

"I don't know you," said the Doctor.

"Oh, you don't know me, eh?" said Toomey, leaning forward to rise. "I don't know you, either. To hell with you!" he added, standing up.

"You're acting like a fool," said the Doctor. "Sit down. I'm going to do business with you."

"Maybe you are. That's what *you* say," said Toomey.

"You're a new card, but I'm going to play you big," said the Doctor. "I'm going to play you like four of a kind."

"What stakes?"

"Twenty dollars a day," said the Doctor, "for a start," he added.

"That's fifty days to make a grand. If I took a drink, it wouldn't keep me in booze," said Toomey. "You don't understand, Doctor."

"I'll give you," said the Doctor, "five hundred dollars down. And after that—you get what you earn. I'm taking a chance, but I need a man, and I think you're the fellow. Sit down. I'm going to write you a note. Do you ever talk soft?"

"Like a lady, Doctor," said Toomey, and sat down again. The Doctor was smiling.

15

THE RESTRAINERS

WHEN TOOMEY LEFT, he paused at the door and jabbed a finger in the direction of Jerry.

"If I was you, Doctor," said Toomey, "I wouldn't have a punk like this hangin' around in the waitin' room. Somebody'll step on him, some day, and make a hell of a mess all over."

"Oh, he's all right," said the Doctor, and the whisper of his soundless laughter followed Toomey out the door.

"The day'll come," said Jerry, through his teeth. "The day'll come when I sock you, and you'll turn over three times before you hit the pavement. You ain't gunna bust. You're gunna splash!"

Toomey went down to his car, with one hand busily smoothing his face, for there were new lines worked into it. When he smiled, he could feel the muscles automatically pulling to one side. If he merely thought of words, his lower jaw thrust out a little.

He drove to the address that had been given to him with the Doctor's speech of instruction flowing through his mind.

"Young friend of ours needs keeping," the Doctor had said, "and he needs to be soothed. There's a woman on the job to do the soothing. Also he has to be restrained, and Ramsey Tay is on the job restraining him. But he needs a lot of restraining, and Ramsey can't last out twenty-four hours a day. He'll need help and you're going to help him."

"How'd you restrain this friend? With a sock in the eye?" asked Toomey, cheerfully.

"You mustn't spoil his face," said the Doctor, with a sigh. "You've got to be tactful."

"That's poison," said Toomey.

"Poison, Wiston? Poison?" murmured the Doctor, reflectively. "When I go to hell, I'm glad I won't be near the sons of the rich men, but I want to be close enough to hear them yell."

With all of this in mind, Toomey went on to the address, a huge cliff dwelling of an apartment house. He went up to the penthouse, where a Japanese with a knife-scar across his yellow face left him standing in the hall and took in his note to Gloria Bender. Her cheerful voice called him in.

He went into a long, low-ceilinged room with old hunting prints on the walls and a smoking stand by every chair. Gloria said "hello" to him; she was re-reading the note from the Doctor and pulling down her dress around the hips as she came towards him. Gloria was one of these platinum girls. Her hair was platinum and her eyes were platinum, too, so that her face was distinguished by the thin, dark lines of her eyebrows and the red of her lipstick. She finished reading the note and gave Toomey her hand, and a good, stiff look. Then she melted her eyes at him.

"Ramsey Tay will be *so* glad," said Gloria. "I'm glad, too. Many hands make light work, and what a work it is!"

She sat him down and brought him a drink. He took whiskey straight, which seemed to worry her.

"The bubbles tickle my throat. I got a terrible sensitive throat," said Toomey, gravely. "That's why I take the hooch straight."

Suddenly she began to laugh. "You're all right, Wiston," she said.

"When I get the right steer, I am," said Toomey.

A big man came softly through a pair of doors. His shoulders were so wide and so stooped, his neck was so long and red, his face was so furrowed, that he looked like a giant condor.

"Ramsey, here's a little helper for you," said Gloria. "How's the brat?"

"He's doin' a flop," said Ramsey Tay.

"Meet Mr. Wiston, Mr. Tay," said Gloria.

They shook hands.

"How long you out, kid?" asked Ramsey Tay.

Toomey looked savagely at Gloria. "Did the Doctor tip you guys off?" he demanded.

She laughed back at him. "Ramsey's a mind reader, that's all."

"Yeah? A mind reader, is he?" said Toomey. "Yeah?"

"Quit it," said Gloria.

"What were things like?" said Ramsey.

"They were giving me everything I wanted," said Toomey. "Giggle water, and everything."

"Ah?" said Ramsey. He explained to Gloria, softly: "Death house!"

"My God!" said Gloria, jumping to her feet.

"Aw, give me a drink, and lay off, will you?" said Ramsey Tay.

She went to get it.

"Get a stay or something?" asked Ramsey Tay.

"Yeah. I got a stay, all right. A hell of a fine stay I got," said Toomey. He darkened his face. "What the hell d'you wanta know so much for?" he asked. "I don't know you, Tay."

"That's all right, too," said Tay. "You wanta learn when you're among friends, is all."

GLORIA BROUGHT TAY his drink, a stiff one, and let the soda foam and hiss into it until he raised a finger. He did not thank her, but waved the glass at Toomey.

"Here's to a wet life, kid," said Tay.

"In your eye," said Toomey, and sipped his drink.

Gloria came back and sat with them. "You better do a flop yourself, Ramsey. Wiston'll take care of him, if he wakes up."

"Yeah, and why not?" said Ramsey Tay. "Have you got a rapper with you, kid?"

"I got this," said Toomey, and he made that flat-of-the-hand pass which caused the automatic to come in view and disappear again.

"See that?" said Ramsey Tay to the girl.

She said nothing, but pushed herself back in her chair and narrowed her eyes. She had lost color and looked nauseated.

"You better have this little honey, too," said Tay. "The sucker's violent, sometimes, and we can't afford to break the skin. Know how to use it?"

He worked an elastic sling off his wrist; a heavy little

leather bag was attached to it. Toomey fitted the thing on his right wrist and then, with a flick, threw the sandbag down between the tips of his fingers. He held it there and made a slapping motion through the air.

"See that, Gloria?" said Ramsey Tay. "The kid knows his stuff. I'm gunna be in the next room. Gimme a buzz if you need me. My God, I'm glad to hand you that louse for a while, Wiston."

He went into the next room and closed the door with a loud jar.

"Kind of a card, ain't he?" said Toomey to the girl.

She kept on watching him, nodding absently in answer to his question.

"I've seen you somewhere, Wiston," she said. "Where was it?"

"Chicago," suggested Toomey.

"Maybe." But she shook her head. "Seems almost as though I could see you—a moving picture, too. Somewhere, in action, raising the devil."

Toomey seemed to consider, deeply.

"Maybe you was in that hop-joint in San Francisco," he said, "when the two Chinks went nuts and—"

"I never was in 'Frisco. That's out," she said. "But Chinks—that means something to me."

"Have a drink, and you'll remember," said Toomey.

She leaned and took the glass from his hand, swallowed most of what remained, and made a face of disgusted satisfaction as the burn and the horror of the stuff went down her throat. She took the bottle from the table, and put it on the floor within reach of Toomey.

"Be at home," she said.

"Maybe I'd know you," said Toomey. "Changed your color, lately?"

"Couple—three years ago," she said. "It's good, eh?"

"It's a honey," said Toomey.

"I've got the eyes for it," she explained. "It's just a fashion with a lot of the girls, but I've got the eyes for it. That's the difference."

"It's a honey," said Toomey. "That's what it is. Been mama here for a long time?"

"Just doing a short stretch," said Gloria. "I'm about done. I'm the one that picked up the brat."

"You could pick him up," said Toomey, "You're right in your three-year-old form."

"I'm all right on a beach," said Gloria. "That's where I work the best. When I come up out of the water, the boys come with me."

"Yeah, I can see that," said Toomey.

"But I don't drape so well," said Gloria. "You can't have any hips, these days."

"That's a hell of a break," said Toomey.

"Dieting takes it off my face," said Gloria, sadly. "I've skipped rope and rolled and everything. It's no good. The damned hips are still there. It's been getting so the boys can't see anything else. One of 'em says he's going to write a song and call it the 'Seashore Blues' and put me back on the stage to sing it."

"Been on the stage, Gloria?"

"I've picked it up and strutted it around a bit," said Gloria. "I've got a small time voice and big time legs. But they don't want hips any more in the show business."

"That's the hell of it," said Toomey. She got up and pulled

her dress tight. "I'm all right coming or going, but it's the profile that beats me, see?" said Gloria. "The damned profile doesn't drape so well, and that's all the boys can see."

"What they want now are two-year-olds," said Toomey.

She filled his glass, drank a little from it, and handed it back to him. She settled back in the chair and laughed and shook her head.

"I've had my day," said Gloria, frankly, "and maybe I'll have it again. I don't cry. I just wait for the damn fashion to change."

There was a noise in the room to the left.

Gloria said: "Hello! He's up again. Better go keep him from doing a nosedive out the window!"

16

WHILE THE RESTRAINERS SLEPT

TOOMEY TASTED HIS whiskey again and went into the room from which Ramsey Tay had first appeared. A big young man strode up and down the floor in slippers and a dressing gown. It was Jack Crawford. He looked like a large edition of his father with less of shoulders and brow. But the chief difference lay in the looseness of the mouth. It could be puckered, but it could never be firm.

He gave Toomey hardly a glance, saying: "What d'you want?"

"I'm the new assistant janitor," said Toomey, "in case anything has to be moved. I may not look big to you, brother, but I can handle a big weight."

He spoke loudly, his face turned towards the door of the living room.

Then he winked and made a gesture at Crawford. He reached that puzzled gentleman and said rapidly: "I'm with you on the inside, from the outside. Put your money on me. But we've got to sell the idea of me to them, in the first place. Stage a ruction. I'll pretend to slap you with this sandbag. Do a flop. After that, they'll trust me with the watch and chain."

A gleam of hope shone in the eyes of Jack Crawford.

Suddenly he shouted: "You're another of those hired stage hands, are you? I'm going to spoil this show for you. I'm going to break your damned neck."

He took Toomey by the collar of his shirt and collar of his coat and shook him.

"You damn fool, if you want it, take it!" yelled Toomey, and thudded the sandbag against the palm of his hand. "Drop, you dummy, drop!" he added in a whisper as Gloria screamed in the living room.

Crawford dropped heavily on his side, winked at Toomey, turned over on his face and stretched his arms above his head. Big Ramsey Tay burst into the room without collar or coat; Gloria came like a rustling wind behind him.

Toomey walked up and down.

"The poor egg tried to choke me, is all," he said. "I pulled his cork."

"You've killed him!" gasped Gloria.

"Only half," said Toomey. "I know my stuff, beautiful."

Tay, without a word, had kneeled and slipped his hand under the heart of the fallen man.

Then he looked up and nodded, with a sigh of relief.

"Ticker's still going," he agreed. "Heave him onto the bed with me, will you?"

"Sure," said Toomey, "but why not let him come to where he is? Why all the baby stuff?"

Gloria came up and kicked the body, lightly.

"Let him come to on the floor. That's where he belongs, the punk!" she said, savagely.

"All right, all right," said Ramsey Tay. "I don't give a damn. You certainly socked him, kid. But go easy, will you?"

"I don't mind his lip," said Toomey, "but if he tries to handle me again, I'll bust him. I used to break dogs in Alaska," he added, with a grin.

The other two went out. Jack Crawford turned his head.

"That was Gloria that gave me the boot?" he whispered.

Toomey nodded. "She's a sweet thing," he said. He sat on his heels beside Crawford. "Have you got any ideas?" he asked. "About where you're going and how you're getting there?"

"You'll be night watch, and we'll simply walk out," said Crawford. "My God—when I'm once on the loose again—some of them are going to sweat in hell! What's your name?"

"Wiston."

"Wiston, you're from my father?"

"Yes."

"How did he manage to get you in here?"

"His brains, and my luck," said Toomey.

He added: "Start groaning. You're waking up, and you're cursing me. You're staggering back to your bed and dropping on it. A lot of groaning and damning."

IT WAS DONE. Toomey went to the windows, closed and locked them, and returned to the door of the living room, which he held ajar.

"Listen, punk," he said loudly. "They been handling you with velvet. But I'm on the job now. If I hear you make one of them windows squeak, I'm gunna come in and sock you. I'll sock you twice, the next time—once to put you to sleep, and once when you wake up again. The third time, you get it three times in a row. You been wrapped up like antique furniture, but I'm gunna handle you like a steamer trunk."

A groan answered him.

He stepped into the living room and slammed the door behind him. Gloria was watching him with large, frightened eyes of delight.

"A cinch," said Toomey. "Nothin' to it!" He flattened out his hand and made a slow gesture in the air, away from him. "Nothin' to it at all."

"How's the brat?" said the voice of Ramsey Tay from the next room.

"Kind of sick, with a lump on his bean. That's all," said Toomey.

"All right. Close my door. I'm gunna sleep about a thousand hours."

Toomey closed the door.

"And me," said Gloria, yawning and stretching up her beautiful round arms. "But I've gotta tell you first that I could love you, you big yegg. I could love you for socking him. I could love that hammered iron mug of yours, too."

"I'll tell you something you wouldn't believe," said Toomey, seriously. "I was a good looking kid, too. Yeah, funny—ain't it? I was a good looking kid. They used to say that: 'The kid's a good looking kid.' The women used to say that. I used to look at myself in the mirror, and I was a good looking kid. Then I started kicking around. But what the hell? I started kicking around, and all that. But I used to be a good looking kid. You wouldn't believe it."

"You look good to me, now," said Gloria, putting her chin on her hand, and watching him with lazy eyes. "You look good to me because you socked him. You're a mean little mug, aren't you?"

"Oh, I don't know," said Toomey. "I'm five feet ten, about."

"Yeah, about," said she.

"You take the average," said Toomey, "it's not more'n five six or seven, or something like that."

"Yeah, something like that," said Gloria.

"Quit it," said Toomey.

"All right, handsome," said Gloria. "Listen."

"I'm listening," said Toomey.

"This is all going to be finished, pretty soon, since we've got you on the job," said Gloria. "And then I'm gunna be full of rocks. And away down south there's sun and palm trees and beaches and gin and everything. Could you love a nice girl, even if she has hips?"

"Listen, Gloria," said Toomey, "you're only in your three-year-old form, is all. Don't let them kid you. The brats don't know nothing. You're only in your three-year-old form."

"You're a mean little mug," said Gloria. "Gee, what a mean little mug you are. I could love you, is what I mean. Gimme a drink, Wiston. What's your first name? No; I want it out of your glass. It tastes better, that way."

HE FILLED THE glass.

"Mick is my first name," he said.

"Irish, too, eh?" said Gloria. "That's not so good with me, but what do I care? It takes all kinds of things to make a life, and what a life you'd make, honey."

She locked her hands behind her head. He held the glass to her lips. She tasted the whiskey, shuddered, smiled at him, tasted it again. He raised the glass and looked at her through the liquor, and smiled before he drank.

"Is that all?" said Gloria.

He leaned over her. Then he paused.

"Give me a hand, Mick."

He helped her up, and took her to the entrance.

"I'm down the hall, two doors," she said. She smiled at him. "If you want anything—tell Togo. He's a good cook. You'll be eating, before long. I wish I'd be there to pour your coffee, Mick, but I'm corked."

Toomey went back into the living room, crossed to the fireplace, and spat into the fire. He took a drink of water and scrubbed his lips with his handkerchief. He went up and down the room, cursing in a whisper.

After a time, the day darkened. He found a bell, rang it, and ordered chops and fried potatoes from Togo. He ate them in the thick gloom of the twilight. Afterwards, he turned on one floor lamp.

He went down the hall and opened the door of Gloria's room. An exquisite fragrance, thin and chill and moonlight, came to him. She was lying face down, arms thrown wide. He closed the door and returned to the room of Ramsey Tay. He was sleeping also; his snores were like so many groans. Then Toomey went again to young Jack Crawford and found him dressed, sitting on the edge of a chair like a football player listening to the coach between halfs. Toomey beckoned to him.

"There's only the Jap," said Toomey. "Are you ready? It's dark now, and there's only the Jap."

"Have you got an extra gun?" said Crawford.

"None of that stuff. I haven't an extra one, anyway."

"We may need it," said Crawford.

"Come on," said Toomey.

They left the living room, went down one flight of stairs,

and took the elevator the rest of the way to the street. Toomey's car was parked nearby. It was raining, but only a mist. The seat was wet. They did not waste time to dry it or to raise the top of the machine, but settled into place and drove off.

"We've got maybe an hour or so, and maybe we've only got ten minutes," said Toomey. "As soon as one of 'em wakes up—and Tay looks like a light sleeper—the telephone wilt start spreadeagling a warning. We have to travel. Sit tight and watch the corners."

"Step on it!" said Crawford. "Oh, to get my hands on Tay! Step on it!"

So Toomey stepped.

17

A MISSION FOR TOOMEY

THEY WENT OUT of town with the slow pulse of the traffic, Jack Crawford sitting low in the car, his coat collar turned up about his face as though he feared to be recognized. He was silent until the mass of cars thinned on the road beyond the city limits, and then his voice came to him again in growling bursts.

Chiefly he talked about Ramsey Tay. He wanted to get his hands on Tay's throat. And he spoke of Gloria, too. He wanted to get his thumbs on her windpipe!

Toomey listened in quiet disgust, murmuring short answers. It seemed clear to him that no matter what life had done to Crawford, such a son was the worst curse of all.

"Now I get hell from the old man," said Jack Crawford, wincing deeper into his seat at the thought. "But I'll take it. I'll take anything, so long as he'll heel me to get back at Tay and Gloria. Smart old codger, eh? Look at the gang of beaks and talons he keeps around him. You're not the dullest of the lot, brother!"

Toomey said nothing. Every word from young Crawford put his teeth on edge. He was glad when the big gray car slid to a halt under the dripping trees before the house of Crawford. It had hardly paused when the front door flew open and the butler came at a run his coat tails flaring out behind him so that he looked like a great bird.

Then he stood bowing before Jack Crawford, looking anxiously into his face, hoping that all was well with him.

"Sure," said Jack. "I'm fit as a fiddle. Lead me to the chief."

When they got into the house, Toomey would have lingered behind, but young Crawford gripped his arm and dragged him on.

"You've got to be with me when the old boy slams me with the first few volleys," said Jack.

That was why they went into the room together and saw Crawford still behind his desk. It seemed to Toomey that he must have remained exactly so during all of these hours. His face was a little more deeply thumbed with shadows, his eyes a little more brilliantly yellow as they shone out of the dark hollows beneath his brows.

He merely said: "Come to call on me, Jack?" And when Jack started striding towards him, Crawford waved him aside and called Toomey. With his enormous hand, he gripped the lean fingers of Toomey and looked up into the face of the younger man with what seemed to Toomey an odd mixture of curiosity and surprise, rather than actual gratitude. It was as though he were striving to use an unguarded moment to penetrate more deeply into Toomey's mind.

He said, simply: "It was through Sewell and the Doctor that you got to him?"

"Yes," said Toomey.

"No other man in the world," said Crawford, slowly, "could have fooled them both." He released the hand of Toomey and said: "Go to your room, Jack. I'll see you later."

Jack slunk out, pausing only an instant at the door, as though he yearned to speak, before he disappeared. And Toomey was aware of the face of George peering at him out of the corner shadows with a brow contorted by wonder and something akin to fear.

It was rather a shock to Toomey. He had expected a warmer demonstration of joy when he brought Jack home; instead, people were looking at him as though he were a strange and perhaps a sinister monster.

He went over to a deep chair near the fire.

"Tired?" said Crawford.

"A little jumpy, just now," said Toomey. "I'll be all right."

"A drink?" asked Crawford.

Toomey nodded. George was already bringing the tray. It gave out one faint chime as the Negro put it gently on the side table. He filled the glass and then took his place behind the chair of the guest. To Toomey it was very strange; he had a feeling that it was the first time in years that George had left his post near his master to stand for the services of another man. And a vein of warmth ran through the heart of Toomey. This was a silent compliment, but the greatest that the house could pay.

HE SIPPED AT the glass which George had filled, and then lowered his eyes to observe the wash of the liquid from side to side, leaving a thick film of oil upon the glass. His hand was shaking, and the sight of that tremor amazed him.

"Do I go back to the Big Fellow?" he said.

"There's a greater thing that I'd ask you to do," said

Crawford. "But you're tired. You need to rest. You're very tired, Toomey."

"Tired, but not so very tired," said Toomey. "What's the new job?"

"We've just discovered," said Crawford, "that Sally Moore, besides being a charming girl, is a very adroit thief."

"Thief?" said Toomey.

"When she left the house, her hands were well filled," answered Crawford.

Toomey stared at him. With an exact remembrance, he drew in every line of her face again. Then, over the house, he heard a dull thundering that developed into the roar of an airplane motor. It was shut off; something whistled through the air not far off.

"The airplane," nodded Crawford, and he added, with a sigh: "They hunt me by air, and they hunt me by land. I have to protect myself as well as I can, Toomey. Yes, pretty Sally Moore is a thief and a very deft one. Oh, she filled her hands well enough when she left my house. God forgive her," he added, murmuring and shaking his great head. "God forgive her!"

"It doesn't sound like her," said Toomey. There was a coldness about his heart like homesickness, as he spoke. "I could think of her using a gun, in a pinch; I can't think of her as being a sneak thief."

Crawford was silent. The great black hand of George stole out past Toomey, lifted the decanter, and filled his glass again.

"What do you want me to do?" snapped Toomey, suddenly. For a sort of despair had come over him, hardening him to steel. "Steel cut steel," he had once heard Crawford say; and that was how he felt now.

"I want you to bring her back here to the house," said Crawford. "I want you to get her from the cottage on the Big Fellow's estate and bring her back here, till we can persuade her to return what she took. It was not money, Toomey. No, but it was a thing of a vast—sentimental— value to me. She knew that I would pay more than money for it. And therefore she writes a letter to me: 'Dear Mr. Crawford, I understand, now, what it means. And you shall have it back when the time suits me, and the Big Fellow goes free.'"

"The Big Fellow!" said Toomey, with a start.

He lapsed back into the chair, muttering: "She loves him, Crawford."

"She loves his money. He has enough hard cash to be worth love, my friend—love from that sort of a woman, at least!"

Toomey stood up.

"I don't want to talk about her," he said.

"I'm sorry," said the voice of Crawford, lowered to a gentle booming. "I know you have a feeling about her, and that was why I mentioned the thing to you.

"I thought you'd rather try to persuade her away from her house, than to have her handled roughly, as my other men might have to do. If they can get at her at all," he added. "The place is guarded, of course. The men of Lawrence Oliver are sure to be patrolling."

Toomey began to pace the rug, and with every turn he made, he felt the red-stained eyes of George following him with that same peculiar glance of bewilderment, that same vain effort to penetrate through a disguise, as it were.

"Once you got her here, what would you do to her?" asked Toomey.

"What would I do to her? Do you think that I'd torment her, Toomey? No, no, my lad! I'd simply keep her here for a few days and try to persuade her. That's all that I could do. You can see that. Or do you lose trust in me?"

Toomey went to the window and pressed close to the glass. Something suffocated him; he wanted air. Outside, he could see that the rain clouds had cleared from the sky, and the haze of the autumn night was a luminous moon-mist.

"Well," he said, "I suppose I'll try to do it. I'll try tonight to get the thing over with."

"NO ONE BUT you could do it—in the proper way," said Crawford. "It would be force, if others tried it. And we don't want force. Whatever else Sally may be, she's a charming thing."

"Aye," said Toomey. An oath came rumbling up against his teeth and was checked there. "And when you have her here—there'll be no harm come to her, Crawford?"

"No, Toomey. I think you have that much faith in me."

Toomey went from the window across the room, in his sudden way, and put both hands on the edge of Crawford's desk.

"I have faith in you," he said. "But I'll tell you this; if I thought a hand were to be laid on her, I'd find a way to cut your heart out."

The yellow eyes of Crawford raised to him; the stern lips of Crawford altered to a smile.

Toomey shook his head.

"I'm sorry I said that," he muttered. "But all at once something went over me. The ice worms began to crawl up my spine. I'm sorry!"

Then he added: "I'll start now. I want to get it over with."

"You want to see her, Toomey, as much as you want to help me," declared Crawford. "And if you manage to get to her, she'll find a way to work on your heart. I never would risk a lesser man with her. She's a crucible that melts the resolution of a man, even if it's like yours, the sort of steel that cuts steel. How it will turn out, I don't know; but if you have faith in me, I have a blind trust in you. Now go."

So Toomey went back to the long, gray car, and slid into the driver's seat; then through the dimness of the moon-mist he drove with furious speed until he was near the place of Lawrence Elliott Oliver.

Into the woods he turned down a blind little forest lane, and left the machine, and walked on rapidly until he came to the high stone wall that fenced in the estate of the Big Fellow. He climbed it. There were iron spikes in a ridge along the top; he had to use care with hands and knees to surmount it, and drop down on the farther side.

In that enemy's country he paused to take note. Few lights gleamed from the great house; only one window glimmered faintly in the cottage face. Through the brush he went carefully around it.

Another window shone at the rear, and when he approached it, he saw two men playing cards at a kitchen table. What was plainly the bulge of a gun showed through the coat of one whose back was towards the window, and the other had the seamed face of a ruffian.

Beyond doubt the cottage was being well guarded.

He returned to the front and looked through that window, after he had rubbed away the mist from a lower corner of the pane. The peephole showed him a small living room with a hooded fireplace opposite him, some big, comfortable chairs, and Sally Moore throwing off a coat whose nap gleamed with the mist of the outdoors.

18

TOOMEY IS TEMPTED

SHE LEFT THE room, throwing the coat over her arm. Toomey, as the door closed behind her, tried the window, and, finding that it was not latched, worked the sash up smoothly, little by little. He could step over the sill easily then. So he pushed down the window behind him. It shuddered from side to side enough to make a small groaning sound that put him more tensely on the alert; but there was no quick footfall of inquiry after the noise.

So he stood by the fire to wait. Fear and something that was like fear were taking hold of his throat. He set his jaw still harder until all his nerves were soothed again. It was a moment later that he heard heels tapping, then the whisper of an opening door that set a window curtain trembling. Sally came in with both hands raised to lift the hat from her head. That was how she stood before him, with the hands still for a moment at her head and her body shrinking small and away from him. She had on a tawny red tweed coat and skirt, and heavy walking shoes. Her hat was sprinkled with the bright splash of drops.

"There's nothing like a bit of wind and rain to blow the city out of the head and the country freshness into the face, eh, Sally?" he said.

She went on taking off her hat and staring at him; then she turned her frightened eyes toward the door that opened into the back of the house.

"Call 'em if you want to," said Toomey. "I've seen that pair of mugs. They look like business."

She put the hat down. Toomey, taking a chair, lighted a cigarette and now she stood by the fire and began to mold her hair with both hands. She had on a jacket that flared out slightly over the hips in the way that only a slender woman can endure. The white of a blouse flowed about her brown throat and over her breast.

Toomey could look at her no longer. He could feel his face growing cold, and his heart was rattling like cartwheels over a log bridge.

"Unless you're going to call the thugs," said Toomey, "sit down and talk to me."

Instead, she picked up the poker and poked with it at the fire until he saw that she was working blindly.

At last she sat down, but she kept her head turned away from him as though the fire offered the more important face. The silence moved on from moment to moment until they could hear the ticking of an old grandfather's clock that stood in a corner of the room; it struck out the seconds with a faintly singing chime.

"Are you going to talk to me?" said Toomey.

She stood up, suddenly, and straightened her jacket with a little tug; and at last she looked at him directly.

"If I call them, you can't get out the door or the window in time," she said.

"Probably not," said Toomey.

"You fooled the Doctor and Sewell," she said. "I've

been talking on the telephone, and I know. You've taken Jack Crawford away. What have you come to do to me, Toomey?"

"I've come to look at you," said Toomey, and forthwith he looked.

She turned away and went toward the door.

"Please come back, Sally," he said.

THERE WAS A long table near the center of the room. She paused beside it, slid one of the books toward her, and flicked the pages with her fingers. Then she came back to her chair.

"You're going to do something," she said. "You haven't come because you want to see me. I know you're ready to do almost any wild thing, but you wouldn't take such chances just to see me."

"But I'm seeing you, Sally," he answered. "And if I had money enough I'd want to buy you. But I haven't money enough; I'm not as rich as the Big Fellow!"

"Do you think," she cried, "that he's anything to me except—"

"Stop it!" said Toomey. "Stop lying. This is better than anything in the world—sitting here with you. But don't lie."

"What do you think you know about me?" she asked him, and her eyes shrank until he could see only their greenness.

"I know that you belong to the Big Fellow," he said, "and I know that you're a little light in the fingers."

"You know those things, do you?" she said, with her eyes still narrowed.

"I'm not going to argue," said Toomey.

"All right," she said. "We won't argue."

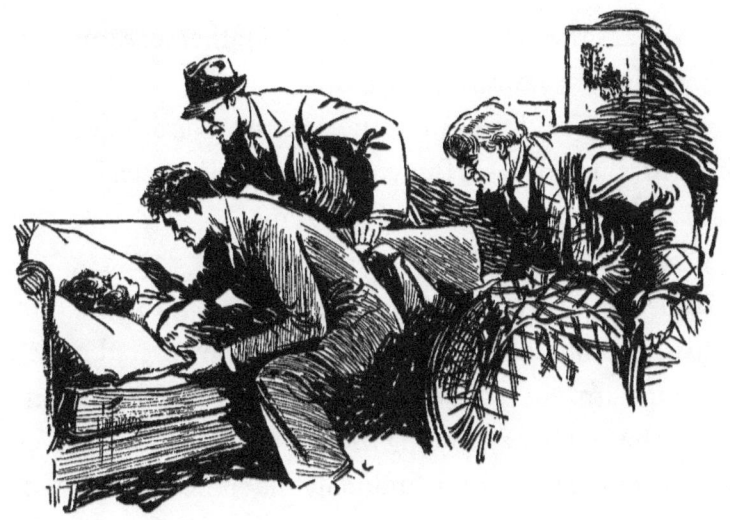

Slip murmured, "Great God—he's brought her too!"

"Is it the truth that you want to tell me?" he asked her, suddenly. "There's something in you. Your heart's bursting to say it. I can count the beat of it in your eyes."

"I want to tell you the truth," she said, "but that's no good. You wouldn't believe me. Crawford has hypnotized you the way a snake hypnotizes a poor bird."

"Tell me one thing, though," he asked her. "Why didn't you give the newspapers the description of me after that night? Did you keep it for the men of the Big Fellow only?"

"I told nobody," she answered.

"Why not? Do you really think that I'll believe that?"

"No, I don't expect you to believe it. But it's the same reason why I don't call out to the two men who are waiting back yonder. Oh, Toomey, how can you be so blind? Why can't you see what everybody knows—that Crawford is the worst devil on the face of this earth, the most—"

He lifted his hand.

"What's the use?" he asked her. "I'd rather lose my right hand than the faith I have in him."

"It's true," said the girl, wondering over him. "He hasn't bought you with cash. But you think that I've been bought, and still you care something about me."

"Yes," said Toomey.

She stood up again and crossed the room toward him, and as Toomey leaned back in his chair she lowered herself onto the arms of it, looking down at him as if for permission. She laid her arm along the back of the chair and kept on looking down at him. Suddenly she smiled. The pounding in the back of his brain ended. A light snapped on for him. He began to look into her more seagreen leagues than ever a sailor peered over from a masthead.

"You're not altogether lying, just now," said Toomey, through his teeth. "You're trying to melt me. But you care a little, too. I've touched some nerve in your brain, I don't know how. Is that true?"

She nodded slowly, never moving her eyes.

"And you want me, Toomey," said the girl.

"Ay," said Toomey.

"There's more to me than you think," said the girl. "I'm putting myself up on the auction block, because I want you to bid a big price, and I have to tell you what I'm like. I don't know much about you, except guessing, but guessing goes pretty far, with me. You like travel, you like adventure, you like the velvet touch; and you want to go like a prince through the world, too."

THE WORLD BEGAN to spread before Toomey. The waves of thought entered him with her voice and laid out the bright, glorious earth without a cloud upon its face.

"You can have everything you want," she said. "You can go as princes go, and be with princes and kings both, if you please. And then you'd like to throw off all the splendor and stand bare-legged at the wheel of a schooner while the wind screams you along. You can have all of that—if you'll come over to our side. You can have everything you want, and me along with it, since I count. I'm a sea lover too. I'll stand salt water, no matter how it roars. And then when you want, I'll go in velvet, too, and never shame you. Oh, Toomey, we can plunder all the happiness in this world. We'll have the fun, and we'll find the jewels, too, where they've been gathering in treasuries for hundreds of years. You can't fold me up and put me away on a shelf to wait for you. You can't shut me into your hand any more than you can shut fire in. But you can take me along with you, and we'll set the world in a flame."

She took her arm from the back of the chair and leaned closer to him, loving him with her eyes. And something about the flash of her smile made him see in a sudden vision a picture of wild faces, the gleam of teeth, the dull sheen of leaf-shaped spear-heads, at night.

"Don't touch me," said Toomey. "If you touched me, I'd be lost. Go stand by the fire."

She got up slowly, and went back and stood by the fire. The light of it flushed and wavered through her hair.

"If I sell myself to the Big Fellow—" said Toomey.

"You've sold yourself to a fiend! You've sold yourself to Crawford!" she said.

"I've never sold myself for hard cash," said Toomey, "and I never will. Wild hawks may go hungry, but they have the best flying. And as for you, I love you so damned much that I love loyalty better."

He stood up.

"I've got a car near here," he said. "Will you come out and watch the moon with me?"

"It's after midnight," said the girl.

"Will you come out and watch the moon with me?" said Toomey.

She put both her hands against her throat, as though to cool the beat of the pulse in it.

"All right," she said, suddenly. And she disappeared for her coat.

She came again, bundling herself into it; Toomey opened the door for her, and they went outside. The mist was thinner; the moon was more; there was a cold sting in the air.

"It's going to be cold," said the girl.

"It's going to be cold as the devil," said Toomey. "Can we go through the gate?"

"It's guarded," said she.

"Can you climb the wall?"

"Like nothing at all," said the girl.

And she climbed the wall, after slipping out of her coat. He gave her a hand up and she went over the top like a sailor. Toomey threw the coat after her. Then he followed, and dropping down to her side, they stood for a moment eyeing the windings of the road. Then they went to the car.

"Crawford loves you," said the girl, "or he'd never have given you this gray bullet to drive."

"Damn Crawford and damn everybody else," said Toomey. "No matter where this drive winds up, as long as it lasts we're nowhere in particular." And Red Toomey himself did not know then, did not know whether he would take her back to Crawford.

19

TOOMEY GOES OUT

HE FELT HER watching him, which was better than having her watch the road. They speeded a little so that he could feel the sway of the big machine and the way the tires bit into the road. He kept watching the road, and the double flight of trees that flowed out of blackness into the head-lights, and dimly past him. He had hardly energy enough to move the wheel.

He stopped the car.

"You drive," he said.

She slipped across into the driver's seat without a word; as he walked around the car, he saw that she was looking things over on the instrument board and on the floor, but she said nothing. When he got in, she started the big car without a lurch. He watched her feel her way flawlessly through the gear shifts. He leaned back deeper into the seat, until the ridge of it came under his head.

"I could sleep," he said.

She kept studying the road with a serious little frown. He saw the autumn red of the dress; her bare hands kept a good steadying grip on the wheel. He felt a foolish loose-ness of body and mind. He could have laughed, except for the effort involved. She drove even more slowly than he had driven, but it still seemed too fast, and something was rising out of his subconscious mind with a warning. It was something about a turn they must make, before long. He felt that he would know, when the time came, and yet he was dimly worried.

The headlights were not the only light, and as the dawn freshened he could see the pale gleam of fields to either side. Trees began to move through a mist; hill-lines flowed away on the left; but still the light that showed her face to him came from the instrument board, shining upwards. He kept running his eyes over the line of her nose and the curve of her upper lip; it was crisply cut, like the mouth of a child. Above, there was the shadow of the hat, and through the shadow, her eyes. They had no color; they were only glimmering; he would have to lean closer to see the color.

"You're a child," said Toomey.

She parted her lips, and made a slight, annoyed sound of clearing her throat. He watched the lips join again. His heart leaped like a trout out of shadows into sunlight. Delight flashed in him.

"You're a child," said Toomey.

She swung the car around a curve. A hill came at them. She shifted down and went up it without rushing the grade. The engine began to stall. She shifted down again. The car poured up the slope with a fluid ease.

Only the brighter stars were able to shine. All the rest were drowned in the soft shower of radiance that was dropping continually from heaven. They went on for hours. Time had stopped.

"You're a child," said Toomey. "Smile for me."

She turned her head a little and smiled. The smile put a

dimple in one cheek but not in the other. He put up a hand towards her face but drew it down again. She was driving well, but she kept her head turned a little towards him, now.

The color was beginning all around the horizon. Light was burning up from the earth brighter than that radiance which had been showering from heaven, and as the color bloomed in the sky, the earth bloomed around them, also. Only the distant hills were black, and beyond these, far before them, the air of celestial space was lucid green. Still the black earth bloomed into the colors of autumn and the upper universe flowered with the colors of the morning.

"Turn to the right," said Toomey.

She turned to the right onto a small road.

"Keep on the small roads," said Toomey. "Turn out the lights."

SHE TURNED OUT the lights. The dim beauty of the dawn poured in upon them. Toomey felt cold. He sat up straighter. In this new and paler radiance he had to look at the girl twice before he was able to see her as he wanted to see her.

That was a surprise. He thought he had been seeing her as she was, but now he knew that an image came between them and that it had to be fitted to the reality.

"Go slower," said Toomey.

She went slower. The road was very winding and narrow. The overflowing hedges rushed like water across the fenders and struck small, harplike sounds out of the wire spokes.

"Love me," said Toomey.

She smiled at the windings of the little road.

He sat up straight and no longer looked at her.

He made a great, vague gesture towards the lucid green above the horizon, and he cried: "We're going on."

He sat deep again, and put his head on the back of the seat. His body rocked with the cradling motion of the car. Divine hands of light were crossing and re-crossing in the zenith.

Then the darkness of memories out of the real world spread like a second night over him. He thought of Crawford and sat up.

"Stop the car," said Toomey.

He got out and went over to the driver's seat while she slid across. When he got in, he recognized the road. She had been weaving endlessly about the country, through all of this time and now he recognized the place they were in, not three miles from Crawford's place.

He went for it like a gray arrow. As he shot the curves, he half wished that there would be a slip, to blot them both out; and when he looked at her, he saw that she was sitting up straight, with her eyes half closed, a half smile on her lips; so that he realized it had been true, all she had said when she was trying to buy him for the other side. She would be a dauntless and a faultless companion on whatever wild way of life he selected.

Then, suddenly, she had altered. She put her hand on his arm.

"Toomey!" she cried.

Before him, he saw the over-arching limbs of the trees in front of Crawford's place, and her voice echoed mournfully through his mind as if through a cave.

He slammed on the brakes. They groaned loudly as he skidded the car to a halt.

"Toomey!" she screamed. "You're not giving me up to—him? You're not—you're not—"

Then she was hanging limply out over the door of the car. He got out and picked up the weight of her body, and started carrying her down the path. She was not light. In spite of her slenderness she was all rounded and the limp burden dragged at his arms; she was not light, but he carried her lightness, for he was all steel again. She was a liar, a thief, and a traitor to Crawford; therefore Toomey was like a steel spring.

That house had eyes which, by day and night, saw all things, which approached. Now, out of the doorway, ran George. He stretched out his monstrous hands to receive the burden. To the wild brain of Toomey they seemed, for the moment, like the hands of a fiend.

"Get out of my way," said Toomey, and stepped on past him.

George was there to open the door, breathing eagerness.

Then they were going down the dimness of the hall, and there was a faint, stale fragrance of cookery in the air. The door opened into the big room which had become, to Toomey, like a chamber in his brain.

Crawford was there, at his desk. Through all eternity he would be there, chained like a damned soul to one place.

Toomey put the girl down on the davenport. He took off her hat, loosened her dress at the breast, put a pillow under her knees to make the blood run back into her brain. He kneeled by her, smoothed back her hair, and kissed her. She was white. He kissed her again, and the color seemed to come back a little into her face.

Someone leaned over them. It was Slip, and he

murmured: "Great God—he's brought her, too!" Then he seemed to flee towards the door.

Crawford came, wheeled in an invalid's chair.

He was saying, softly: "George, carry her upstairs to—"

"Don't let him touch her," said Toomey.

SHE WAS BREATHING, audibly, a faint moan with every breath. Out of the middle of his body, all strength flowed away. He was hunched and crumpled on his knees like a child. His body was loose. His brain was loose, also. It refused to work. It was like an exhausted muscle. And under the heaven-wide vault of the mind the voice of Crawford seemed to be booming like a gong, saying: "She's a thief! She's a traitor! It's all right—what you've done to her!"

But it was not Crawford's voice. A voice of judgment, then?

Two men came to carry the girl out. Toomey looked at them and shook his head. Their faces were not right; their hands were not right to touch her.

"I'll carry her. You show the way. She's coming back to life," he said.

He gathered her little by little, and the touch of her brought back his strength until he could lift her lightly.

He bore her down the hall, up the glimmerings of a staircase, and then into a small room, all bright with glazed chintz. There was a bed in it with four posts of slenderly sculptured mahogany. Into the soft whiteness of that bed he laid her. He kissed her eyelids, and they fluttered under his lips.

"Get some women in here to take care of her," he said.

The brutal faces of these men stared at him with fear,

or a neighbor of fear. One of them had on his head a cap, which he touched in a salute.

"Yes, Mr. Toomey," he said.

Toomey went out into the hall, and as he closed the door behind him, he heard the voice of the girl cry out, like a sobbing child: "Toomey! Toomey!"

He hurried down the hall.

He was on the stairs when the voice came again, with a wailing shriek that tore his heart into agonies: "Toomey! Toomey!"

Toomey fled down the stairs and into the big room at the bottom of them, where Crawford and George were waiting. As he slammed the door behind him, all distant sounds were shut away, and he spilled his weight into a chair by the fire—the chair where he had sat through so many great moments before.

"Gimme a drink," said Toomey.

He saw George shaking his small head slowly from side to side, smiling. He had three gold teeth in front, which helped his smile to flash.

"Don't smile at me," said Toomey.

"No, Mr. Toomey," said George.

He took the glass from Toomey and filled it. Toomey drank that, too, and it was just like water, with a stale taint in it.

"Now everything has been done," said Crawford. "An angel from heaven could have done no more than you've managed. You must go to bed and sleep, Toomey, my son."

"Tell me one thing," said Toomey.

"All that I can say to you," answered Crawford.

"I want to know just one thing. Was it right?"

"It's as right as justice," said Crawford. "It's as right as the best justice that I can imagine."

"I can't think," said Toomey. "But you know. You understand. My brain won't work. Crawford, you have to be right."

"I'm right," said the gong-like voice of Crawford. "Right! And they're in my hands, now utterly. They've been stopped and blocked and beaten at every turn, and the Big Fellow's in my hands. Toomey—I'm going to make you so rich—"

Toomey sprang up.

"Quit it!" he said. "The main thing is—was she the Big Fellow's mistress?"

"Yes," said Crawford. "Why?"

"Because," said Toomey, "if there were any mistake about that—why, even if her body's tainted, there's purity like heaven somewhere about her soul— God, God, I love her— But she's a sneak-thief and a traitor."

"She's a sneak-thief and a traitor," said Crawford.

"I only want one thing," said Toomey. "When the time comes, I want the killing of the Big Fellow. And I won't want any tools for the job."

He walked out of the house. Slip was in the small front room, biting his nails.

"You drive me back to the Big Fellow," said Toomey.

20

THE POKER CHIP

ON THE WAY, Toomey slept, his body bumping loosely about, but he wakened just before he reached the cottage.

He found the eye of Slip fixed on him.

"How d'you manage it?" asked Slip, half in envy, half in pure malice. "Where d'you find the sort of luck that you ride?"

He was pulling up in front of the white house on the hill, as he spoke.

Toomey got from the car without speaking, and went up the path. Filthy curses, kept under the breath, came hissing after him. Then he tried the door, it was locked. He rapped on it, twice. After a time a footfall came, and Bushmill opened the door. He stepped back, almost fell back, against the wall.

"What the hell!" said Bushmill. "You back? I thought your job—"

"Ask Slip," said Toomey, and walked straight on into the sitting room, where the Big Fellow sat with a rosy face by the fire, nursing a tall highball in the fat of his hand. His smile froze into a puckered crust when he saw Toomey.

Toomey went to him, took the glass from his hand, and threw the contents in his face.

"You damned swine!" shouted the Big Fellow. He got up and ran blindly about, with his hands pawing at his burning eyes. He fell over a chair, crashed against the wall, and thumped the floor.

There were two boxes of cigars open on the table. Toomey threw them into the fireplace. Bushmill came back and stood in the doorway. He gripped the two doorjambs and looked from the Big Fellow to Toomey.

"You beat him up for exercise, eh?" said Bushmill.

It is a very good trick when you can take a gun out under the flat of your hand. Toomey took his out, in that way, and slapped Bushmill across the face with it. Then he dragged the loose body down the hall, with the heels bumping, and dropped it on the front porch.

"Come and get him!" he called to Slip.

The voice of the Big Fellow came shouting down the hall, begging some one to save him from Al Toomey.

Toomey closed the door and faced the Big Fellow.

"Go upstairs and put on two sweaters," he said. The Big Fellow looked down to the gun which Toomey still held, and saw the blood on it. He turned gray-green and went slowly up the stairs. When he came down Toomey drove him grunting and cursing and groaning across country.

The morning was bright, the ground black and wet; the honest sweat took the poisons from the body of Toomey, though it could not take the pain out of his heart. And as he ran he admired the change in the style of his prisoner; for the soggy bulk of the Big Fellow had been burned out and refined and hardened until he stepped out with an excellent, springing stride. There was plenty of reach and go to his pace, and the whisky he had drunk under the more friendly ministrations of Bushmill had not altogether taken his wind again.

In fact, when they went down a slope Toomey had to stretch and strain a little to keep up with the sweeping stride of the taller man. That and the moisture of the ground gave him a fall. He had stepped on the surface of a stone not only smooth but further polished with sweat-like dew, and he skidded and rolled straight past the Big Fellow.

He sat up, he got to his knees, stunned, like a prize fighter in the ring prepared to rise, but waiting for the count to proceed. But Toomey could not gain his feet for an instant, and in that instant he saw Lawrence Elliott Oliver catch up a weighty stone and poise it in his hand. There was plenty of burden in that rock to crush the skull of Toomey; and here was freedom for the big man, an instant gift.

The hand with the rock wavered in the air, but it did not strike. It slid out and dropped harmlessly to the ground even before Toomey was up, his gun in hand.

The Big Fellow was shaking his head and blinking like a man just come out of a plunge in cold water.

"Why didn't you slam me with that stone?" asked Toomey, scowling.

"I leave murder for rats like you, who are used to it," said Lawrence Oliver, and strode off toward the house.

Toomey went with him, silently. One of the greatest blows of his life had fallen upon him.

ALL THAT HE had heard and all that he knew of Lawrence Oliver had built up in his mind the picture of a man capable of taking every possible advantage. It would not have been murder, but a mere stroke of self-defense if Oliver had struck him down. And yet the blow had not fallen. The thing amazed him, utterly.

What was there before the Big Fellow so long as his captivity endured? His very life was probably not secure; and yet he had failed to strike the blow that would mean what he called "murder."

The thing did not fit in with any preconception. It was not of this sort of a man that Crawford had talked. It was rather the nature of Sally's Big Fellow.

In a torment, Toomey came back to the house. They had not run the rest of the way. There was too much on his mind.

Before they went in, he said: "Big Fellow, it seems that I've made a few mistakes about you. I thought you were a yellow hound to the core of the bone. I was wrong."

The Big Fellow made no answer, but went straight on into the house. And Toomey, following him in a brown study, wondered more than ever. He had perceived the sketch, the vague outline of a certain manliness in Lawrence Oliver, from the first moment; and for that purpose, more than merely to torment him, he had insisted on the rigid training, wondering if he could melt away the loose bulk of the exterior, and the softness of mind, and leave instead the hard strength of a real man.

It seemed, now, that he had succeeded. But to Toomey the thing had all the strangeness of a miracle.

When he got into the house, the Big Fellow started up the stairs for his bath, but Slip stopped him.

"Here's a little present for you from Crawford," he said.

Lawrence Oliver tore open the envelope and shook out into his hand—a yellow poker chip!

The sight of it was enough to drain all the strength out of him. He fell up against the wall with a groan. His eyes closed, and his face became loose and weak, as though he had received a stunning physical shock. The poker chip fell out of his nerveless fingers, and rolled away across the floor.

"He knows—everything," groaned the Big Fellow. "Tell him it's enough. My God, does it matter to him to have my body a prisoner, when he's got my reputation in his hand? Tell him I surrender—unconditionally!"

He turned and went slowly down the hall, then, like a very old man, up the stairs, one at a time.

Toomey went into the living room, with Slip. Bushmill was there, nursing his bleeding face with a handkerchief; his eyes avoided Toomey with a murderous sullenness.

"It's over," said Slip. "He's chucked in the sponge. The Big Fellow's given up, Bushmill."

Bushmill made no answer.

"You run over to Crawford," said Slip, "and tell him the good news. We'll be through with this job before another day's out, unless I'm mistaken. Brains—that's what the chief has. He takes this fellow Toomey and blocks the other gang all the way around. But the chief drops his own acid on Oliver. Two postcards and a poker chip. What the devil story can be behind that?"

He laughed as he spoke. Bushmill got up, gave Toomey one villainous glance, and then left the house. The sound of his automobile purred away into distance.

"Watch the Big Fellow," said Toomey. "I'm going to sleep."

He lay down on the flat of his back, on the rug. In the old days he had learned to sleep like that, on shipboard.

The Big Fellow was not what he had seemed to be. That much was plain. And there was something disturbing, also, in the fact that Crawford had plied him with what appeared to be some subtle sort of blackmail. The whole thing was a monstrous whirl before the brain of Toomey.

21

SOMEBODY IN THE BRUSH

WHEN TOOMEY WAKENED, the last light of the autumn sun was on his face and on the wall beside him. The cold had seeped in across the floor and was numbing his body. Slip leaned above him.

"Get up, Toomey," he said. "Bushmill's back with orders. The game's about finished, I guess."

Toomey sat up, kneeled, rose to his feet, and stretched himself. The numbness left his body with the groan that came welling up out of his throat. The dimness and the confusion had gone partially from his brain, also. There only remained the fact that a new value had to be assigned to the Big Fellow.

Suddenly he said to Slip: "You hate me, Slip."

"Yeah, the whole heart of you," said Slip, quietly.

"Then tell me the truth. Is the Big Fellow a hound—a wholehearted hound? You can't lie to a man you hate, Slip."

A struggle appeared in the face of Slip, a contortion that spoiled the beauty of his perfectly made features.

Then he said, slowly: "You get the silent treatment—by order." And he turned on his heel and left the room.

Toomey followed. There was only one "by order" that would mean anything to Slip, and that was the direct order of Crawford. And it was very strange that none of the men had talked to him—not Slip, not Bushmill, nor the others he had met in the house, including George. They neither talked about Crawford nor the Big Fellow, nor about anything else of importance. And more than once voices had been stilled or subjects violently changed when he came near.

And the first suspicion came like a cold, quick frost upon the mind of Toomey.

Suppose, then, that Crawford was not what he had seemed; that the Big Fellow was right; that Sally Moore—

He gritted his teeth. For his brain was whirling again, and he knew that he dared not continue the process of thought that was beginning in him.

The Big Fellow sat in the kitchen, reading closely a letter that was spread on the table before him. Bushmill stood in a corner. Slip was near the window. He beckoned to Toomey, and when Toomey came near, murmured: "I had a look at a bird that was walking up there through the brush. He seen me looking through the window, and he started off. There was something about the way he sneaked off, Toomey."

Toomey frowned.

"If the Big Fellow's people have spotted this house—there'll be trouble—there'll be big trouble," he said.

"They'll get him or die for him," said Slip. "That's the kind of people who work for him."

He had added that in a murmur, and now he glanced at Toomey with quickly narrowed eyes, as though he had said too much and regretted the deductions that might be drawn.

"Toomey!" said the Big Fellow, in a peremptory voice.

Toomey crossed the kitchen and stood in front of the table, sneering down at the prisoner. The Big Fellow was writing rapidly. He came to a conclusion, signed his name with a huge scrawl, and then looked up as he folded the paper.

"Toomey," he said, "I've just signed away the results of a long life of labor. I'm signing it away because you've had your grip on me. I'm signing away money that's gone partly to build fat on my own body, and partly to help a good many friends. They'll be destitute, now. And you're the guilty one. The rest of 'em are nothing—Bushmill and Slip and the rest. You've been the right hand man of Crawford. You came like a hunting beast and got me. You've kept me. And though it may seem childish to you, there's a small scruple of religious faith in me that tells me you'll burn in hell for what you've done. That's all I wish to say."

He extended the folded paper.

"Here's the order that Crawford wants. I suppose it goes to you?"

Toomey turned his back.

"Take it, one or the other of you," he said.

"I'll take it," said Bushmill. "It's my job to deliver the note. The stuff will come out to you, here, in a suitcase or something, I suppose. They won't turn the junk over, I guess, until they can put it in your hands, Big Fellow."

Bushmill went to the door.

"I'll be seeing you later," he said. And for one instant of loathing, his glance rested on Toomey. Then he was gone.

"SUPPER TIME," SAID Toomey. "Who's the cook?"

"I'll be the cook," answered the Big Fellow, with amazing good cheer.

He got up and began to stir among pots and pans.

"Kind of takes a weight off you, eh?" said Slip, regarding him with a malicious grin. "Kind of takes a weight off, now that the junk is off your hands?"

The Big Fellow turned from the stove with an odd smile.

"My dear boy," he said, "the fact is that when a thing has been thrown over the shoulder it's far better to walk on and forget about it. Don't you agree?"

Slip scratched his chin.

"Game, eh?" he muttered to Toomey.

But Toomey was beyond speech, lost in thought.

He went into the living room, and walked rapidly up and down, filled with considerations.

The Big Fellow was not as he had been before. The sogginess was gone from him. Perhaps it was partially the exercise through which he had been dragged; perhaps it was the succession of shocks which he had received on this day that reacted as stimuli rather than as depressants. But he was altered.

There remained the fact that he owned Sally Moore. That made up for the rest of the differences. Nothing could alter that, to the mind of Toomey. He had to set his teeth in that idea, and cling to his belief in Crawford as best he might. But the whole horizon of his faith was terribly shattered, and threatening to collapse in upon him.

The Big Fellow had people who were willing to die for him—that was the opinion of Slip. Crawford had hired thugs. Toomey knew their faces and their hearts. In Big Fellow the girl believed—Crawford she hated and feared.

And he, Toomey, had left her screaming his name, that day.

The sweat rolled out on his face.

And then he heard a mellow song come rolling out from the kitchen. The Big Fellow, singing:

"I've got to be right," said Toomey, softly. "I can't be wrong."

He was called in for supper, and ate at the table with the other two. The Big Fellow made the conversation, talking of riding in Ireland, and horses which could "jump a house." But toward the end of the meal Slip looked inquisitively at Toomey and said: "I wonder why I can't be friendly with a guy like you, with all the nerve?"

"I don't know," said Toomey, "but I don't want any part of it."

"No," said Slip. "It's the same way with me. Only, I sort of wonder, is all."

"So do I," said Toomey.

"It's funny, ain't it, how I wanta carve you?" said Slip.

"Yes, it's funny."

"And some day," said Slip, slowly rubbing his hand on his trousers, "I think I'm gunna do it."

"And that's that," said Toomey.

"Yeah," said Slip, "and that's that, and don't you forget it."

When supper was finished they stacked the pans and dishes and ran water over them; the other two men went into the living room, but Toomey told Slip that he would go outside.

"I'm going to walk a beat," he declared. "You never can tell. Something may break wrong for us. You saw somebody in the brush."

"Walk your head off and be damned," said Slip, cordially.

So Toomey went out into the cold of the night and walked around and around the house. It was not the first time he had done it, for his restless nature was apt to keep him pacing like a beast of prey behind bars.

So he knew these rounds, even in the midst of the thick darkness.

He had made them so often that he could have made his way through a milk-white fog, soundlessly, avoiding the stumps, the rocks, the shrubbery. He knew every outline, however dim, and that was why he stopped short presently.

For at the rear of the house he saw two shrubs standing.

What else could they be? And yet he knew perfectly well that there were no bushes on that spot. He watched them breathlessly, for an instant, and then, though he would hardly believe his eyes, they moved out of sight toward the back of the house.

Vague expectations are the hardest realizations; but Toomey knew in his soul that the men of the Big Fellow were on hand to deliver an attack!

22

THE CAPTIVE

AS HE APPROACHED he heard only the faintest of noises, but Toomey knew it was the creak of the rust on the hinges of the kitchen door.

When he got to the corner of the house he saw the door opening again.

"We can do it ourselves, Gregg," whispered a voice. "Stick here and we'll do it ourselves."

"We're only scouting," said a voice that breathed from the kitchen door. "They're both in the next room. We gotta make sure of 'em, this time. Sit tight, Rush. I'll bring the others here in a minute."

The whisper itself was a ghostly thing that almost died before it reached the senses of Toomey. Like a ghost, too, a man went down the low kitchen steps and lost himself in the black of the night. Toomey got up with his gun and came to the kitchen door.

"Rush!" he whispered.

Something stirred inside. Toomey pulled open the door, slowly, and stepped inside.

"Rush!" he breathed.

There was a shifting of darkness inside of darkness. He stared like an owl at it.

"What's the matter?" whispered the shadow.

Toomey used the heel of his gun to strike for the whisper. The man dropped into the spot of light that Toomey put on the floor with the torch that he carried in his left hand. He was only partially stunned. His face was twisted with effort. He lay tugging to get something from under his body. The gun-butt had torn his scalp, so that blood began to sluice down the side of his face. Toomey kneeled off the small of his back, took some twine off the kitchen table, and tied his hands behind his back. Then he switched off the electric torch that he had left lying on the floor to light his work.

He fumbled, found the gun that Rush had finally managed to drag out, and laid it aside.

"You can sit up," he said.

The captive sat up.

"So this is this, eh?" said he.

"Shut up," said Toomey. "If you yap again, I'll conk you."

They waited in the darkness. Toomey could have called for Slip, but he was afraid his call would warn the enemy. The running blood began to tap-tap on the floor. Beyond the kitchen door Toomey heard at last what he was waiting for, the muffled impact of approaching feet. He lifted his gun. He could sweep that doorway as though with a hose.

"Gregg! Look out! They got me!" yelled the captive.

There was a noise like scattering leaves before a wind. Toomey lifted his gun in the darkness, held it suspended, but changed his mind.

From the hall came the startled voice of Slip, demanding what had happened.

"Come and see," answered Toomey.

IT WAS THE Big Fellow who brought in a lamp that quavered in his hand as he looked at the bloody face of Rush.

"Where did he come from? What's happened?" asked Slip.

"He's a windfall," said Toomey.

"Damned amateur kid," said Slip. "What's popping?"

"Go out and see for yourself," said Toomey. "There were some more of 'em, and this kid warned 'em away. He was game to stay and take it, but he yelled to warn the rest away."

Slip cursed with surprise, and ran out the kitchen door, pulling a gun. They could hear his footfalls crunching, far away, as he ran here and there like a hunting dog.

By the light of the Big Fellow's lamp, Toomey bandaged the head of his victim.

"Who put you boys on this job?" asked Toomey. "Where you from?"

"Over in Dennyford," said Rush. He made a face as the pain bit into him. "We come from over in Dennyford. Gregg spotted this house, and a coupla nuts hangin' out in it. We thought that we'd come over and see what we could find in it."

"Is that all?"

"Ain't that enough?"

"All right," said Toomey.

When the bleeding head had been tied up, Slip returned with a report that nothing could be seen near the house.

"See if this guy is on his own or an agent," said Slip. "A lot depends on that."

They took Rush into the living room and put him in a

chair, while Toomey offered him a large shot of whiskey. Rush set his teeth and shook his head.

"You can make me take the needle," he said, "but you can't *give* it to me."

"Been hearing stories of fancy poisonings?" asked Toomey. He sipped from the glass himself and once more offered it.

"A kind heart, eh?" said Rush, grinning all on one side of his face, and taking the glass with an avid hand, he tossed off the liquor.

He looked like one of those pictures of college "men" that magazines put on their covers, his face was so clean-cut, and his jaw had such a nice forward swing to it, that any prize fighter would have said to his manager: "Get that guy for me! I could do a nice, short number with that bird."

"This your first time at murder, Rush?" asked Toomey.

"That's damn good whiskey, brother," said Rush.

"Is Gregg your team captain?" asked Toomey.

"It's good whiskey, but there ain't much burn to it," said Rush.

"And who talked to Gregg?" said Toomey.

Rush leaned back in the chair against his tied hands.

"Listen—" began Toomey, then paused.

He put the poker in the fire, where the draft pulled two tongues of flame together. Then he stood before the fire and sunned his back in the warmth.

"How does the head feel?" he asked.

"Okay," said Rush, watching the poker in the fire.

"It's been a rotten day," said Toomey.

"I don't mind rain," said Rush. "It's the damn frost that I hate."

"Look," said Slip to the Big Fellow. "This is okay, all right."

Toomey took the poker out of the fire and looked at the orange-red tip of it. He stood over Rush and lowered the poker at his brow. Rush shuddered his head from side to side for an instant. Then he steadied himself and looked up the line of the poker into the face of Toomey.

"Talking?" asked Toomey.

Rush locked his fine, clean-cut jaw. The point of the poker singed his eyebrows.

"Quit it," said the Big Fellow.

Toomey looked over his shoulder. "All right," he said.

He sat the poker up beside the fireplace and dusted off his hands, vigorously, though there were no ashes on his fingers.

"What's the idea? Give him the medicine!" exclaimed Slip.

"Look at the Big Fellow," answered Toomey.

For Lawrence Elliott Oliver had become very gray all over, except the hollows of his cheeks, which were white. There was a tremor, also, running through his big body.

"Are you sick, Big Fellow?" asked Toomey.

The Big Fellow stared at the prisoner, without a word.

"Wait a minute. I'll make the brat start right in yapping!" vowed Slip, snatching up the poker.

"Let him alone!" shouted the Big Fellow. "He—I'm to blame for him."

"He lies!" cried Rush. "I don't know a damn thing about him. I—"

He paused. Perhaps he saw that his own vehemence had simply betrayed his secret farther into the hands of the enemy. So he lay groaning in the chair and looking with anguished eyes at the Big Fellow.

"Belongs to you, Oliver?" asked Toomey.

The Big Fellow went closer and laid his hand on the shoulder of the lad.

"I'm sorry, Rush," he said. "You're too young for work like this. Why did they let you come?"

"Because I begged 'em!" said the boy. "It was me that seen something phony, here. It was me that got four gents together. We all been scouting every inch of the country—and I seen something here, and watched two days, and I thought I seen you out in the open, this same day. Oh, Big Fellow, if I was any good, I'd of done something for you more than take a rap on the bean."

"It's all right, Rush," said the Big Fellow. "You've tried your best."

"If they'd just charged in!" groaned Rush. "If they hadn't minded me, and just charged in—only I didn't want 'em to come sneakin' through the door and get planted. But they could have scattered and tried the house from three sides—I—"

He checked himself, groaning again.

"All your age?" asked Toomey. "The rest of 'em your age?"

"Yes," said Rush.

Toomey looked at Slip. "That's better," he said.

"Yeah, that's better," said Slip. "But even if they were a pack of kids, they may know where to pass on the dope they've picked up. We may have a whole pack of thugs on our shoulders before morning, Toomey."

"Who do you know?" asked Toomey of the boy.

"Nobody," said Rush, his teeth clicking.

"Tell them, lad, tell them," said the Big Fellow, hurriedly. "God knows I appreciate how you and the rest have been hunting for me, but if you don't tell these fellows, they'll tear you limb from limb. They're devils, Rush."

"They can tear me, then," said Rush, panting with fear and determination. "I ain't going to squawk. I've said enough. Only, Big Fellow, if I could've gone home and told the old man that I'd done a little something for you, I'd have been a great man around the house. The whole town would've thought a lot of me!"

"What town?" asked Toomey.

"No town, damn you!" said Rush, savagely.

"Nothing, nothing," said the Big Fellow. "Village up the river, is all. I've done a few things for the people there, and they're grateful. That's the whole story."

"And they started out to comb the countryside for you when you disappeared?" asked Toomey, sharply.

"It looks like it," said Lawrence Oliver, shaking his head.

Toomey took a turn on the floor.

"It's safe to let it drop till the morning," declared Slip. "Just a lot of country blockheads. They won't get anything started before morning."

"Talk to Rush and get everything out of him, but don't roughhouse him," said Toomey. "I'm going to work on the Big Fellow. Go on out into the kitchen," he commanded, and the Big Fellow went obediently before him to the rear of the house.

23

TOOMEY HEARS A STORY

THE STALE ODOR of food was in the air. The embers in the kitchen stove sent up small puffs of smoke through the intervals between the plates, as the wind thrust its fist down the chimney, now and again.

"Sit down," said Toomey, pointing towards a chair at the table.

The Big Fellow sat down.

"I've never talked to you," said Toomey, "because you turned my stomach."

"That goes with me," said the Big Fellow, calmly.

"Because I'm a rat?"

"A *murdering* rat."

"All right, but you'll talk to me now."

"I suppose so," said the Big Fellow. "What about?"

"The village up the river."

"That's nothing to you."

"What's it to you?"

"Nothing much. There was a flood. A lot of the poor devils were wiped out. Lost their shops and houses. A whole street of 'em."

"And what did you do?" asked Toomey.

"I gave them a hand, that's all."

"What sort of a hand?"

"I fixed up their houses for 'em, and loaned them money for a new start."

Toomey considered, through a cloud of cigarette smoke. With all his might, he was striving to believe nothing good about this man, and yet belief leaked into him, constantly.

"Good works today," he said, "to make up for crooked work in the old days. Is that it?"

The Big Fellow stared at him.

"What do you mean by that?" he asked.

"What I say. Trying to save your rotten soul, eh?"

"I'm as bad as the next man," said Lawrence Oliver, "but not so much worse. My conscience doesn't keep me awake at night."

"No? Then there's damned little conscience in you. I could tell you a story."

"Could you? Well, fire ahead. But make it short, Toomey. It nauseates me a little to talk to you. I've seen the brute in you too often."

"Maybe you'll see it again, too."

"If you have your way, of course I shall. But I'm about to buy my way out of your rotten hands, I think. What's your story?"

"Why, it's about two men who walked up into the Alps, a long time ago, and went hunting, and there was an accident, and one of 'em was shot through the hips. And the other one went off to try to get help. Know that story?"

The Big Fellow looked at the smoking stove with a frown.

"Are you driving at the time I was hunting with Craw-

ford and he was shot, through his own damned careless-
ness?"

"I'm driving at that time."

"Well," said the Big Fellow, "I suppose that story is still
floating around, here and there. People made a lot too
much of it; they still do. It was a hard pull carrying him
down, I admit; and the storm in my face was pretty bad.
But it wasn't killing me. I was standing it all right. It was
the hot, close air when I got into the rest house. That was
what made me keel over, I think."

"Carried him down?" said Toomey, slowly. "You carried
him down?"

"Why, what did *you* hear?" asked the Big Fellow. "People
have talked a good deal about it. Things get garbled. Of
course, I carried him down. I forget how many metres.
Enough, anyway. It was the blizzard that made the hard
going."

"You lie!" exclaimed Toomey. "You didn't carry him
down. You let Crawford lie out there in the bitter cold of
a blizzard while you got yourself drunk—"

Something in the face of the Big Fellow stopped him.

"Wait a minute," said he. "Did Crawford tell you that?"

"It's the truth!" exclaimed Toomey.

"Well, then," said Lawrence Oliver, quietly, "the society
of mountain climbers that gave me the medal didn't know
what happened, I suppose."

"What medal?" exclaimed Toomey. "And what society?"

"I've got the medal at home. I don't wear it on my watch-
chain. Too big for that. I forget the whole name of the society. Something about St. Bernard in it. I could remember,

in a minute. Did Crawford tell you that I left him up there to freeze?"

TOOMEY WAS SILENT. The blood about his heart had begun to congeal.

"Because he *would* have frozen, all right," said the Big Fellow. "The wind blew the heart out of me, even when I was walking and carrying his weight. And he was no feather. But I got him in too late. The doctors couldn't save his legs. Not really. From the waist down he turned into a monkey, poor devil. God knows I've tried to forgive him for a good many things, knowing what life's meant to him. Because I remember him when he was a Hercules. My weight, but twice as strong. No wonder the human withered out of him and the devil took its place."

Toomey pulled a deep breath between his teeth. He took the edges of his knuckles and ground them across his forehead. And belief still slid into his soul!

"Well," said Toomey, "I've got to talk to you about another thing. How long has Sally Moore been—your mistress?"

"Mistress? Ever since she was knee high to a grasshopper," said the Big Fellow, grinning. "She was a lively brat."

He looked up into the tense face of Toomey and suddenly cried out: "Mistress? What d'you mean, you foul-mouthed fool? Mistress? Moore's little girl—my mistress?"

He stood up, slowly.

And a frenzy came over Toomey as he answered: "You lie again. I see the whole thing's a lie, by this last one. You kept her in your house. You rented her out to be a spy in the house of poor Crawford. You made her steal like a sneak-thief from him. And what's the good of your lying, when she's back there, safe and sound?"

"Back where?" said the Big Fellow. "Back where?"

He had turned gray-green. He came around the table towards Toomey.

"She's safe in my house!" said the Big Fellow. "And I know it! The wild, silly girl had to show her courage—she had to prove that she was her father's daughter by being secretary to Crawford for a while, knowing that he was sharpening a knife for me. But she's safe back on my place, now, and my men know they have to watch her and protect her as if she were my own child. God knows that she's the nearest to a child that I have in the whole wide world."

"Oh, God," said Toomey. "Oh, great God!"

"But what do you mean?" cried the Big Fellow. "Back with Crawford? He'd burn her body like a match. He'd burn it inch by inch. Sally back in the hands of that fiend? Toomey, you don't mean it! It's a new way of deviling me. You don't—"

"Go back in the other room," said Toomey, suddenly.

The Big Fellow looked at him with eyes half dubious, half anguished. Then he obeyed the order.

Toomey followed to the door of the room.

"They're both on your hands," he said. "Watch 'em. I have to jump across country."

"Wait a minute!" exclaimed Slip. "What the devil's the idea? There may be a load of trouble around here tonight, and I don't want to be left alone to—"

He stopped, for the front door had banged behind the flight of Toomey.

24

WITH THE EDGE OF STEEL

ACROSS THE NIGHT Toomey drove the long gray car until the tires groaned against the road, and the wind screamed at him, and the thunders of the exhaust trailed away behind.

When he stopped in front of the Crawford place he wondered who would see him first, and he sat for an instant in the seat, trying to clear his mind. But he could not clear it, and a red madness kept pouring in on him out of the corners of his brain. He was afraid to let his judgment work. All he could do was to see Crawford at once and have the thing out face to face—in some manner!

He went down the path and climbed the steps. The door opened as though conscious of his coming. The butler, a long face set on a shining triangle of white, was standing aside, greeting him, reaching a vague hand for the hat that Toomey had not brought.

"Go straight in, sir," said the butler. "Those are his orders. You are always to go straight in."

Toomey, his hair blown wildly on end like flames, entered the quiet and the sheen of the big room once more. It was as always—George in the corner—Crawford at his desk, writing. The two seemed to be frozen in place, like insects in dark amber.

"Have you brought it over, Toomey?" asked Crawford, eagerly. "There must be a suitcase full of the stuff that we've made the Big Fellow disgorge!"

"I didn't bring anything," said Toomey.

He halted on the rug in the middle of the room and looked down for an instant at the weltering blues and reds and yellows; the Persian carpet seemed to smoke and burn beneath his feet. Or was it because his brain was on fire?

Then he looked up, and it seemed to him that the glance of Crawford was swinging significantly away from George and back toward him. With small, irregular steps, Toomey began to approach the desk.

"Crawford," he said, "it's Sally. I want to see her."

That was not all he wanted; but she was the beginning and the end of his questions.

"Ah? Sally?" said Crawford, letting sympathy pour richly forth from his softened voice. "I'm sorry that you've heard about her. It's a shock to you, Toomey, my dear lad. I know that. I know that you're fond of her—and so am I!"

Toomey stared into those yellow eyes. They were the gates that opened upon a strange country of the soul—a heaven, or a hell.

"I have to see her," said Toomey. "But I haven't heard about her—not since I brought her here."

"I wondered how you could," said Crawford. "Was it simply instinct that brought you back? Ah, well, instinct works like a set of wireless to tell us about the people we love. Poor Sally! It was the shock, Toomey. We were a little rough-handed. It was the shock that upset her, I suppose, and then—"

It seemed to Toomey that two hands of ice were laid against his temples and began to freeze his brain.

"D'you mean that she's dead?" he asked. His voice staggered. "Is that what you mean, Crawford?"

Crawford shook his head, slowly, rather as one who agrees in a sad thing than one who denies it.

"I hope not—I hope it's not the last of her life, Toomey. But the shock brought on a fever, and the fever got into her brain. And the brain is very delicate food for fire, Toomey. It's easily consumed."

"I think my brain's on fire now," said Toomey. "I've got to see her."

"I suppose you feel that way," sighed Crawford, nodding his lion's head in sympathetic agreement. "Naturally you feel that way. Poor fellow! I'd like to be there, too. I'd like to sit there in the darkness and touch her. That's the pity of it. We have the feeling that by mere physical contact we can be of use. But we're wrong, Toomey. We're terribly wrong. There are times when even a mother can't be near her sick child."

Toomey dragged a hand across his forehead.

"You mean that I can't see her?" he said slowly.

Crawford shook his head, adding: "Only the two nurses. They move like pale ghosts around the room, making no sound. They have what even affection can't give to us. They have understanding. They know what to do to help Sally. They understand how the ice-packs must be arranged about her head. They know how to soothe her—exactly what to say. No, Toomey, you mustn't see her. And the more affection you have for her the more reason there is for you to stay away."

"I can't go into the room? I can't even look at her from the door?" asked Toomey.

"All shocks, good or bad, are equally upsetting to her," said Crawford. "They might be fatal."

He lifted his head, and a strange light came into his eyes.

"The least touch may destroy her," said Crawford, softly, almost huskily. "The least touch might also unbalance her reason forever. No, my dear fellow—you mustn't try to see her. You mustn't dream of it!"

TOOMEY DREW IN his breath with a gasp.

"Crawford," he said, "no matter what you say, I've got to put my eyes on her. And if she's as you say—"

"*If* she's as I say?" echoed Crawford, the old brazen thunder ringing deeply from his throat again. "If? Are you doubting me, Toomey? Are you—actually doubting me?"

His glance flashed aside, toward George. It seemed to Toomey that there was the sting of a whip cut in that look.

"I've got to doubt you," said Toomey. "And I have to find out about that night you were left to freeze in the Alps, and why the Big Fellow was given a medal for heroism on that occasion?"

"Ah?" said Crawford. He smiled. "Has the Big Fellow tried the old cock-and-bull story on you? It's a wonder that he's waited so long. I knew, sooner or later, that he'd bring out the story of the medal; God knows what it cost him in bribery to buy it. I don't suppose he told you how much of a cash investment it represents?"

But as the voice flowed on, easily, it suddenly broke,

and came to a harsh stop. The lips of Crawford pinched together.

"You lie!" cried Toomey. "By God, you've been lying from the first day, and I've been the fool and the tool you've used as you pleased!"

Those yellow eyes narrowed a little, and yet Toomey suddenly could see more deeply into them than ever before. He could see the strange country of the mind which they guarded; and it was a hell!

"You know, do you—at last?" said Crawford, and he lifted one finger.

"I know," said Toomey. "And now—"

He had reached for his automatic as he spoke. He had it in the flat of his swift hand when he felt, rather than saw, the shadow of the blow that was looming behind his head. He tried to whirl about. George—he had forgotten George. In his madness, he had turned his back on the great Negro.

Then the shock struck him beneath the right ear and hurled him sidelong to the floor. He lay in a loose heap, his head twisted oddly about under his shoulder.

He was paralyzed. He could not even lift his eyelids, which remained a trifle apart, but his mind still lived as vigorously as ever. He lay there with his right hand still on the automatic, unable to stir the weight of a finger, but conscious, terribly conscious. He thought of two things: Sally was already deep in the Crawford hell; and he himself would taste the same terrible region. It was not fitting that he should die under a single stroke. It would not be pleasing to Crawford, who would prefer to unravel the strings of his heart with every agony.

His mind leaped away to every picture that had flashed before it since he left his rooming house and stood on the corner. He saw Crusty Mallow, and Bushmill, and Slip, and the Big Fellow. Now that the curtain of darkness had been drawn from before his judgment he could see, with all the bitter truth of a clear winter morning, that the Big Fellow was a man rich in kindness, in gentleness of heart, in compassion for others. The proofs had been heaping up all the time before his eyes.

The man had been unnerved, at first, and soggy with easy living and whisky; but when Toomey's regime burned the fat from body and brain, he had become once more something of what he had been in that other time, when he was capable of carrying the weight of a huge, helpless man down the Alpine heights.

And Toomey had ruined him, at the last. He had ruined Sally, too. The mightiest labors had all been poured into the hands of Crawford—and Crawford was a devil on earth!

In one second, the racing brain of Toomey had covered all of those truths, and understood them all.

"Have you killed him, George?" said Crawford.

"Yes, sir. I reckon George killed him," said the Negro. "I had to hit pretty hard, sir. There wasn't taking of no chances with him. If I'd missed the spot, he'd of blowed up this whole house, and you and me with it, I guess, Mr. Crawford!"

"Were you afraid of him?" asked Crawford.

George heaved a great, groaning sigh.

"Mr. Crawford," he said, "when you give me the look, and I started sneakin' up on him from behind, I felt like I was walkin' up on a black panther, like I seen once watchin' me out of a heap of shadows in a zoo one day. First there wasn't nothing inside of that nice big cage. And then there was eyes, and then there was the body all coiled up and soft and slimsy like a pile of velvet. And then I seen that it was just a black streak of lightning layin' easy and restin', and gettin' ready to use itself. And ever since I've seen Mr. Toomey, he sure made me think of that cat!"

"AND YET THERE'S the end of him," said Crawford. "A wonderful machine, George. A very wonderful machine. But the brain broke down, at last. It allowed him to come here and doubt me to my face. Love did it, George. He loved the girl as she loves him, and that love has ruined them both. God pity them."

"Yes, sir," said George. "God pity them!"

"Bring him here and put him on the desk," said Crawford. "I want one last look at his face."

The mighty hands of George lifted Toomey and laid him out on the cold of the polished desk.

Crawford said, quietly: "All steel—all hammered steel. Look at that jaw, George. Look at that nose. Not a pretty fellow, but all edge. Steel that cuts steel. God knows he cut through enough harder things than steel, for me!"

"Mr. Crawford, sir," said George, "maybe George might ask why would you go and keep him? Why wouldn't you go and buy him, sir? Like you've done others?"

"Because he's not like the others," said Crawford. "He's fought his way around the world, but he's fought clean. And I can't keep clean fighters. Sooner or later, there's dirty work to be done. And a clean man wants a clean plate to eat from. Well, it's good-by to him. Those eyes are as dead as fish, this moment, but a little while ago, it would have taken all your manhood to face them, George. Take him away. Hold on—by God, he's still breathing."

"No, sir," said George. "I sure busted his neck. I sure heard the bone crack."

"Look for yourself," said Crawford. "He's breathing. Look out for him now, George. He may be shamming this faint, even! Be careful in the name of God! It's gun cotton you're handling there—it's raw nitroglycerine!"

"He ain't more'n one part alive in ten," said George. "Look here!"

He lifted the arm of Toomey and dropped it. The arm swung idly, loosely down.

He picked up the body of Toomey. "He's a dead one," said George, and dropped Toomey flat on the floor.

It seemed to Toomey that the back of his head was smashed in, and that bones were broken all through his body. Then he heard Crawford laughing, softly, like the laughter of a man who tastes his pleasure gradually. Rage burned away the pain in Toomey, and suddenly he could move, not that he stirred so much as a finger, but he knew that he was capable of motion.

"You're rough with him," said Crawford.

"Panther livin', or panther dead," said George, "it ain't every day that George gets a chance to handle 'em any way he wants. Look, if he ain't still breathin', but he's breathin' mighty small. He don't need much breathin' for the little part of him that's left alive. There ain't as much life left in him, Mr. Crawford, as you could pinch between two fingers."

"Take him away," said Crawford. "Take him down below.

Take him where Flannigan is. We'll finish off the pair of them together. How is Flannigan now?"

"Kind of moldy," said the Negro. "He ain't feeling too smart. He's just kind of moldy and rotting away, like you would say. He don't even talk no more, but sets in a corner with his head on his knees."

"You keep his hands tied?" asked Crawford.

"Yes, sir. I keep 'em tied. But there ain't no will in him to use 'em anyway."

"And Crusty?" said Crawford.

"Why, he's fixed up fine and comfortable," said George. "You know we been takin' good care of him, sir."

"Let him go to the devil now," remarked Crawford. "He's nearly well, the doctor says, but let him go to the devil. The only reason I wasted any time or attention on him was because Toomey, here, wanted him saved. You might chuck him down there with Flannigan and Toomey. Perhaps, George, they'll all be the death of one another. A regular three-cornered murder, which the police will find the traces of in some old deserted house, near here. Take Toomey away. But bring me a glass of whisky first."

"Whisky, sir?"

"I'm going to have one glass if it burns my heart out. A glass of that stuff Toomey liked so well."

George crossed the room and filled the glass.

There was a chance now for Toomey to roll to his hands and then to his feet, but he dared not take that chance. How fast his reactions might be, now, he could not tell, and well he remembered how George, like a monstrous bird, had swooped on Crusty, on that other day, and struck him limp.

Crawford held the glass in his hand, as the Negro picked up Toomey again.

"Toomey," said Crawford, "to all that's left of you, I drink. You've made me rich in hard cash, and you've smashed my old enemy flatter than a worm under my heel. Here's to Toomey, and steel cut steel forever!"

25

BACK FROM DEATH

GEORGE STRODE FROM the room. When he came to the threshold, he threw the body of Toomey over an arm as rigid and mighty as an iron bar while he opened and closed the door. Then, turning across the hall, he pulled wide a door that let up the cool, earthy smell of a cellar.

To carry a burden down those narrow steps would not be easy, because the thing borne in arms would blind the bearer to the steps he was taking. But it was a simple problem which George solved in a simple way. He merely dropped the body of Toomey, took him by the hair of the head, and slamming the door behind him, began to drag that inert form behind him down the steps.

A light burned in the cellar below them, somewhere, but it threw only the faintest glimmerings, here. Dimly uncertain as that light were the thoughts of Toomey. Now might be the time to attempt to throw himself at the giant. But when he rolled his eyes up, he saw his hair clutched by a hand almost as bulky as his head. Moreover, there was no certainty in his body. There was no surety that his muscles would answer his nerves swiftly and surely.

Like a sack he was dragged, therefore, down to the cement floor of the cellar, down a narrow hallway, and so through another door into a dismal little room where one small, frosted globe shone from its wall fixture like an evil eye.

Toomey was dropped. He let himself fall loosely, spilling half over on his face. In the corner what had looked like a heap of old clothes unfolded itself, and shoulders and head of a man rose out of it.

That was Flannigan. A smudge of unshaven hair was like a black mask across the lower part of his long face; the skin about the eyes and forehead seemed to have been painted white, so great was the contrast.

He sat on a ragged old quilt that was thrown over an equally ragged tick filled with straw; his head had been resting on bony knees that were drawn up high, his arms, tied at the wrists, embracing them.

"Here's company for you, Mr. Flannigan," said George.

The little eyes of Flannigan blazed.

"It's Toomey!" he cried. "Is he dead?"

"Mostly dead," said George, "but not quite. He's going to lie down here with you in the coal, for a while, and keep you company, Mr. Flannigan."

The laughter of George filled the room, thundered and re-thundered through it.

He put back his head, and let the noise roll out in a vast flood. Toomey, never moving, scanned the walls and the floor, as far as he could see without stirring his head. The place had been used as a coal bin; that was why the walls were so dingy and the floor so black, and there remained a small heap of the coal covered with dust and cobwebs, near Toomey. On that heap his glance fastened.

"I'm glad he's here," said Hannigan. "I wanta see him rot

"Here's company for you, Mr. Flannigan," said George.

an inch at a time till he falls to pieces! He's why I'm here. He's the reason!"

"Yes, sir," said George. "He's the reason for a mighty lot of things, Mr. Flannigan; but I guess he's done his last trick. He ain't going to move much, but I'll just make his hands sure."

He leaned, and picked up from the floor a length of cord that lay in the black of the dust, like a coiling snake. It was only a moment, but it was the chance for Toomey, since during that instant the back of the great Negro was turned, and his bulk, bending over, obscured the vision of Flannigan.

So Toomey rose to hands and knees and reached for the largest lump of coal that his eyes already had selected. It was in his hand, he was rising with it, when Flannigan uttered a sharp little cry like that of a dog when it sees game afoot. Big George, straightening, whirled about, warned by the cry and the wildly staring eyes of Flannigan; and blindly Toomey struck at the head of the Negro.

It seemed to him that his unresponsive arm hung for ages in the air. It seemed to him that the warding hand of George rose through the air as slowly as a fish floats up through green water. In reality, the movements were a mere flash of time, though they seemed slow to the convulsion of his brain.

The blow landed on the side of the Negro's head. It was like beating a weight against a wall. The two great hands of George lifted, reached, closed on the throat of Toomey as he hammered home a second stroke, this time at the base of the jaw.

The hands fell from Toomey's throat. The eyes of George rolled. His whole body sagged forward.

A THIRD TIME Toomey struck him, falling; and that vast bulk spilled inertly across the floor. His own weight knocked the air from his lungs with a prolonged gasping sound, and he lay still.

Flannigan, agape, his eyes rounded by the miracle they were beholding, watched Toomey lean above that fallen, helpless body, with the black lump poised. A blow now would shatter the skull, and that was what Flannigan expected to see. To his bewilderment, Toomey snatched up the stout length of cord from the floor and caught the hands of George in the noose of it With other loops, then, he secured the feet and drew them up until they met the hands. Hands and feet he lashed together with many windings.

He said, as he worked: "Flannigan, they've had you lined up for a grave. Will you help me if I turn you loose?"

"Turn me loose from this," gasped Flannigan, "and I'll walk on my knees around the world for you!"

In a moment, Toomey found a knife in a coat pocket of George. What was more to him, he found his own automatic. He dropped the gun into a pocket while he slashed the twine that bound the wrists of Flannigan together.

George was groaning with every breath he drew, now, soft, deep, snoring sounds. And Flannigan began to rise, bracing his hands against the walls in the corner, struggling up little by little on legs that shuddered with the effort.

Toomey kneeled by George. Wild, yellow-stained eyes rolled up sidewise to stare at him. The great mouth was loosely open, drooling.

"You hear me, George?" said Toomey. He took out his automatic and smacked the heel of it into the palm of his other hand.

"I hear you—Mr. Toomey," groaned George. "You better kill me. The way you kill me'll be a lot easier for me than Mr. Crawford's killing! Oh, God, I'm a worthless fool nigger. I had a wildcat to handle, and I took and turned my back on it!"

"You're going to talk," said Toomey. "Where's Sally? Where's Sally Moore?"

The yellowish eyes rolled. There was no answer.

Toomey lifted the automatic and weighed it with two or three short movements.

"I'll bash your face in bit by bit, George," he said. "D'you hear me? I'll bash it in little by little, till you tell me where she is!"

He raised the gun with a quick jerk, as though to strike.

"Wait!" gasped George. "She's back in the attic of the big barn. She's back there."

"What are they doing to her?"

"I don't know, Mr. Toomey. Jack, Crawford's son, is back there with her, and he—"

Toomey snarled like a wild beast. Then, tearing a piece from the covering of the ragged mattress, he wadded it into a ball and forced it into the mouth of George, driving it well in behind the teeth. Frightful, strangling eyes glared back at him. He bent lower for an instant, however, until he could hear the drag of the labored breath. The man would not strangle unless panic gagged him still more.

"You ain't going to leave him there?" said Flannigan, reeling on his uncertain legs. "Toomey, you ain't fool enough to leave him there, are you? Here—let me—"

He picked up the fallen chunk of anthracite and swayed it above his head as he staggered forward, his grin wrinkling the blackness of the hairy mask. Toomey took him under the pit of the arm and turned him sharply about.

"He told me what I wanted to know," said Toomey.

"There was no bargain made. And anyway, what's a bargain with that brute? A hog is a better thing!"

"Come on with me," said Toomey. "He stays where he is. Are you sick, Flannigan? Can you walk? What's the matter with you?"

"I've been thinkin' of dying for so long," said Flannigan, "that I can't get back to life in a hurry. I'm gunna be better in a minute, though. Don't quit me, Toomey. I've been a rat—but for God's sake don't leave me in here. Kill me yourself—but kill me outside. I been buried in here—and waiting!"

"I'm not chucking you away," said Toomey. "Come on with me. Stiffen yourself a little. That's all. Don't make a sound when you walk. Come along. That's better."

SO HE HALF urged and half supported the cadaverous frame of Flannigan down the hall. They reached the steep flight of steps and went slowly up them, testing each with their feet for fear of starting a noise of creaking.

At the door above they paused again, staring at one another through the dimness. For every door represented to them a threshold that might divide life from instant death.

Then Toomey pushed the door open. What he heard was the booming voice of Crawford, that seemed almost at his ears. He started to jerk the door shut, before he realized that the great voice in reality came from a distance. So he glided out into the hall with Flannigan behind him. The teeth of the Irishman were clicking together rapidly in the greatness of his terror.

They heard Crawford saying: "Toomey is ended, my friends. You've been jealous of him, Bushmill. So have the rest of you. Now he's ended. He served a turn, and after that he had to be put away. It's a little matter that you'll know more about, later on. Pass the word around."

Toomey, stealing rapidly along the rear hall, heard the voice disappear behind him, and began to breathe again. They had reached a door that opened on a small back porch, with a brilliant electric light shining over it. Switches were fixed against the side wall, however, and the first down extinguished the lights in the hall, while the second covered the porch with darkness. A moment later they were outside, across the porch, walking on grass.

Gasping sounds came from Flannigan; he was weeping with joy, and stifling the sobs.

Straight before them, they saw the outline of the barn, almost as massive and widespreading as the house itself; off to the left in an open field was the huge outline of an airplane. That was the tool which Crawford used, as he had said, to defend himself from attacks by air.

Flannigan gasped, at the ear of Toomey: "Where you going, Toomey? Head off here to the side. There's a light up there in the barn. There's men around the barn, too, likely. Come off here—"

"I'm going into that barn," said Toomey.

"Going—inside?" breathed Flannigan. "Are you crazy?"

Toomey stopped, and faced him.

"You go along your own way," he said. "The nerve has been spilled out of you. You couldn't help me, now; so go and help yourself."

"What I mean—" said Flannigan.

But Toomey walked off and over his shoulder he saw the tall silhouette waver, for a moment, then move away into the darkness over towards the trees.

And so Toomey went on, more and more slowly, pouring all the strength of his senses into the power of the eyes, trying to penetrate the blackness around the barn. He had his reward presently, a reward that made him drop behind a bush, for around a corner of the barn he saw a shadowy form move. A moment later a second man rounded the opposite corner and passed the first one. They were marching on their beat to keep guard; and Toomey could trust that the wardens posted by Crawford would be vigilantly alert on patrol!

He waited till they were out of sight, then ran to the front door of the building, and tried to slide it back or push it in. It was locked. He sprang to the nearest window. Locked, also.

He tried a second. It stuck fast, then suddenly yielded upwards with a loud screech. Toomey went through the gap like a cat, pulled the window down, and waited, breathless.

26

JACK CRAWFORD
SHOWS HIS HAND

FOOTFALLS CAME RUNNING, and excited voices. A flashlight shot through a neighboring window, and, cutting right and left in bright sabre strokes, showed Toomey neatly ordered bridles and well washed English saddles hanging on their pegs.

He lay down flat, his back to the wall, and waited.

At once, through the window just above him, the flashlight played again, and showed all the hanging straps, and their black-painted shadows falling behind them.

Then the window sash was pushed up, groaning. A man's head and shoulders leaned in, while Toomey, supine, covered the fellow with a raised gun. Again the flashlight played up and down the length of the long room.

"I don't see nothing," muttered the man who was leaning in.

His flashlight went out like a blessing, to Toomey.

"Better climb in and take a look around," said another voice.

"Climb in yourself," said the first speaker. "There ain't anything inside there."

"I heard a window."

"Yeah. Maybe Jack opened a window up above."

"That noise didn't come from high up."

"There ain't anything in here."

"Here's something coming. Look sharp!"

"Hello, Dick?" called an advancing voice.

"Here!" said the voice of the man who had opened the window.

"There's news," said the newcomer.

"About what?"

"About Toomey."

"That's all there ever is. News about him! You'd have to keep a newspaper out every day to cover what that bird does. I'm sick of hearin' about him. You'd think that old man Crawford didn't have nobody else working for him than Toomey."

"Well, Toomey ain't working for him now."

"Quit it. He'll work for Crawford till he flops."

"He's flopped."

"The hell!"

"He's flopped, I say."

"Who flopped him? Some of the Big Fellow's agents?"

"George flopped him. Busted his neck for him. George socked him, and you know he can sock."

"George socked Toomey! How come?"

"I dunno. The chief didn't say. But the word's around that Toomey's out of the picture. You know—it goes to show that no matter how high they stand, they can all flop. The chief wants all the boys to know. He says it proves that steady service is better than brilliant work."

"I'll tell you what it shows," said the other. "It shows that

Toomey took a tumble and found out about Crawford. He thought Crawford was straight, they say."

"Yeah. How could he be such a dummy?"

"I dunno. I'll tell you what I think. This here Toomey, he was one of these here enthusiasts. You know. Guys that get nutty about something. They go all out and keep themselves under the whip. They may lead all the way around the track, but likely they pull up lame before the finish."

"Toomey!" muttered a voice, "seemed like nothing could ever stop him. He's gone, but he ain't gunna be forgotten in a hurry."

The window was drawn down, and the voice became an obscure muttering, that passed on down the side of the building.

Then Toomey rose and found the door that he had located when the flashlights were whipping about the room. When he opened it he stepped into the warmth and pungency of the stable section of the building. He heard horses stamping, here and there, and the rustling of hay under the lip, and the grinding of it between monstrous teeth.

He wanted a flashlight, now. He wanted it almost as badly as he wanted life, for every moment was urging him on with a frightful insistency. Before long, Crawford might begin to wonder why the Negro lingered such a time in the cellar of the house. And when he discovered that Toomey was gone, all the hornets would pour out of the hive, ready to sting to death whatever they found.

But he had no light, except the feeble flicker of a cigarette-lighter. When he cupped that with his hand it showed him his way, finally, but it was not the handy thing that a flashlight was.

There was a door on the left. He found that, put out the lighter, and found himself in a square hall, out of which a stairs arose, a stairway with open, iron steps. Up that he went, blessing a rigidity of metal that could not creak underfoot.

AT THE TOP of the stairs, he pushed against a swinging door, which let him into a vast darkness.

He ventured to let the flame of the lighter flicker again. More than half of the second story of the barn was used as a mow, bales of hay being piled in it. But off to the right appeared several doors. Toward these he went in the darkness that surrounded him when the flame was extinguished again. And it seemed to Toomey that a voice arose out of the floor at his feet, like a fountain of fire, the voice of Sally pitched on a high note of fear.

The knees of Toomey buckled under him. A keen pain slid up his right arm. It was from the force with which he gripped the automatic.

He went on, sliding his feet out before him to avoid any obstacles along the floor. Then a man's voice began to speak, wonderfully close at hand, as though he were walking toward Toomey through the blackness. It was Jack Crawford, and his talking guided Toomey to a narrow pencil-stroke of light that widened as he came nearer. It was the crack at the edge of a loosely fitted door. His touch found the knob, turned it—and found the lock had been turned.

Cold sweat poured over his face. He sank to his knees. The key had been turned and withdrawn, so that through the hole, as through a wide gunsight, he could look into the room. It was fitted up as a servant's bedroom, with a narrow iron cot, white-painted, a grass rug on the floor, a calendar picture of a smiling country beauty on the wall above the bed. And in a chair in the center of the room, her arms tied to the sides of it, was Sally, with Jack Crawford opposite her.

Toomey could hardly have known her face. Fear had puckered or drawn it until it seemed ten years older. She was slumped to the side, as one who cannot draw back and must shrink in some direction. And Jack Crawford, his hands on his knees, was leaning toward her, talking in a soft drawl. Even in profile, as Toomey saw him, he was his father's son, with less of thought and more of beast about the jaw and mouth.

"You've talked a lot," said Jack Crawford. "And I've been patient, eh?"

"Yes," whispered the girl.

"But as I've just told you, I'm tired of lies. You're going to speak the truth. You understand?"

"Yes," she whispered again.

"The old man is damned hot because I've lingered the thing out, like this. When I answered the telephone, just now, it was from him, and he said that I was to push things through in a rush. He wants me over there. And I'm going to be through, too. I told him that. I told him that in five minutes I'd have everything out of you that we wanted. Is that clear?"

"Yes," she said.

"Now, listen to me," said Crawford.

She sat up straight. A highlight wavered up and down

her throat as she swallowed. Suddenly she seemed to Toomey not the formidably clever girl that she could be, but a mere child. He half rose, to try the door with his shoulder; but a great doubt withheld him.

"In the first place," said Jack, "you're going to tell me what's in the book. What does the writing in it mean?"

"It—it's a pay book," said Sally Moore.

Jack started.

"You know that, do you? You think you know that? What sort of a paybook?"

"Of your father's—his record of payments—to—to crooks!"

"With their names?"

"Yes," she faltered.

Crawford stood up.

"Now, then," he said, "you can see that we've got to have the book. There's no other way. We've got to have it. You hear me?"

"Yes."

"Answer me. Where is it?"

Fear swelled her eyes. She said nothing.

"Why, you're a fool," said Jack. "Come, out with it. Where's the book? I've asked you that a thousand times before, but now I'm going to learn."

"I'll tell you—when the Big Fellow's free!" said the girl.

"Still trying to bargain?" sneered Jack. "Well, you're calling my hand, and now I'll show it to you."

HE TOOK A little vial out of his pocket, uncorked it with exceeding care, placed it with equal caution on a small deal table, and dipped a slender glass rod into it. When he raised the glass tube again, a small drop of brightness trembled like a liquid diamond at the tip.

"Here's some stuff," said Jack Crawford, "that will make that pretty face of yours melt away—the way water would melt sand. Understand? It'll rot that face of yours away before my eyes. Now—talk!"

He leaned over her, the glass rod poised just above her face.

"No!" screamed Sally Moore.

Jack recoiled a little.

"Not so loud, damn you!" he said, looking suddenly around towards the door. "Well, go ahead. It's nothing to the way you'll screech when this stuff begins to eat into you. Not a thing in the world to the tune that you'll sing then! Now—will you talk?"

He leaned above her once more. With horror her eyes followed the glimmerings of the pendant drop.

And then, suddenly, the quivering went out of her, and she turned to stone.

"No," she said. "You can burn me to bits. You can burn the eyes—out of my head, but I won't speak till you've made him free. I won't!"

"All right," said Jack Crawford. "Then take—"

Toomey smashed the lock of that door with a forty-five caliber slug of lead.

She was screaming. Toomey hurled himself at the door. It flung him back like a pair of great stiff-fingered hands. He went at it once more. The screaming had not ended.

Was the stuff burning her, then?

Crawford was shouting. He was threatening to shoot if the door were broken down. He might as well have threatened a wild beast. For Toomey cast himself at that door like a diver at open water. The whole frame was torn from its hinges, and he catapulted into the chamber with the wreckage.

A gun boomed in his very ears, twice. He was lying on his stomach, with the gun stretched out before him and he saw Jack Crawford crouched down like a sprinter ready for the start, his thick lips grinning away from the white flash of his teeth.

Toomey fired. The man wrapped his arms around his body. He fell in a heap and he kept turning and turning, kicking himself around and around, leaving a thick, smeared trail of blood behind him.

Toomey slashed the cords that tied the girl. His hands and the knife did the work, blindly, for he was straining his eyes at her face. There was no spot on the skin, no deadly red blur or white, leprous marking to tell where the acid had taken hold.

Like one falling asleep she lay with her head resting on the topmost rung of the chair.

He took her by the shoulders and jerked her to her feet. This was a time for her to faint, when the whole barn would be filled with people in a few seconds! There was no tenderness in Toomey. He felt nothing but impatient rage. Jack Crawford bumped against him, and staggered him. He looked down. The man was like a wounded caterpillar, twisting about on itself. Toomey lifted the automatic and put it near the man's head.

Two hands grappled his wrists.

"No, no, Toomey!" she pleaded. "It's enough. Don't kill him—if he can live!"

And then all the sense of danger and of battle swept away from Toomey. He looked at her with eyes of a calm interest, as though her words had been read out to him from a book of the fables of long ago. *She* had pleaded for the life of Jack Crawford! The taste of that moment would never be out of his mind so long as he lived.

27

THE FLIGHT IN THE GRAY CAR

THE THUNDER OF feet beating on the iron of the stairway was filling the barn when Toomey and the girl ran out. He led her to the right, running sidewise, his hand stretched far out before him to feel the way. Behind them, the shaft of light from the open door helped illumine the barn floor in one direction, only, and that was towards the stairway door. Yet it gave to the two of them faint glimmerings of the rest of the shadowy interior.

They were among the bales, they were out of them. They were skirting between the big pile and the wall on the farther side, when the first men entered, slashing at the darkness with their flashlights. They showed the shadowy rafters above, the sleek gleam of the bales of hay, and several tenuous arms that swayed down across the open loft door—ropes for the hoisting of grain or hay. Toomey saw them last of all, and with the greatest hope.

They could not get down the stairs. A steady stream of people would be flooding up and down that way, for a long time, and in a few short moments, the searchers would spill all over the loft in their man-hunt.

First, they had spotted the open door, as matter of course. They headed for it with a rush, while Toomey made the girl slink with him between the double walls of hay and wood towards the loft door. They came to it. He handled the ropes, and tried them with a sailor's deftness. A pair of grappling irons was hitched to one end. He showed Sally how to stand on the irons, and started to swing her out over the sill.

More people were pouring up the stairs, beating the door open with the flat of their hands. The flashlights ripped the darkness open with a thousand strokes, like the flights of brilliant glow-worms through summer night. And now there rose a voice such as Toomey in all his wanderings never had heard before. It had the shrillness and the pitch of a woman's scream, but it had the volume and the throaty harshness of a man in agony. It was Jack Crawford; yelling: "Toomey! Get him for me! He killed me. He killed me! He murdered me. Get him for me. Oh, God, get him for me, boys, and I'll love you. I'll make you rich. I'll give you all the old man's dough. Get that Toomey!"

Sally swung clear of the sill. Toomey prepared to go down with her, holding onto the up-passing rope as a brake on their descent, when the grappling irons, striking the side of the barn, rang louder than the clapper of a great bell. And the sound drew a battery of flashlights upon them.

"There!" screeched a voice. "It's Toomey himself!"

A gun boomed, and another; and as the rope burned through the hands of Toomey and they swept towards the darkness of the earth below, it seemed that a river of noise was pouring towards the brink which the open door of the loft afforded. If the thundering reached that lip of blackness before he and the girl were running at full speed, he could guess the end that would come to them both!

They struck the ground with a great jangling of the irons; then they fled. From above, shouts struck at them like stones. A bullet nipped the ear of Toomey as he whirled Sally around the corner.

"Straight back towards the house!" he gasped.

For the pursuit would expect that direction least of all, perhaps.

They heard iron thunder of feet upon the stairway inside the barn. One of the horses began to neigh. It was a stallion, and his whinney sounded to Toomey as had the screaming of Jack Crawford a moment before. Other horses answered. There was an increased uproar of tramplings that resounded from the hollow wooden floors of the stable. And human voices ran through this torrent of noise like burning oil on fast-flowing water.

Yet all of those sounds were still muffled as Toomey and the girl raced towards the big house. Then, as they gained that additional shelter, the human noise of the pursuit came booming out into the open.

Inside the house, Toomey heard the lion's roar of Crawford raised. He was shouting for someone to find George. Right under the windows of Crawford's big room—which to Toomey was so like a chamber of his own brain—they raced. It was a sad temptation to leap for one of those windowsills, pull himself up, and with a bullet darken the evil brightness of that great mind forever! But seconds and half seconds counted for the salvation of their own lives.

They rounded the front of the house. He heard the whistling gasp of the girl's breath, but she ran on with the lightness, with the swing, with the speed of a boy.

They swerved into the front path. They passed the gate.

And there was the long, low, powerful outline of the gray car. A figure leaped out from before it and shouted. The circle of a flashlight's glare staggered across the two of them as they ran; and, still running, Toomey fired at the light.

A YELL ANSWERED him. The light dropped. It continued to spill its brilliance down the sidewalk, while he who had held it ran as fast as a dodging snipe.

They were in the car. The starter rumbled, paused. The engine would not start! He tried again, and now with a whirr and then a soft roaring the engine caught hold; the exhaust started snoring and rattling, and snoring.

He had the gear in first as the stream of the pursuit came beating around to the front of the house. And all their clamoring went up like a cry of hounds as Toomey sent the car ahead with a jerk and a lurch.

Now he was in second, and shooting forward. Now in third, and racing.

What did the popping of guns behind them matter? It seemed to Toomey that they were travelling faster than the bullets could!

He used on the first corner a skid turn that snatched them to safety more quickly than a frightened deer could leap. Still the car gathered speed. He let it out, straightening the curves, while the massive machine swayed rapidly from side to side.

"Which way?" said Toomey.

She lay back in her place, her head supported against the edge of the cushion, that kept jouncing it up and down.

"The Big Fellow!" she answered.

The Big Fellow, first, then.

The men of Crawford would be able to guess that the Big Fellow was the destination; they would tumble into automobiles and follow as fast as they could drive; but the hope of Toomey was that he could distance them so far that he would have time to disarm Slip and take the Big Fellow into the car, before the others came up. But every second counted, and that was why he kept the big car straining like a racing greyhound at every bend of the way.

"Stand up!" he told the girl at last, as they were sweeping up a tall hill. "Stand up and look back and see if any headlights are coming."

She stood up, accordingly, holding to the top of the windshield and the back of the seat. She staggered as the car reeled and heeled on the swerving road, but she maintained her post just for a moment. When she sat down, she said: "Away back—away back, Toomey, there are three cars coming. I could see their headlights bobbing. And others coming after them. They may not be Crawford's cars."

"If the headlights are bobbing, they're Crawford's cars," said Toomey. "And they're racing. That's why the lights seem to jump. Are they very far back?"

"Miles—miles!" she answered. "Toomey, what changed you? What was it turned you to the Big Fellow? What brought you out against Crawford?"

"I learned a little of the truth; George taught me the rest by putting a lump behind my ear," said Toomey. "Sally, why didn't you try to tell me the truth long ago?"

"Would you have listened? Would you have let me talk against Crawford?" she asked.

"No," he admitted, gloomily. "Crawford was a saint, until today. I wouldn't have listened."

They shot down the last stretch of road, and he swung the car to a skidding halt in front of the little house on the hill.

He was up the steps and beating at the front door, long before the girl was out of the car.

"Who's there?" called the voice of Slip.

"Toomey! Open up!"

A footfall came, gliding; the key grated in the lock, and the door opened. It showed Slip faintly outlined against the dim light that reached the hallway from the living room.

"Time enough that you came back," snarled Slip. "Two bums for me to look after, while you go off joy-riding, eh?"

Toomey laid the heavy muzzle of his automatic in the pit of Slip's stomach.

"Heave up your hands, Slip," he commanded, "then turn around and walk back down the hall!"

28

WHILE THE SEARCHLIGHTS HUNTED THEM

IN AN INSTANT a gray mask was drawn about the mouth of Slip—not fear, but rage.

"The doublecross, eh?" he said. Then, seeing the girl over Toomey's shoulder, as she hurried in and closed the door behind her, he added: "Price, one female! What a cheap guy you are, Toomey!"

He turned on his heel, with his hands raised shoulder high, and walked down the hall, and into the living room. The Big Fellow was standing up, staring at this strange procession as though it had been a troop of ghosts, and young Rush, lolling in his chair, rolled his eyes at the phenomenon.

"Sally—what does it mean?" gasped Lawrence Oliver.

"It means that Toomey's on our side. It means we're going to win," she said.

"Toomey? On our side? Toomey?" cried the Big Fellow.

"Stop batting your eyes," said Toomey. "Come to life and fan him, Big Fellow. We've only got seconds. Sally, cut Rush loose—that youngster, there. He's a friend of the Big Fellow. Is this the loot you were going to turn over?"

For all across the table were scattered little packages of

greenbacks and the stiff, folded paper of readily convert-ible bonds. A suitcase, still partly full, lay open on the floor.

"Aye," said the Big Fellow. "That's all the blood that they could drain out of me on the spur of the moment. Enough to sink me. There's close to three millions in that little heap."

Rush was loose.

"Rush," said Toomey, "take that same cord and tie Slip, and tie him hard, too. Sally, get that stuff back into the suitcase. We're jumping from seconds and trying to grab our lives. They're after us, man! They're after us, Big Fellow. Look alive. Come on with me!"

He was busy with his hands, in the interval, stuffing a gag into the mouth of Slip, and as he finished the task, he heard a roaring come out of the air and sweep down toward the earth, until it seemed as though the airplane were plunging straight at the little house. The motor shut off. They heard the rushing sound of the huge body and wings cutting through the air.

"That's Crawford's best bet, and it's too good for us," said Toomey. "Try the back way. We might be able to cut across the fields before they get out of the airplane and scatter around the house."

They reached the back door with a rush. Big Fellow, leading, had jerked the door open, when a shaft of light from an electric torch struck fairly across them. They heard a voice yell, a gunshot; a bullet flew through splintering wood, but a dozen feet from them.

The Big Fellow leaped back, slamming the door. It remained shuddering rapidly from the force of the impact; that same shudder was in the heart of every one of them.

The kitchen was dark, but each knew how the other looked at that moment.

Toomey turned and ran back into the front of the house. To left and right, ahead and behind him, eyes of light winked on and off, throwing against the house flashes that peered for an instant into the darkened rooms.

From a front window he stared to the left and saw them coming—car after car, with headlights that swerved and staggered with speed. The vanguard of Crawford's men had nailed the fugitives in place. The rest of the army would soon take the house. They walked back into the living room where Slip, bound hand and foot, regarded them with eyes of baleful content.

Each acted according to his particular nature, now. Toomey began to walk up and down with a quick step that paused now and again as some thought struck him, and was gone again. The girl sat down and let her glance drift after Toomey. She was rather flushed than pale, and there was nothing unusual about her except that her eyes were a little wider than usual. The Big Fellow leaned against the wall with his arms folded, and a spot of white in the center of his cheek as though a finger had been pressed hard on that place, and just removed.

As for Rush, he was white indeed, and perceptibly shaking. By the twitching of his mouth it was plain that he would find it hard to speak, and yet the set of his jaw proclaimed that he was fit for action. Set him in motion, and he would soon be himself.

Outside, they could hear the moan of brakes and the grind of tires on gravel as one car after another came to a halt.

More flashlights struck across the house. The Big Fellow suddenly straightened. He waved his hand in a quick gesture.

"Well," he said, "what Crawford wants is that stuff—and me. More than anything else, he wants that. He can have it all and me with it. You've all done your best for me. And all I can do is be the ticket that lets you out through the gate." **HE TURNED INTO** the hall with a long stride. Both Rush and the girl looked at Toomey; and Toomey, his head bent low, peered from under contracted brows after Lawrence Oliver.

"Come back here," he said, suddenly.

The Big Fellow turned.

"We can't do anything," he protested. "You can see that for yourself. What they want is Lawrence Elliott Oliver, and they'll have to have him—and his cash, too. But that's all right. If they have me, they'll probably go easy, knowing that you're on the loose, and that you're my friend. You'll be my insurance policy while they have me, Toomey."

"Shut up, will you?" said Toomey. "We want a chance to think. What you say is all damned nonsense."

The Big Fellow looked at Toomey like a little child at an old wizard. Then he came softly back into the room and sat down. He put his head against the back of the wall, and closed his eyes. He had been willing to face death; now it was as though he had been reprieved after standing in front of the firing squad. The others gave him one glance, and then carefully avoided his face. They had seen his courage, and they did not wish to dwell on his weakness.

And all of them were cold at heart, for death was in the

air; the thin, stale smell of food was like the smell of death, to all of them.

Toomey began to pace the floor again.

Then he went to the front room and again looked out. The gray car stood there waiting for him, like a friend. If once he could put its power in motion they, as though closed into the handle of a hurled spear, could be flung off to safety, perhaps. But there was terribly small chance of that. Out there in the night were watchers upon every side. They were gathering to make their plans, now. They might rush the house; or they might decide to buy out the fugitives; they might choose any one of many possible courses. And here and there in the brush, or streaking the night with a pale cone of brilliance, a flashlight winked and was out again, to show that danger lived in the darkness.

Toomey went back to the living room. The Big Fellow's eyes were still closed, but the girl, and Slip, and Rush, all stared at Toomey.

"If we make a rush for it," said Toomey—" you and I, Big Fellow—we'd draw a lot of attention to ourselves. And the girl and Rush could go the other way as safe as you please."

The Big Fellow nodded, swayed forward in his chair, and stood up. He looked sick, but he was ready. A sudden outpouring of admiration made Toomey cry: "You're a good one, Big Fellow. By God, there's a heart in you! Are you ready to take the dive?"

"Yes," said Oliver.

"I'm ready too," said the girl, standing up.

Toomey lifted a finger at her. "You stay here!" he commanded.

"It's no good, Toomey," she answered. "I won't stay behind. You can't make me."

"Nor me," said Rush, stammering a little.

Toomey glared wildly at them. Then he turned his back, and resumed his pacing. He squatted suddenly on his heels, and stared at the floor.

"I'm the one who destroys everything for—" began the Big Fellow.

"Oh, shut up, shut up!" said Toomey.

They were silent.

"The car is the trick," said Toomey. "To grab that, and make a run. But they know we're depending on that car. The minute it moves, twenty lights will be shining at it, and twenty guns pumping lead. The car's no good, and yet we've got to use it."

"Anything they don't expect is the right thing to do," said the girl. "If we could *seem* to use the car, and then do something else—that sounds silly, I know."

"Why, we can put our ghosts in it," said the Big Fellow, sourly. "Bullets can't hurt ghosts, so we'll put our ghosts in it."

"Or a dummy?" said Toomey.

"A dummy!" cried the girl, jumping up.

Toomey looked at her vaguely. Then something snapped on a light in his brain.

"A dummy's going to start the motor, eh?" said the Big Fellow.

Toomey left the room. He went up to his room, got a suit of the clothes of Crusty Mallow, and came again down the stairs, dragging pillows. They hardly understood, but they fell to work. One end of a pillow was stuffed up into a hat, and the other end put inside the coat. A second pillow fattened the coat. Papers were crammed up the sleeves of it.

"THAT OUGHT TO do," said Toomey. "Now, then, I'm going to take this doll and get to the car with it. I'm going to put it into the front seat, the driver's seat, and lean over and press the self-starter. As the motor starts, I fade into the brush on the other side of the driveway. In the meantime, you two have sneaked on your hands and knees, inch by inch, till you're in the same brush. The minute that motor turns over, there's going to be a lot of noise and light— noise enough to cover the sound that we make in smashing through the brush and getting out onto the road. When we're on the road, we dive for the nearest car. They've got cars enough, out yonder. We get one of those busses, and step on it. That's all. How does it sound to you?"

The Big Fellow began to laugh, shakily.

But the girl said: "It's a beautiful idea. It's as good as done."

"Yes, *we're* as good as done," said the Big Fellow. "But something is better than nothing. If we stay here much longer we'll be having snakes in the house with us."

Every moment of the darkness, in fact, seemed to make the danger soak more intimately into the house.

"Listen to me, Rush," said Toomey to the boy. "You're going to stay here until we've made the demonstration in front of the house. And when the shooting starts, you stand at the back door, and count up to ten; then open the kitchen door and sneak from the brush uphill. They'll be too busy in front to pay much attention to you."

"I won't sneak," said Rush. "I'm going to stick with you!"

Toomey scowled at him.

"We've got to get at a car, and there may not be room for you," said he. "We don't want you on our hands. You'd only clutter things up."

"Yeah. I know. I'm no good. I'm a bust," said Rush, faintly.

"A bust? You showed me that the Big Fellow is a white man," said Toomey. "You saved your pals from breaking their heads against a wall. You took your medicine. You're the gamest kid I ever bumped into. All right, you stick. Now get the hell out there into the kitchen, and wait for things to happen."

He thrust Rush into the hall.

"It's like seeing the sun shine at night—having Toomey on my side of the fence," murmured the Big Fellow.

Toomey walked down the living room, stood over Slip, and looked down into the keen, malevolent eyes, bright as the eyes of a bird of prey. There was no fear in Slip, but only an endless malice.

Toomey went back into the hall.

Those night noises which begin with the evening, when the fall of temperature twists at the boards, started creaking through the little place like footfalls. And footfalls they might of course be. They went down the hall to the front door, and pulled it back; and at the same moment a beam of light swung across their faces from outside the house!

29

THE ROAD TO PORTHAVEN

IT WAS LIKE a breath of wind, that beam of light. And they were sere autumn leaves, whirled by it, as they backed against the walls. Looking back, Toomey saw another flash cross the windows of the living room.

"Doesn't mean anything," said Toomey. "They didn't see us. They're just spraying the house with light, now and then. They've got electric light *and* brains, out there."

He crouched beside the door.

"Don't move," said Toomey. "Don't move till the next flash, and then go out across the porch and down those steps and think you're snakes moving. Go right straight across the road and into the brush. And don't once get up to your knees. Understand?"

"I understand," they muttered, in a chorus.

Toomey looked to the west, which was the direction in which the house faced, and he saw that streak of lucid green which he had noted in the morning, but now it was smoked over and growing darker with the night.

"Why couldn't we all go on into the brush?" said the Big Fellow. "Why couldn't we all go through, and then try to rush a car and take it?"

"Because we'll make more noise than elephants, getting

through, old son," said Toomey. "We need something to cover that noise, and to draw the boys in from the road. Because they have men out there with the automobiles. You can be sure of that."

"The damned police!" said the Big Fellow. "The State police, too, that everybody's so proud of and always talking about; they're never where they're wanted. They're no damned good."

"Hush, Big Fellow," said the girl.

"Are you all right?" said Toomey.

"I'm all right," she said. "I'm sort of sick at the stomach, but I'm all right."

"Give me your hand," said Toomey. He found it in the darkness.

"You're okay," he said. "You're not shaking. Move steady and soft, when the time comes. That's the trick. Steady and soft."

A blinding flash of electric light whipped across the doorway, lunged down the hall, showed the glistening varnish of the banisters, and was gone. Toomey crept out on the porch, and heard the breathing of the others behind him. If the holder of that torch should swing it straight back across the house front again—well, one has to die some day!

The bulky burden of the dummy was one great trouble. He managed it as well as he could, but the bottom of the thing was always dragging. It rubbed against the painted wood and made a sound like a rasp—to his ears. It dragged on the gravel of the road, and sounded to him like the crunching noises of a big automobile.

The small rocks bit into his knees and into his left hand, as he crawled.

Then he literally banged his head against the rear bumper of the car! He had forgotten the huge length of the machine. The bumper gave off a dull, singing note from the impact. He actually forgot himself far enough to curse aloud, in a whisper, at his folly!

But no guns spoke. No light played. Yes, there it was, a sudden swordstroke across the night. He lay flat on his belly beside the car and was aware of the flash of that stroke through the darkness. A wind breathed, as he got to his feet. It seemed that a legion were whispering together in the night. He glanced up at the stars. There were thousands of people, in places, watching those stars, wearily, carelessly; they could not realize the breathless delight of their privilege in being able to look in safety at those great diamonds in their bed of blue-black velvet.

He settled the dummy in the driver's seat, pulling it well over against the door. Then he reached far over and in. He pulled out a bit of choke. He waited. The thing was for the engine to take hold at once. Whatever happened, he must not simply flick the starter with his finger, but press it hard. He must give it a good shove, then turn, wheeling to the left, and dive for the brush—dive for it, as if it were water.

So he leaned farther and bore down on the self-starter. The engine whirred, with a powerful impetus, and Toomey flinched away.

He was stooping, beyond the car, when lights—three or four brilliant spars—struck the automobile. And then a great gong-like voice boomed through the night. Crawford himself had been borne to the scene to take command in this all-important battle!

RIFLES BEGAN TO rapid fire. No, there was a machine gun. Nothing but machine guns could make that staccato roar. The clanking of the bullets against the metal body rang behind him, and Toomey dived for the brush. Into it he went, came up to hands and knees, and ran forward again. Bullets were raining. Perhaps they had seen him, for the shots were cutting through the shrubbery just over his head. He could only hope that these were the spill-overs that had whizzed above the machine.

Someone yelled again, in a screech as high as the voice of a frightened woman: "A fake! A lousy fake! It's a dummy!"

He should not have used pillows to stuff the dummy. He thought of that as he ran through the circular patch of brush. He should have realized that the rain of lead would tear the cloth apart and send the down of the pillows into the air like steam from a boiler.

Then he was on the road beyond the circle. A bulky man was running in the same direction before him. The girl followed at the heels of the Big Fellow. Those shoulders of the Big Fellow were like the shoulders of a prizefighter. He thought of that, too, as he ran for his life.

From the tail of his eye, he saw other men rushing in from the roadway towards the firing. The roar of the guns stopped, suddenly. Only an occasional explosion, that sounded strangely foolish and futile.

The Big Fellow had headed for the nearest machine—there were four or five of them drawn up. And an image jumped up and came around the back of that phaeton, shouting: "What in hell—"

The Big Fellow fired while he was still running. The man behind the car fell on his head and knees and then doubled up in a knot, like a wounded caterpillar.

The Big Fellow hurled his suitcase into the back of the car and wrenched the door open. The girl was running around the machine, around the head of it, as Toomey got into the driver's seat. He found the key in the lock. That chance, also, he had not thought of until his hand touched the edge of the metal. The starter whirred; the engine throbbed. The girl was there beside him, slamming the door shut on her side as he slipped the gears in. They engaged with a shocking jar. He had forgotten to throw off the hand brake, and the engine stalled!

The firing from a distance had stopped. But voices were yelling, here and there, it seemed from the throats of a regiment of men. Heels beat on the gravel of the little country road. As he pressed the starter again, the automatic of the Big Fellow began to boom from the back seat. Somebody yelled as if in protest. The girl had thrown off the hand-brake. With incredible slowness, first speed pulled the car ahead. Second dragged it on, till it quickened, suddenly, and then he could throw in high. Ah, what a difference between this and the gray car, the long, low metal monster that seemed to love to spring forward like a deer!

Guns broke out behind them. The bullets thudded through the back of the car, with ripping, hammering sounds. The Big Fellow gasped.

"Bad, Big Fellow?" cried the girl.

"Stung, that's all," said the Big Fellow. "Nothing—nothing! Damn 'em! Nothing! And we're away! We're away, Toomey. Give it hell! Hit the road for the Big Noise."

"We're going across country," said Toomey. "They'll head us off on the other roads. They'll be on a telephone, in five minutes, and have men watching all the main roads. We're going across country."

WHERE?" SHOUTED THE Big Fellow.

"You've got to say," shouted Toomey. "Start the brain working. Crawford has hornets everywhere; there won't even be a chance to get to police. Where can we go?"

"Porthaven!" said the girl. "There's your motor boat waiting there at the dock, and it's always tuned up and ready to go, Big Fellow."

"It's twenty miles!" cried Lawrence Oliver.

"Damn the miles. We've got to get there," said Toomey.

"Go on, then!" cried Oliver.

"Out to sea," said Toomey. "Crawford rules the land, but we'll find out if he owns the sea, too!"

Then he groaned. "Look back, Big Fellow. See if they're gaining. I've got to turn on the lights, and that'll show 'em the way. I can't see. And the damned car's a baby. It's a rotten pile of tripe. I've got to have light to see by."

"You can't have it," said the girl. "You can't hold up a lantern for 'em. If we smash, we smash, and that's that!"

"If we smash, we smash," said Toomey.

He felt like a child to which a parent has given permission. Half the responsibility was gone from him, and all he had to do was to keep the accelerator pressed down to the floorboards. For if they crashed, they crashed, and that was that.

The road wound narrowly; he straightened those bends as much as he could; the rear wheels scratched like the paws of a dog, as they skidded again and again on the gravel.

She was light; she was terribly light; every bump made her hop and lose her grip. She was sickeningly light, and weak! Then a powerful headlight wavered, steadied on them from behind.

"They're walking right up on us," said the Big Fellow, calmly.

Toomey felt his brains go numb with an electric shock. It was still a mile, almost more than a mile before he could make a turn. The girl gave directions, but he was guessing at the actual road; only those lights from behind, drawing nearer, helped him with far flung glimpses of what lay ahead.

A rifle, unheard, must have spoken behind them, for a bullet sang at his ear.

Then he saw the turn to the right, a swale at the side of the road, a slight rise for the entrance to the lane. That lane was a thin, winding ribbon across country, and tapped a main road five miles away.

It was madness to take that turn without slowing the car, without taking his foot off the feed. But he kept the feed jammed clear down, and took the turn as a madman would. There was a lucky bank on the left. He caromed off of that and shot down the road into blackness that was a solid wall.

Now he could make out the way, a winding hint of a way through the night. It was useless to watch the road itself, very much. The starlight glinted vaguely on trees and hedges beside it. He split the difference and took the way between. In the first half mile, he smashed through brush on one side, and then brush on the other. He heard the Big

Fellow beginning to curse. Now and then there were bad bumps. The road seemed to rise at them and stop them with an extended hand. But if they smashed, they smashed, and that was that!

Still no lights followed them from behind. There was no great flare of a headlight. They had gone a long distance before a pale glimmer stole over the hedges at the sides of the road, like the gleaming of the dawn, and he knew before the Big Fellow spoke, that a car was rushing after them.

30

THROUGH A WALL OF BLACKNESS

THEY FOUND THAT the menace came rapidly up behind them. Toomey, in despair, turned on his own headlights. They were already caught by the lights from behind, and he felt it made little difference to him. But something roared over him. Something like a fabulous bird sailed on stretched wings not thirty feet above the road, across the upper glow of the headlights.

It was the airplane, of course. A machine gun crackled, distantly, hardly distinguishable above the roaring of the great motor in the air. The windshield smashed. Bits of broken glass blew back against Toomey. The wind hurtled against his face, moving his head from side to side.

He flashed off the headlights again. The girl, silently, was picking up fragments of the broken glass. The Big Fellow, in the rear seat, was silent also. It seemed to Toomey a miracle that they were still quiet, when yells were working in his own throat, trying to get past his locked teeth.

They hurdled a bridge. The body of the girl rose, fell. Her head struck against the wheel, beside his hand, and she slid in a loose heap to the floor. She interfered with the working of the feed. He reached down and moved the weight of head and shoulders away.

She might be dead. But if they smashed, they smashed, and that was that.

The Big Fellow leaned across the seat and stretched down to pick up the girl. His elbow bumped hard against the shoulder of Toomey.

"Get out of my way!" shouted Toomey. "Get—out—of—my way, you thick-headed fool!"

The Big Fellow was no longer trying to lift the limp body of the girl. He disappeared into the back seat again. Her head and shoulders slid over against the foot on the accelerator, again. He cursed. The wind whipped the curse off his lips, entered his mouth, blew his cheek into a straining pocket.

What were they doing? It felt like seventy or eighty. Hardly eighty, but it felt that way. And still the lights from behind drew closer and the hedges gleamed more brightly on either side.

The black bird sailed out of the sky again; the machine gun whirred louder than the motor. The bullets sang like wasp-wings in incredible flight. Then the phantom was gone.

This was the true sport, the real hunting practice, to course your game across the fields with dogs, while hawks stooped at it from the sky.

Was Sally being cut by the remnants of the glass on the floor?

She moved, she rose, she slid back into the seat again. He said nothing. Presently she stooped and began to fumble for more bits of the glass that jangled on the floor of the car. But now with one hand she kept a firm grip on the back of the seat. She kept throwing out bit after bit.

"Are you cut?" he shouted.

She put her mouth close to his ear. Her thinner voice seemed to cut through the windy roar without trouble.

"A bump—I'm all right," she said.

"Sally, are you all right?" thundered the Big Fellow.

"Shut up!" cried Toomey. A sort of hysterical madness poured up through his brain. "Shut up! Shut up! Shut up! Damn you!"

Before him, lights flowed smoothly, with ridiculous slowness, in a double column up and down the length of a main road. He came closer and could see the sheen of the metaled roadway. Behind him, the headlights were no longer pale, but brightly glowing.

There were fifteen miles on that good road—unless the cops stopped them! Fifteen miles, Sally said.

HE SHOT ONTO it, the car leaping high over the crest and landing with a stagger, in front of a machine that swerved out, almost struck a car coming in the opposite direction, and skidded badly. Toomey was going full blast, by that time, and the wind in his ears muffled the shouting.

They could not shell him from the air on a crowded road.

So he switched on his headlights again. The traffic grew thicker. He went through it like a snake through grass. He never touched the brakes. If they smashed, they smashed, and that was that. When the cars were jammed hub to hub, he drove straight at them, and miracles happened, holes opened.

Once, when blinding lights shone towards them, he ventured a single glance at the girl. She lay back in the seat, her body braced, with a streak of blood down her face, but she was smiling at the glory of the speed.

People who play the game are better than those who have to fight it. In the back seat, the Big Fellow was fighting the game, now. Toomey knew it. The nerves that whiskey had rotted away had recovered enough to stand all of this without breaking. Ten days ago, the man would have been a screaming lunatic long before.

You can shape a man, thought Toomey. And you can improve him with hammering, the way you improve steel. Good hammered steel is what you want in this world. It takes a better edge, too, and it holds against the thunder-shocks and jars of life.

Fifteen miles down a broad, smoothly-metaled roadway!

He began to relax.

"Report!" he shouted.

"Not in sight!" yelled the Big Fellow.

A little later: "Report!" cried Toomey, again.

"One car coming like hell on fire."

"They're after us!" said Toomey, to his soul, and pressed vainly down against the floorboards. The car was giving all it had. What gibbering idiots, what childish fools would make a car incapable of more than seventy-three miles an hour?

That was all that they were doing. Seventy-three! Oh, for ten minutes on the long gray armor-piercing shell that he had been seated in that morning!

But the miles were leaping past them. They were flying away. The speeding car from behind shot up to within a hundred feet. Then came another welcome traffic jam, and Toomey went into it almost gladly. His fenders were ringing like musical instruments when he came out on the other side. Let them follow him through that sort of white water!

No, they did not follow. They stretched out over the next half mile, before the shooting pair of headlights came upon him again.

Then, before him, he saw a state policeman skidding, a man who sat bolt upright, his hands on the wide guiding-bar of his motorcycle. He jounced up and down a little, as he took the bumps. He swayed far to this side and to that as he cut in and out among the cars. Now and then, he turned his head with the stern air of authority. This was a knight who rode in the service of his lady, the law. But he was of no use to these three fugitives. What would the men of Crawford think of shooting down one officer for the sake of capturing a fortune in hard cash, and honor in the eyes of their master?

So Toomey went by that man of the law like a hawk past a fledgling dove.

He saw the head of the officer flick towards him, and felt the burn of anger behind the goggles.

ON THEY WENT. They only had three or four miles on this road, before they made another right turn. Then he heard the snort of the motorcycle as it came shooting up alongside. The policeman, heading in front of that guilty fugitive, raised his hand with an imperious gesture, waving Toomey to the curb, putting on the brakes directly in their path.

Toomey veered to the left, almost frightened a passing car into the ditch, and shot ahead. A mile or two were left when the Big Fellow shouted: "Coming again!"

The wind, by a queer freak, ripped at the eyelids

of Toomey, made them flutter, half blinded him. But if they smashed, they smashed, and that was that!

He glanced at the girl, in the flare of passing headlights, and this time she was leaning forward into the hurling of the wind, and laughing a little.

They have a saying among the Arabs, when the queenly mare walks out of the tent in the morning, and lifts her head to look towards the horizon: "Now she is saying: 'When will a real man, when will my master come over the edge of the earth to me?'"

Toomey thought of that.

"When he comes up, show him your gun, and wave him back. Shoot into the road in front of him, if you have to!" called Toomey.

The girl relayed the message, as the speeding motorcycle came grandly up again.

It drew alongside. The lips of the policeman moved vainly, incapable of making rounds that would penetrate the Niagaras of noise that floated past the ears of Toomey.

And then the talking of the policeman stopped. He was jerked to the rear.

"Is he pulling a gun?" shouted Toomey.

The girl relayed, and the message came back from the Big Fellow: "Yes! A gun! A gun!"

Then: "He's starting full speed again."

And immediately afterward: "There comes the other car. By God, they've almost run the policeman down. He's shaking his gun at 'em—"

Toomey heard no more; or, hearing, he could not decipher the significance of the syllable, for another wide pool of cars had formed on the road before him, and almost literally he trampled through that confusion. As he shot by, they swerved out a little, instinctively, to escape from the way of the monster.

He reached the end of that broad roadway, so far as it was serviceable on this night of nights.

He swung right, and the Big Fellow cried: "Coming again!"

"The policeman?"

"The car!" called the Big Fellow.

And once more they were plunging through narrow, winding ways, hurling towards Porthaven, without lights, through a wall of blackness which, after the main highway, was more impenetrable than ever. Toomey found a ditch that nearly wrecked them on the right, and, straightening again, almost tipped them over in a similar ditch on the left. But after that, something cleared his eyes. The wind began to blow at their backs. The hurricane he had been facing was therefore less by a half, and still that accelerator was down on the floor when the girl cried out, and pointed.

Then she leaned over to him.

"The gasoline reads empty!"

He listened without understanding.

"What?" he shouted.

"No gasoline!"

No gasoline—and he had simply driven them out into a more complete wilderness, where the gunmen of Crawford would be able to deal as they pleased; and from behind them, the old monotony of the pursuing headlights began to waver.

31

BEHIND THEM A BLACK SHADOW

WELL, THEY COULD go until luck stopped them. Gasoline registers are not always perfect. They make mistakes, too! This was one of those mistakes; it had to be.

They shot on through blackness. They saw a string of lights, regularly spaced as beads. That was Porthaven, and beyond it another dimmer, double patch of lights—a ship with its image moving beside it over still water. The sea was not more than a lake. But Toomey would have preferred the dark madness of a storm to hide them from the hawks that hunted from behind.

The airplane seemed to be gone. That was one comfort.

They reached Porthaven. They passed the scattering outlying houses with brief roars of the exhaust as the echoes were thrown back from solid walls. Then they struck the center of the town and bored through it toward the waterfront. At the main intersection the traffic cop blew his whistle till it screamed, but Toomey was making a skid turn to the right, with the glare of the pursuing headlights not a block behind him. "Pier Five!" said the girl.

The sour smell of the sea came into his nostrils. He saw pier number three, turned right, and saw five. He jammed on the brakes till they screeched, and the car went skidding and stuttering to a halt.

"Straight out to the head of the pier!" called Sally.

He was out, and snatching the suitcase from the Big Fellow. Then he sprinted, and, looking back, saw the flaring headlights of the Crawford car behind him, as it slowed to a halt, with dark forms leaning out of it.

Even burdened as he was with the suitcase, he ran before the girl and the long legs of the Big Fellow. Out of the shadows at the end of the warehouse stepped a figure with a glint of a steel shield on its breast.

"What's the hurry?" growled this image of the law. "There ain't any steamers sailin' from this dock right now, gents. Hold up! You will, will you?"

For Toomey, running straight on, had given no heed, and the policeman swung his nightstick. Almost casually, almost as in play, Toomey picked the good hard ridge of the jaw and lodged his knuckles against that shelf, still running, leaning his weight with the punch. The policeman dropped. Toomey barely saw him fall, as he ran on.

Half way down the pier he looked back. All was shadow, shadow, with the sea-water swelling softly about the piers, shadows also. But he could see little forms of men dashing after him.

He paused. The girl and the Big Fellow caught up with him.

"Go on!" he yelled, and, pulling the automatic, he sent three shots breast high down the passage.

Then he turned and fled after the others.

When Toomey reached the place, he saw the ladder that went down to where a long, narrow racer was moored. The girl, already in the cockpit, labored at the levers. The Big Fellow was almost beside her.

Toomey looked back. There were no longer many men following. Only one figure ran toward them from the base of the pier, with straddling legs. That would be the policeman, he felt sure. So he threw down the suitcase and followed after it.

Sally was busy at the wheel. The rope was cast off, by the Big Fellow, the propeller growled in the water, they started with a lurch almost like that of an automobile.

High above them, as they slid away, appeared the form of the policeman. He had his gun in his hand, by this time, and he took aim, shouting all the while at them to stop, or he'd sink them! Sally solved his indecision by simply doubling around the head of the pier, and by the time the man of the law had reached that vantage point they were on the extreme verge of a revolver's range.

Even so, they heard the gun pop behind them, futilely, several times, but no sound of a bullet came near them.

The Big Fellow spilled back on the seat with one hand trailing to the deck, one arm dangling overboard. The wind caught his hat, whirling it far. He lay without moving.

The girl, too, was crumpled up, but it was with laughter!

Toomey stared helplessly at her. Yes, it was laughter, unaffected and real. She jumped up from the wheel, and waved her hand. She shouted and cheered, and Toomey looked up at her with delightedly shining eyes.

"There's blood on your face," said Toomey, grimly. "Quit the nonsense, and wash your face. There's blood on it."

She dipped up salt water and washed her face, and dried it with Toomey's handkerchief. The Big Fellow sat up, with a groan. He took out a cigar, sank his teeth in it, scratched a match, and then threw the match away.

"**DAMN YOU, TOOMEY,**" he said. "Traveling with you is traveling with a conscience. Traveling men shouldn't have any conscience. And now where are we going?"

"Across to the other shore," said Toomey.

"France or England?" said the Big Fellow, grinning.

"Down the coast," said Toomey.

"And that's a pity," said the girl. "Now that we're started, it's a crime to turn back."

"You're thinking of old cognac and Armagnac, and things like that," said the Big Fellow.

"Toomey doesn't like hard liquor for ladies," said the girl, "so Sally doesn't like it, either."

She looked gloomily at Toomey.

"If I ever started hating you, Toomey," she said, "I could have a good, old-fashioned hate, I'll tell you. He doesn't like to see girls smoke, either, Big Fellow. At heart he's a missionary, and I've got to represent the Heathen Nations."

"You represent 'em, all right," said the Big Fellow. "Sally, how fast will this boat step?"

"She'll do thirty-five. She's doing it now."

"Doesn't feel like it," said the Big Fellow.

"There's a bit of a following breeze," said Sally, "and the water's calm. You feel speed more when a boat is jumping the waves, and that sort of thing."

"Look back here," said the Big Fellow.

They looked back. The lights of Porthaven had drawn together to a handful, like a great star-cluster in the heavens.

"See that?" said the Big Fellow. "A boat, back there? Isn't it a boat?"

There was a very small swell, yet it was enough to bring into view or hide, moment by moment, a slender streak of shadow, far behind them.

"It's a boat," said Toomey, instantly. "And a fast one, too."

"Swing off your course," said the Big Fellow. "Slide out toward the sea. We've got to find out if they're following us."

They veered to port and they began to quarter the little waves. Presently they could see that the stranger had altered its course, also, and swung out toward the sea; It was drawing nearer. One had only to look carefully at the skyline in order to see it very clearly.

"It's a speed-burner," said Sally.

"Can we get to land ahead of it?" asked the Big Fellow. Toomey looked forward to the black cloud of the shore-line, then back to the shadow that drifted behind them. He shook his head.

"It's no good. That bird is walking the water," he said. "We can't get to the shore ahead of 'em."

"Can we duck them, in any way?" asked the Big Fellow.

"You can see for yourself," said Sally. "They're walking right up on us."

"Machine guns, I suppose," said Toomey. "Can't, we get away from 'em, Sally?"

"If we had wings, we could," she answered. "Or if we could go slow, by daylight, through the shallows, we could dodge 'em. I know the shallows, all right."

"It's your boat, Big Fellow," said Toomey. "How does

Sally happen to know all about everything so much better than you do?"

"She's been pilot. I've been the absentee owner, most of the time. She knows these waters like a book."

"The shallows, Sally," said Toomey. "Where are they?"

"You can see 'em, out there on the point, running out this way. You can see the shine of the foam, yonder. The current's boiling through the rocks, right now."

It was only a glint across the face of the water, a long, narrow streak of pallor that extended well out from the shore.

"Well," said Toomey, "if the rocks can be run by day, they can be run by night."

"By day, slow, dead slow," said Sally, hastily. "And then you've got to know them by heart."

"You can do it by night, too," said Toomey.

"I can smash the boat to smithereens, and drown the lot of us," said Sally.

Toomey turned to the Big Fellow.

"Sorry, Big Fellow," he said. "I thought she would be game!"

Sally turned a wild glance toward Toomey, then headed the craft straight at the glimmering line of the shallows.

32

A DROWNED MAN ON
A DROWNED SHIP

THE BIG FELLOW got up to look the better. He sat down again, suddenly.

"Never stop riding your luck when it's under you," said Toomey, gravely. He looked across at the girl, and she glanced back at him. He wondered how great the fear in her might be, but not a sign of it appeared in her. She thrust out her chin, and hunched her shoulders a little.

He paused, and Toomey said, harshly: "What seems to you?"

The Big Fellow was silent again, chewing at his cigar.

They were coming closer, now, and they could see, now and again, pale leapings among the rocks, uplifting tentacles, and the bald heads of the rocks themselves.

"How much will we save—how far would they have to go around?" asked Toomey.

"Couple—three miles, maybe," said Sally. "And out there's the mist. They'll never catch us in that sea-mist. It's not a fog. It's just a mist!"

Toomey could hardly make it out, at first, but then he was aware, beyond the point and towards the open sea, of a pallid streak, like smoke, that extended with the curve of the horizon.

Something showered into the water, near them, jets rising; the far-off purr of a machine gun reached them. The Big Fellow was instantly on the deck, lying low. The girl, at the wheel, sat straighter.

"They won't get us," said Toomey. "They want us so badly that they hope they can stop us before we get into the rough of the water and the rocks."

"How it's leaping!" said Sally. "How—"

She ducked her head, as a flight of bullets sang over them. Toomey looked back and could make out the flare of the bow wave that shot out on either side of the speed boat that followed. It was so near that now he could discern the confused shadows whose heads appeared behind or above the windshield. The machine gun spat winking fire, but Toomey could not hear either the explosions or the noise of the bullets, for with a sound of roaring, and an engulfing voice, like a thousand mighty beasts swallowing, they were among the rocks.

The machine gun fire ceased. Toomey flashed on the headlight and it showed them the heart of the madness that lay before. The current, swinging towards the shore and focused and confined by the outrunning line of the rocks, gathered the strength of a river in the spring of the year. Over the smooth-backed rocks it poured with polished swellings, but where jagged surfaces, sheer walls met it, it turned to thunder and to spray, bounding high into the air. Toomey was helpless; motor boats were an unknown world to him. Their lives lay in the hands of a girl.

All of them were half drenched the instant they were

Toomey followed and the sea sucked down the little craft.

well committed to the shallows. Sally, her teeth bared, crouched lower, the wheel constantly in motion between her hands. They grated the sides of the boat, again and again, with a sound like the sliding of a steel sword-blade against a parrying weapon.

A mighty geyser picked them up, dandled them in the air, and smacked them down again, crashing. The eyes of Sally glanced around in an agony, but it was only a glance. She headed right on into the maelstrom. They glanced, like a cast spear, between the rocks. A great upwelling of the water heaved them again, and smote them down on a boulder. Underneath, they heard the mortal wounding of the boat, the rending of the fabric of that slim hull. Then they slid out into the safe waters beyond, and the white veil of the fog passed over them. Each became to the other a ghost.

"She's filling," said Sally. "She's getting water-heavy underneath. I wonder which way the land lies beyond this smother?"

"Where's your compass?" asked Toomey.

They sat hushed. The salt sea-mist cut at their faces. All in a moment, it became wonderfully cold. If they tried to probe the fog with their headlight, they merely blinded themselves and raised a luminous wall of white before their eyes.

EVERY MOMENT, THE speed boat sank lower and lower in the water. Little ripples from the waves ran along the gunwale and came creaming over the side. The sea was lipping them, now, getting ready to open mouth and swallow.

"There ought to be land!" groaned Oliver. "There's got to be land. Right ahead! We've gone ten miles—twelve miles. My God, suppose we're wrongs—suppose that we've been driving straight out to sea, all the time?"

No one answered him, because there was no answer to make.

Then, over them, right over their heads, it seemed, crashing down on them out of the sky, so that they all winced down, they heard eight strokes of a loud bell, the beats coming in closely joined pairs.

Sally veered the boat sharply to the side, an instinctive dodging that let in a great sheet of water. But now, through the fog, they saw the looming hull of a ship, an immense blackness along whose hull they shot, with wonder growing in them all the while, for yonder was the cable dangling out from the bows, the huge anchor cable that bound the great vessel to the ocean bottom.

"The Rum Row," said Sally, with a sudden gasp. "Rum Row! That's what I did. I came right out to sea, and this is Rum Row!"

The cockpit was full of water as they reached the ship's ladder. "A line!" groaned the Big Fellow. "If we get a line, we can keep her up."

The girl and the Big Fellow were up the ladder, first. Toomey followed, but there was no chance to salvage the speed boat. Beneath him the sea sucked down the little craft with a bubbling sound. A blinding brightness struck the girl in the face, as she climbed up the rail. A voice roared out: "Who's there? Who's there? Answer up bright and smart or I'm gonna let salt water into some of you."

"Friends! Friends!" cried Sally.

"That's a lie," said the harsh voice. "I ain't got no friends, and I don't want no friends—"

"We're off a sunken boat."

"Ah, ha, and oh, ho!" said the roaring voice. "Aye, and that's a different story. You're off a sunken boat and you're on a sunken ship, so come on board and all be damned along with me."

They climbed to the deck and into the presence of a huge old man who waved his torch over them. Toomey repaid that compliment. It was a face that dripped all over with masses of white beard, but all the face that was visible about the eyes and brow was flaring red, and the pungency of rum stole from him onto the air.

They could see him the more easily because at this height above the face of the water, the mist was wonderfully thin. It was a mere blanket of white wool that hugged the ocean, and only films of mist floated around the superstructure of the ship. It was one of those old three-castle fortresses that still tramp the ocean, shuffling the seas before their swelling bows. It might be of two thousand tons. The central "castle" rose just beside them; their eyes and the dissolving light of the torches could barely reach to the after, structure, or to the forecastle.

"Who's aboard, my friend?" said the Big Fellow.

"Who'd be on a drowned ship except a drowned man?" said the sailor. "Or if you're askin' my name, I'm Joe Hearne. And all the rest is gone."

He laughed and waved them onto the deck. "We've been drifting last night, and we drifted clean out of the line, and now the captain and all the rest, they're off to get a tug to tow us back to place."

His face grew more sober.

"You got a look of government men about you," he said.

The Big Fellow laughed heartily, and clapped Joe Hearne on the shoulder.

"We're not government men," he said.

He turned to his companions.

"Is this pretty soft?" said the Big Fellow. "We spend the night here; and when the crew comes back with their boat, we'll hire it for the trip ashore. Does that sound good to you, Toomey?"

Toomey nodded.

"Them that hire will fire," said Joe Hearne. "Are you hungry, mates? Why, them that are shipwrecked are bound to be hungry. You're wet, too, the most of you are. Come along with me, and I'll fix you."

"He's a little bit twisted in the head, the poor old man,"

said the girl to Toomey. "Did he say that he was a sunken sailor on a sunken ship, or something like that?"

"Nobody but a crazy man would man the ship, this close in shore, I suppose," said Toomey. "She's probably far out of the line and a government cutter might come along and pick her up with whatever she has on board. Anyway, we're out of the eyes of Crawford, and that puts me at rest with the world."

She caught his arm.

"Don't speak of him, Toomey," she said. "I've been thinking of him like a great squid, reaching his arms for us through the fog, fumbling for us, ready to draw us under, when we're found."

Joe Hearne showed them cabins where they could take off their clothes and wring them out and put them on again. No one catches cold from salt water, he said, and when they were dressed again, they'd find that he'd cooked them up a snack in the galley. He was no "doctor" he said, but he could work in a galley, at that.

They followed all of this advice, duly, and met again in the captain's cabin, to which the voice of Joe Hearne was calling them. He had fried a platterful of ham and eggs and cooked them a great pot of coffee, and there was a wooden trencher filled with slices of bread. Joe Hearne himself, as they sat down, lifted a glass filled with the red amber of rum.

"Here's to all of them derelicts that drift in a derelict ship!" he called. "Here's to sunken ships, and sunken men and—"

He tossed off the drink. "Lord, Lord!" said Joe Hearne. "In ten seconds it's one bell, and here I stand!"

33

CRAWFORD'S MEN

WITH THE FIRST taste of hot food, their troubles fled far from them. They began to laugh at their own bedraggled appearance. On the forehead of the girl there was a small, purplish bump. Her coat clung tight about her shoulders. She looked like a starved street waif, except for her laughing face. Toomey, also, looked rather like a drowned rat, but the Big Fellow, in spite of the fact that his collar had melted, his necktie was crumpled out of shape, his coat a mass of wrinkles, still remained the magnificent man of affairs in a strange way. A light seemed to shine in him.

He had planned the immediate future. Crawford, he said, was now in the throes of a fury, like a tiger shark, and he would spare no pains to set his terrible hands on them all, if he could. To have lost money was like losing blood of the soul, to Crawford, he said, but to have lost Toomey was far worse. For the empire of Crawford was built of people, not of mere cash.

While Big Fellow talked, the world was an easy way before their feet. Then the bell clanged once, forward, and Joe Hearne returned to them. He was delighted to see that the food had disappeared so quickly.

"I ain't a 'doctor,' rightly," said Hearne, "but I sailed

before the mast, and there ain't a man that ever sailed before the mast that don't learn cookin' by what the dirty 'doctor' of a squarerigger *don't* do to food."

"How d'you come to be a sunken sailor on a sunken ship?" asked the Big Fellow.

"Why," said Joe Hearne, calmly, "this here is the 'Mary Rose' that sunk in Fairhaven, five years back, and the crew drowned, and I was one of the crew."

"They all drowned," said the Big Fellow, "and you drowned with them, after that, you all come back to life again, eh?"

"They all drowned," said Joe Hearne, "and I climbed up to the top of the derrick mast, and when I sat on top of the derrick mast my head and shoulders was above the water, and I seen the other drowned men floatin' around me. I seen Terry Wells with his mouth wide open, laughin' at what he was seein' in hell, and I seen the Welshman grindin' his teeth, and Scotty twistin' his mouth to one side. I seen them all mostly floatin' close to me, till the wind come up, and blowed them away, and the gulls come and looked me in the eye, and the wind blowed, and the waves, they slapped me, and they shook me, and pretty nigh shaked me off'n that mast, and me not a swimmin' man. So's my head was mostly under water, and I done my breathin' like a swimmer in a race, and my wind was tuckered out, and a boat come along and says the boatswain in her: 'They is all lost, poor devils, and every man drowned!' and I sings out that I was drowned, but that I could still speak for myself. So they hauled me in."

"Well," said the Big Fellow, "they hauled you in, and what did they do to the 'Mary Rose'?"

"They raised her," said Joe Hearne. "I'd been with her eight years, and I helped at the raisin' of her, and the scrapin' and paintin' of her, and I've been with her ever since, which is nine years more, because a drowned ship and a drowned man take kindly to one another, as you can see for yourself. Why not have some rum?"

"I need it," said the Big Fellow.

They had rum all around, except the girl.

"Rum and whiskey are illusions of this sinful world, Big Fellow," she said. "I'm leaving them behind me. I'm steering for a better life, or being steered there, and that amounts to the same thing."

The rum was the true Jamaica, sweet and powerful. It went coldly down, and promptly set the brain boiling. The Big Fellow began to sing; Joe Hearne was so delighted that he clogged a dance with his stiff old legs, and the girl got up and went tipping back and forth across the cabin opposite him, while the onlookers shouted.

SALLY ANNOUNCED THAT she was going to walk herself dry. Toomey left the rum and the smoke of the cabin and went with her to walk briskly up and down on the after deck.

Two bells rang forward; they could hear the hobnailed boots of old Hearne running again to join in the merriment. Presently he and the Big Fellow were booming a duet.

"You're not happy," said the girl.

"It's a rotten business," said Toomey. "I told Crawford that I was his man. I gave him my hand and I meant it. Now I've chucked him. I know he's a hound, but still it's a rotten business. I've done most things that are crooked, Sally, but I don't break my word every day in the week."

She had no answer to this, for a time. Then she said: "No, you're not meant for a crooked life, Toomey. All you want is a good fight, now and then, to keep your blood circulating. You couldn't get enough fighting inside the law, so you've lived outside it, a good part of the time. That's all."

He considered this, looking with a troubled eye over the blanket of mist that covered the sea. Wisps of it curled on high, here and there, but almost everywhere they could see the stars, which pricked the fog with feeble little spear-points of light.

"How do you feel about things, Sally?" he asked her.

They walked two turns in complete silence.

"I don't want to think," said the girl. "Don't make me think. If I don't have to think about settling down, and being rooted to one place, and pouring tea for old fools— and then receiving neighbors... or that sort of thing— Toomey, good people drive me crazy... They don't see themselves clearly... It's all a baby game of pretending. I hate it. There's no good in it...No good for me, I mean... Nothing is good for me that's dull..."

"You know something?" said Toomey.

"Fire away."

"I feel like taking you by the nape of the neck and shaking you, hard."

"I was so afraid that you wouldn't feel that way!"

She began to laugh. They kept on walking up and down, and the singing poured out to them from the cabin. Three bells struck. There had been a long silence between them.

"You know that cabin I was in?" she said.

"Yes."

"There's a big mackinaw hanging up there on a nail. D'you mind getting it for me?"

He left her, silently, for he felt that it was merely an excuse to get rid of him. He went to the cabin, found the mackinaw with his electric torch, and came out again.

The mist seemed to have risen a little higher; he could not see Sally Moore. He flashed the torch on. It showed him the wet, gleaming deck, the after peak, the midships structure, but no sign of Sally.

He flashed out the light again, and set his teeth.

"I wonder if she thinks that I'll follow her?" thought Toomey.

Nevertheless, after hesitating, he conquered his angry pride and climbed up the ladder to the extreme stern of the ship. He looked down the black hole of the companion way. A smell of onions and potatoes, rotting, came up to him.

Something bumped the lee side of the ship; the waves could not strike it there, so he looked over the rail and made out, very, very dimly through the fog, the long, slender lines of a boat. He gave it one flash of the torch, which showed him a powerful looking launch, with a rope ladder rising from it to the rail.

He went down that ladder to the cockpit, where he surveyed things with a few winking glimpses of the flashlight. There were empty cartridge shells on the deck. Two big machine guns were mounted, one peering forward, and one aft.

Toomey went up the ladder again like a wild cat. He dropped from the after structure to the after deck and ran forward and up the opposite ladder until he was on the deck of the dining saloon.

Nothing had happened. The Big Fellow was there, sipping rum. Up the deck Toomey peered, and down it. Nothing was in sight, so he stepped through the open door and said, rapidly: "Up! Up! They're here."

The Big Fellow rose with a gun in one hand and the suitcase in the other.

"Who?" he whispered.

"Crawford's men," said Toomey. "Where's Sally? Has she been back here?"

"Look out! Behind! Behind you!" shouted the Big Fellow.

Toomey did not pause to turn and look. He simply leaped to the side, and felt the concussion of air from an explosion fan his head. Opposite him appeared Bushmill and another man Toomey never had seen before, and opened fire.

The Big Fellow threw up his hands, flinging the suitcase far across the cabin, and fell on his face.

34

TOOMEY'S BOX

THE OTHER DOOR opened, with Slip on the threshold. It is hard to make one gun cover two doors. But Toomey did it. He shot across his body towards the malignant, rejoicing face of Slip. He turned the gun to the other side and tried a snap shot at Bushmill. The man fell inside the door. His companion's face disappeared. The door where Slip had been standing had been slammed suddenly from without.

Toomey shuttered the windows, one by one, expecting every instant to see the gleam of a gun outside. Then he leaped to where Bushmill lay, caught him under the armpits, and dragged the body in, simply because it was easier and quicker to do that than to throw him out.

As he got the fellow inside and dropped him again, face down, a voice barked out something, down the deck passage. A gun sent three bullets splintering through the cabin door. But Toomey snatched it shut and locked it again.

They were snug. No one, at least, could look in on them, for the moment, though there might be a thousand devices for routing them from the place.

He sprang to the Big Fellow.

Lawrence Elliott Oliver lay face down, his head in a pool

of his own blood. Toomey turned him over. There was a frightful crimson furrow ploughed across the upper part of the forehead; and the blood flowed freely.

He had to be dead. That bullet must have mashed its way through his brains. And yet dead men do not keep on bleeding. When he looked closer, Toomey understood. The shot had not pierced the bone. It might have fractured the skull, he might well die of the wound later, but chance had made it a glancing rather than a mortal wound.

He took some water from the table, sluiced it over the wound, and ripped off a section of the tablecloth to make the bandage. Under the painful pressure of it, the Big Fellow came to a sitting posture with a groan.

"Shoot, Toomey!" he gasped. "Damn 'em—"

Then he came to himself, and groaned more loudly.

"You're nicked, but you're not broken," said Toomey. "Lie back on the floor till you feel better. Here's a slug of rum."

He held it to the lips of Lawrence Oliver, and the Big Fellow poured it off at one swallow. He looked up once, half confidingly, half questioningly, at Toomey. Then he obeyed orders implicitly, and lay back.

Toomey went to Bushmill and turned the body over. The fellow was not dead. His eyes were open, and he was blinking rapidly. But death was not many steps away from him. It had been a center shot. Blood poured down over his clothes. Toomey started to take off the coat.

Bushmill shook his head.

"What's the use of any funny business?" he said. "I know I'm cooked. I know I've got it, so leave me be. When I conk 'em between wind and water, like this, I know where they're goin', so I know where I'm goin', too. Gimme a shot of rum, if you'll waste it on me."

Toomey poured out a brimming bumper from the jug and handed it over.

Bushmill embraced it with both hands, took a deep drink, and rested his back against the cabin wall. The blood kept pouring from him. Toomey took the rest of the table-cloth and flung it across his body.

"Makes you kind of sick, eh?" said Bushmill, quietly. "Same with me. Kind of grips me, when I see blood. Gimme a cigarette, will you?"

Toomey gave the dying man a cigarette, and lighted it for him.

"Thanks," said Bushmill. "You're O.K. But Crawford has you down in the book, and that's too bad. He has you down in red, Toomey—and *that's* too bad."

He took another drink of rum.

"God, this is luck," said he. "I might of choked in salt water. I might of laid out on a frosty night and got the cold into the wound, instead of sitting here warm and easy and drinkin' rum, and just bleedin' it out. I was born lucky."

His fat face puckered with a contented smile.

"You won't die that way, Toomey," he said. "Not by a damn sight."

"What happened to Sally?" asked Toomey.

"Go to hell," said Bushmill.

Toomey made a step towards him, and stopped. Bush-mill grinned.

"The gentleman burglar, do he sock the guy that's down? He do not. You poor sucker!" said Bushmill, sneering.

Suddenly a white patch appeared in the center of each cheek, and his eyes rolled.

"I slipped a notch, that time," he said, taking another drink.

TOOMEY FILLED THE glass.

"That was neat," said Bushmill. "I put out the light of the Big Fellow. And I just had the gat on you, brother, when you snipped off my branch to wither in blooming damn dust."

He grinned, tried to inhale the cigarette smoke deeply, and shook his head when pain stopped him.

"Let me tie the wound up," suggested Toomey.

"Shut up," said Bushmill. "You can't help me. You can only bother me. I'm dyin' the way I wanta die, setting up and looking the world in the eye over a slug of booze, with a cigarette in the other hand. What's better?"

Toomey nodded.

"It's been a swell life," said Bushmill. "I don't ask for any better. I don't want my money back. The till can keep what I've paid over the counter. I've had the money's worth. I've had my fun, and I been paid for it. I've had my booze, and I've had my women. You know the best of the lot, Toomey?"

Toomey said nothing.

"You got a hard mug," said Bushmill, calmly. "You got a real hard mug. If anybody had to put me out, better have a hard mug than some young punk that bought his first gun yesterday and got famous on me, today. You know Japan, Toomey?"

"I know it," said Toomey.

"Yeah, you would. You wouldn't miss high spots like that. I was only there once. It was cherry blossom time, too. That's the time to be there. Always laughing is what the damn gals are. And they walk around with flowers in their hands. It's funny. Gimme a drink. It leaks out as fast as I get it down."

Toomey filled the glass again.

Bushmill slumped, suddenly, and most of the rum spilled out of the glass. With his elbow resting on the floor, he managed to bring the drink to his lips again.

"Damn comfortable—" he said. "Here's to… good old world… may it never be older… or wiser…"

The glass clinked, and then rolled across the floor. Bushmill dropped to his side, with his head pillowed on his arm, exactly as one who falls pleasantly and easily asleep. Toomey pulled an edge of the tablecloth over his face. The Big Fellow had heaved himself up on one elbow.

"GAME," SAID THE Big Fellow. "Dead game, that one."

"Dead game," agreed Toomey. "How are you?"

"Things whirl. I'll try to stand up—"

"Stay where you are."

A voice called through the door, the voice of Slip: "Hey, Toomey!"

"Here, Slip," said Toomey.

"We've got you, you rat. Come and fight it out like a man!"

"One to four or five?" said Toomey. "You're a red rag, old son, but I'm not a bull. Where's Sally?"

"Where we want her—damn you!" said Slip. "We've got her, and we'll keep her. You hear?"

"I hear you talk," said Toomey.

"Want to hear sense?"

"Love to."

"If we get the coin, Toomey, we'll let you and the Big Fellow get by, if he ain't dead."

"He's not dead," said Toomey.

"We'll take you back safe—to Crawford."

"That's a comfort," said Toomey. "And he'll give us tea, I suppose?"

"Whatcha want?" demanded Slip. "The world with a fence around it? I'm giving you a break, and you don't know it. I'm giving you a chance. I'll take you safe, back to Crawford."

"Thanks," said Toomey.

"Big Fellow! Big Fellow!" called Slip. "You hear him turning down a swell offer like that?"

"I'm hearing you, Slip," said the Big Fellow. "You bark like a dog, because you *are* a dog. Don't bother me."

"Damn their hearts," said the snarling voice of Slip. "Toomey, I told you that I'd have the carving of you. A gun's not what I want, for working on you!"

Toomey went to the dumbwaiter that communicated with the galley below. He peered down the shaft. He tried the rope, and the waiter rose softly.

"Sally, you talk to the fool!" said Slip. "Here's Sally, Toomey. Talk to him, Sally. If I gotta turn loose on him, I'm gunna burn him up."

"Toomey!" called the voice of the girl.

"What happened, Sally?" he asked.

"They came up out of the deck, and grabbed me," she said. "They seemed to come right up out of the deck. Toomey, do you hear me, dear? They mean murder. Don't trust 'em. Fight—"

Toomey distinctly heard the sound of a blow. He ran at the door like a maniac. Then his senses came back to him.

He sat down in a chair and tried to light a cigarette; his hand shook the match away. When he had lighted the smoke, deeply inhaling, he poured out some rum, but then pushed the glass away.

The Big Fellow got up, staggered, and fell into a chair at the table.

"Steady, Toomey," he said, putting a hand on the arm of the other.

Toomey struck the hand away. He looked at the Big Fellow with red-stained eyes.

"They hit her, Big Fellow," he said. "They hit—*her!* They hit her in the face. I heard the punch. They knocked her silly. She's a girl, Big Fellow. They banged her in the face!"

"Toomey!" called the voice of Slip, at the door.

Toomey went suddenly to the dumbwaiter, and measured the width of the shaft.

"You see the game's up, you fool," said Slip— "We'll smoke you out in five minutes, if you don't give in. Understand?"

Toomey slid the dumbwaiter to the top of its shaft. That left room for his slender body to slide through. He was half way in when the Big Fellow came to him.

"Toomey, you're not running out on me, are you?" he stammered, softly.

Toomey glared at him, shook him off, and disappeared down the shaft.

HE WENT DOWN to the bottom and found nothing. He pulled the draw rope and came up again, feeling the wall on the way, until he located the catch door. When he opened it, a flash of his electric torch showed him the ranged pans and pots of the galley. The glitter of them fairly hurt his eyes.

He slid through the door and into the galley. With both hands stretched before him, he found the door, opened it, came out in the narrow passage of the lower deck. He went along it with his hands still stretched before him, his head down. That is the best system when one feels the way in the dark. The hands will serve for eyes.

He came well forward. The whole ship was suddenly silent. No doubt, Slip was devising ways and means of "smoking" his men out of the cabin. Perhaps he would do it literally.

At the front end of the passage, a soft murmuring from the forward deck, reached the ears of Toomey. There was a man's voice, and the lighter murmur of a woman.

Toomey knelt and took off his shoes, then he went with shadowy silence down the companion to the fore deck. He could see them now, dimly enwrapped in ghostly arms of the mist, and yet through those arms the stars of the horizon were shining. There were two forms on the deck, and one man walking up and down before them. Toomey slid forward a little every time the walker reached the end of his beat, and turned. After every slip forward, he paused, almost flat on the deck, with his gun ready.

The ship was coming to life, it seemed to Toomey. There was hardly a sign of a swell on the sea, and yet now and then a tremor ran through the body of the old freighter and it swayed a little, so Toomey thought.

Then the mere sound of a voice froze him to the deck,

for he heard Crawford saying: "The crazy fellow—what happened to him?"

"I banged him on the head and dropped him down the forward hatch," said the guard, pausing in his walk.

"You ought to have brought him here," said Crawford.

"He's just a nut," said the guard. "He can't do nothin'. We got Toomey and the Big Fellow sealed up in a box. Only question is, how you gunna crack the box open?"

Now Toomey was aware, towards the prow of the ship, half lost against the darkness of the bulkwarks, of a form that seemed loftier and vaster than human. Above the hugeness of the shoulders was an absurdly small head. It was George, the Negro. His presence explained how Crawford had been carried on board the ship.

"There's no hurry," said Crawford. "As a matter of fact, I've never enjoyed moments more than I enjoy these. And it's romantic, Louie, to sit here at sea with a pretty girl beside me"

"I'd tie that bit of romance with rope, if I was you," said Louie. "It's a kind of a she-Toomey, is what it is. I wouldn't have none of that pepper in *my* soup."

"You hear that, Sally?" said Crawford. "He doesn't think much of you."

"I think too damn much of her to leave her hands and feet loose at the same time," said Louie. "She ain't safe. There's some of the Toomey wild cat in her, chief."

"Let her be free for a little while," said Crawford. "Use all gently, Louie, when fortune is going your way. Sally, how shall I open the box and take out the Big Fellow and Toomey?"

She was silent.

"I might soak some waste in oil and burn down a door with it," said Crawford. "Or I might blow the doors open, at the same time. But that would mean fighting. And why should I fight when there's probably a better way?"

"You'll bargain with them," said the girl. "If you try to smash them—they'll destroy the Big Fellow's money before they let themselves be taken!"

"I've even thought of that," said Crawford, chuckling. And the music of his voice made a charm through the air. "I've even thought of that. Bargains are easily made—and broken, Sally."

"They'll find a way to make you keep your word," said the girl. "Do you think they're foolish enough to trust you?"

"They've got to die, Sally," said Crawford. "If it's the end of my own life—they have to die. Mr. Big Fellow, because I've had him marked all these years, and Toomey because I'd never have a quiet moment if he were at large."

"That's sense," said the guard, pausing again in his walking up and down.

On the flat of his belly, Toomey wriggled forward with his gun.

Then, from deep in the hold, a wild, powerful voice arose in a sea chanty.

"There's the nut," remarked Louie, with a laugh. "Singin' songs, he is. He thinks that it's springtime, somewhere. Listen to him, will you? The poor sap!"

A voice called from the top deck.

"Chief! Hey, chief!"

"Yes?" said Crawford. "What's the matter?"

"Don't it seem to you like the ship's riding kind of low and tippin' to the right?"

"You're drunk," said Crawford. "Is anybody guarding the power boat?"

"No," said the man from the top deck. "There ain't any use. We got 'em in a can, ain't we? But it looks like, to me, that there's a kind of a cant to the lie of this ship. She don't sit straight!"

The song of the madman rose nearer to them, as though he were climbing the companionway up from the hold, "What's that?" exclaimed Crawford. "By heaven, I felt the ship stir, then, as though it were lying down on its side."

In fact the whole deck had canted to the side, and Toomey made that his moment. He rose to hands and knees, and leaped. The stroke of his gun butt merely glanced off the head of Louie, but with force enough to knock him flat and send him rolling.

"Sally!" cried Toomey, and saw her flash to her feet.

"Help!" shouted the mighty voice of Crawford. "It's Toomey!"

And from the bridge of the ship, instantly a strong light flashed down.

35

THROUGH THE WHITE DEATH

STRAIGHT INTO THE light Toomey fired. The light went out, and a yell arose, tingling.

"Back down the lower deck—find the boat—get into it—cast off!" gasped Toomey, and fled aft, swarming up the companion.

"Big Fellow! On deck!" he yelled as he ran.

Then he dropped down beside the awning that covered the starboard railing of the upper deck. He heard the rushing of footfalls. The door of the dining saloon opened, casting enough reflected light to bring into some relief three men who were running forward. The Big Fellow appeared at the open door, gun in hand.

Toomey, with time to spare, fired twice. Two men spilled to the right and to the left. The third man, smaller than the others, leaped over them and ran straight on towards the spitting gun. It spat no longer. The next bullet jammed. Toomey rose, weighed the gun in his hand, and hurled it. The shadow swerved and the missile flew harmlessly.

It was Slip, Toomey knew. It was not an illusion, that sense of a glistening thing that was in the hand of Slip. It was the knife that he had promised, and Toomey dived headlong along the deck, as though into water.

Something tripped over him and went down, but lightly, lightly. He heard a little whine of eagerness and rage; as he got to his hands and knees he saw Slip leaping in again. The man was a feather. Any gust of wind was able to blow him about. Down the deck came the beating of heavy feet—the Big Fellow running to the rescue. But this wild cat might claw out the life before help came.

There were only seconds left to him, Toomey knew, before the Negro, George, would come bounding up from the foredeck and end this fight with a stroke of his hand.

Toomey rose, striking straight out.

The blow was true enough. It should have knocked the little devil headlong. Instead, there was simply the bobbing of a weight at the end of Toomey's fist as Slip received the blow and came on in.

The knife played like a snake's tongue. Toomey, trying to dodge it, felt the whole length of it buried in the tough, twisted muscles of his left shoulder.

But it is better to quench a deadly fire with the bare hands than to let it spread. And Toomey received the shooting agony of that wound with a dim pleasure. Before the knife could be drawn out, his fist found the head of Slip again, and again.

The little man went down. He could have used a gun, all this while. There was one in his hands, now. It was simply that he had preferred the knife. Carving was what he wanted to do. Toomey let him lie.

There was not even a moment to pause. Footfalls were beating here and there, and the voice of Crawford, louder than a brazen trumpet, was thundering: "Two more of you come here to help me! The crazy man has opened the sea cocks and we're sinking! Get to the boat. Drop everything else to get to the boat, before Toomey—"

And the wild voice of Hearne suddenly issued from the hold and rang out along the decks:

"Whiskey is the life of man,
Whiskey for my Johnnie!
Whiskey is—"

The voice went out like a light, as a gun barked. That was George at work, no doubt; and the appearance of poor Hearne was what kept the giant from coming aft into the battle.

Toomey and the Big Fellow were already aft. Into the dining saloon, Toomey dipped and got the suitcase. Forward, there was wild confusion. Running was difficult, except to the bare feet of Toomey. For the old freighter was heeling over fast.

DOWN THE COMPANION to the main deck they rushed, and speeding aft, they leaned over the rail and saw, down the long slope of the side of the careening ship, the vague, vague outline of the power boat. It slid towards them as Toomey shouted. He set the good example by swinging himself over the side and sliding down the iron plates as if down the steepness of a toboggan. He flung the suit-case before him into the cockpit, where it burst open, and flung out a litter of paper wealth from side to side. Toomey himself followed. It was not a long drop. But as he came to his feet the Big Fellow landed with force enough, as it seemed, to drive through the bottom of the boat. Sally followed.

The propeller churned. They started, but as they gathered way, great round eyes of light fell on them; guns began, and yelling voices.

The very first blast of lead put out the lights in the cockpit. Still Toomey could hear the clangor of the bullets and the quick, vibrating sound of the metal hull, as the lead clipped its way through it.

The power boat swerved far off to the side, into darkness.

It gathered more speed. It leaped off like a running horse over an increased swell, and still the gunfire continued. A bullet sang past the very ear of Toomey, and made him duck.

But now the shooting stopped.

"Toomey!" cried the voice of the girl. "Are you hurt?"

"I'm scratched. That's all," he said. "Big Fellow?" she called.

"Just a little smear across the head," said the Big Fellow, with wonderful calm. "Where are we going?"

For it was hard to see. The mist which had held over the sea only seemed to have spread up into the sky itself. They could see no stars. All was a white smother, from a point so near the water as this.

"We've got to go back," said Toomey. "There's no other boat on that old freighter. We've got to go back!"

"Bring in cold snakes to warm by your fire? Is that it, Toomey?" asked the Big Fellow.

Far, far off behind them, it seemed to Toomey that he heard a long cry, like the blast of many faint sirens in the distance. It was long-drawn, but then it ended sharply.

"Did you hear that?" said Toomey, gasping the words out.

"I heard it," said the girl. "We're going back."

"God knows what we'll do—if we have to pull a boat-load of those devils out of the water," said the Big Fellow.

"Crawford," said the girl, as she swerved the power boat in a swift half-circle. "He can't swim, of course."

And she sent the boat back like an arrow, straight towards the point from which they had heard the strange cry.

Presently Toomey said, huskily: "Start cutting in a circle. We've gone too far. You've got a horn. Use it—then listen— then use it again."

She cut the speed down, and began to circle, carefully. She sounded the horn. Toomey leaned over the side, to hear better any answer that might come. The motor hummed softly. Not another voice came to his ear.

The horn sounded again. For an hour they cruised, Toomey listening, straining his frantic ears, while the Big Fellow bailed. They seemed to have been shot through and through twenty times, and the water kept rising into the cockpit. They were so waterlogged that even the small waves made them heel over crazily.

And still no human voice came out of the white mist to answer them.

"All right," said Toomey at last, faintly. "I guess—we'd better try to get to the shore."

Still the girl circled for minutes. At last she said. "The lighting system's smashed."

"Here's a flash," said Toomey.

The flashlight showed an instrument board fairly splin-tered by bullets which miraculously had missed human targets. And, worst of all, the compass was broken to bits. They had to cruise blindly through that white death, and guess their way without even a touch of wind to aid them to find a course.

They cut down to slow speed. Silently they drove on.

THE FLASHLIGHT GAVE illumination enough for the Big Fellow to bind up the wound in Toomey's shoulder, clumsily. And the face of Lawrence Oliver showed white and strained. There was no joy for their escape—for what were they more than a mere morsel, compared to what this remorseless sea had swallowed from before their eyes?

They hardly bothered to sweep together the contents of the suitcase and cram them, as in contempt back in place.

And then they voyaged on, with the motor purring softly, the water splashing over the side, as the Big Fellow and Toomey bailed.

The motor sputtered, failed. The girl used the flashlight to examine the cause.

"Gee," she said. "The tank was punctured, I suppose. We're a derelict now. Here, I'll take my turn at bailing."

Her voice was quite brisk and cheerful.

The dawn light began. It showed them to one another as pale ghosts. It showed the power boat with its nose declining into the water, its stern thrusting up, foolishly. They got out life preservers but did not put them on.

The light increased. A wind rose, without breaking the mist at once. And the first clear glimpse that Toomey had of the girl was her body leaning out so that the full blast of the wind would strike her. Toomey could see the faint smile. Dogs smile like that, when they lean out the side of a car to get the blast of the air—like the joy of running without the effort.

She was insatiable. There was no give to her, no wear-out. She was all supple steel and whalebone, and fire.

"What are you smiling about?" he asked, suddenly.

The smile went out. She said: "Nothing, Toomey. Nothing."

He never would know her. Only for an instant at a time could that wild Bedouin belong to him. Action, fierce action, was her only lord and master.

The swell increased. The wind cut at them, and grimly fingered Toomey's wound through all of its depth. The Big Fellow put both hands over his head, where the bandage passed. He said nothing; he endured.

The girl, suddenly yawning, stretched out flat on the cushion, and was instantly asleep. The wind kept plucking at her. It worked some of her hair loose and blew it across her face. It set her coat and her skirt flapping like two sails. But nothing mattered; she slept.

All in a rosy glory the full morning came on them, and with a gesture brushed the face of the ocean clear.

There was no land in sight—all to the west was the bright steel face of the water, and no more.

Then a column of smoke climbed over the western horizon with the dawn, and grew, and a great liner drove her prow like a knife, straight at the little boat. The whistle blew, a long, yelling blast. Toomey was waving Sally's coat as a distress signal. The great ship stopped with a shudder of water all up and down its side. A boat swung down. Dreamily Toomey saw the six-legged craft walking in the water. They were taken on board, and still it was all a dream.

36

THE BRIDE OF A SAVAGE

IT WAS TOO early for a crowd to be present. The angry officer listened with disgust and disbelief to the story which
the Big Fellow told. But the captain was a different matter.

The amiable Lawrence Oliver was closeted with that
dignitary for hardly ten minutes, before they came hurrying out. There were two big, empty suites. Why should
they not be used? It was only a pity that the ship was not
heading back for the western shore, but all the comfort that
the "Imperia" could give would be theirs. Clothes would be
found for the men. As for the lady, were there not dainty
shops aboard?

Toomey, when the doctor had finished with him, found
his bed in a glory of gold and lavender and fluttering
tasseled curtains. He fell on the bed face down and slept
the round of the clock, and rose, and bathed, and shaved,
and breakfasted on beefsteak, and slept again.

It was twenty-four hours after his arrival on that ship
before he climbed into a neat fit of borrowed clothes and
looked for his travelling companions. They were in the
living room of the suite, the Big Fellow reclining on a
couch with a mass of pillows behind his back and head, and
the golden heads of a pair of bottles of champagne frosting

in a bucket of ice, nearby. Sally Moore wore a gray dress. It wasn't exactly gray, either. Perhaps it was the color of the belt that set it off. The bump on her forehead, through some miracle, had been made to disappear. There was something about her fingernails, perhaps, or in a new way of holding her head, that made Toomey think of strange women and strange lands.

She poured out a glass of champagne, and offered it to him.

"Champagne's filthy stuff," said Toomey. "I'll have some Rhine wine."

He rang the bell for the waiter.

"Toomey, the boulevardier," said the Big Fellow. He folded his hands over his stomach and smiled at Sally, and Sally smiled back at the Big Fellow.

"That rotten cigar of yours is spoiling the air," said Toomey.

The Big Fellow stamped it out in an ash tray and folded his hands behind his head. He continued to smile at Sally, who smiled in return at him. The Big Fellow began to wobble one foot up and down, like a small boy in a moment of excessive comfort.

"Who've you been practicing on, Sally?" asked Toomey. "Or is that your Paris mug?"

She looked down at the soft, pink sheen of her fingernails.

"Oh, I'm a very simple child," she said. "Very!"

"Toomey," said the Big Fellow. "Monsieur Toomey, the boulevardier. You ought to have a flower in your buttonhole, Toomey, my lad."

Toomey lighted a cigarette. He took a long look at the Big Fellow. Then he took a long look at the girl.

"It's going to be a nice trip," said Toomey.

"Nice for a wedding trip," said the Big Fellow.

The waiter who had gone for the wine, returned with it in an ice cooler and pulled the cork. Toomey was aware that signals were being made behind his back; that back grew straighter. He tasted the wine. It was a good Rudesheimer. He closed his eyes as the waiter went out. A thousand thoughts mounted to his brain with that fragrance, a thousand images formed, dissolved, vanished, like reflections in bubbles.

He sat down and sipped the wine.

"There's smoke in the air," said Toomey. "You can't taste wine when there's smoke in the air."

"Monsieur Toomey," said the Big Fellow, "the boulevardier."

He chuckled with idiotic pleasure. The girl chuckled, also.

"Monsieur the newly married man," said the Big Fellow.

"There's not going to be a marriage," said Toomey.

"Monsieur will not marry. He declines. With pleasure and regrets, he thanks mademoiselle, and declines," said the Big Fellow, and began to laugh.

The girl laughed too. Toomey looked twice at her, but it was true. She was laughing. Toomey poured out another glass of wine. "The lousy gin and whiskey take a while to get off the palate," said Toomey. "When do we eat?"

"After the marriage, monsieur."

"Damn!" said Toomey.

"Monsieur Toomey, the boulevardier," said the Big

Fellow, "will not marry on an empty stomach. So? He shall have a pretzel, then. Sally, pretzel for monsieur! A delicacy, with Rhine wine, monsieur."

The Big Fellow laughed till his eyes were wet. He kept bobbing his foot up and down. "Big Fellow, you idiot," said Sally. She laughed also, till her eyes were wet.

"If you laugh, he'll ask you why," said the Big Fellow. "Monsieur Toomey, the boulevardier—"

"Oh, shut up, will you?" said Toomey.

He yawned and stood up.

"I'm going on deck," he said.

"Mademoiselle, mademoiselle!" called the Big Fellow. "Accompany monsieur. He will make the promenade. Quickly!"

She was silly and weak with laughter, but she was into coat and hat in a minute, and caught up a pair of chamois gloves. Toomey said at the door: "Thanks, Sally, but I'd rather be alone."

HE WAS AMAZED to find her at his side, in spite of that. He walked straight forward and stood at an open bow window, where the wind was a gale. Sally leaned against the gale also. She kept looking at him, and holding on her hat. The cold wind hurt his wound unendurably.

He went up to the boat deck, and to the games deck above. The wind screamed, but Sally kept beside him. He went to leeward and found a sheltered bench, and sat down. The wind beat the waves down, it covered the ocean with gray wrinkles, and the black image of the trailing clouds of smoke hardly showed at all. There was something wrong with the burners. The smoke was thick as soup.

"Well, Sally," he said, "it's no go. You can see that. It's no go at all."

"No," she said. "It's no go."

He took in a quick, short breath.

"We couldn't get on together," said Toomey.

"No," she said. "We couldn't get on together."

"We're too much alike," said Toomey.

"We are," she said. "Much too much alike."

"We're both savages," said Toomey.

"That's it," said the girl. "Both savages."

"Haven't you got any ideas of your own?" said Toomey.

Her elbow was on her knee, her face on her hand, a little averted. The angle of her head was one of thought. Her hair fluttered like windy sunshine at the nape of her neck.

"Everything you say is so true," said Sally.

"It doesn't make me a damned bit happier," said Toomey.

"No," she said. "It doesn't make me any happier, either."

"The fact is, Sally," he said, "that I loved you—at one time."

"Ah, and so did I! I loved you, too—at a certain time."

"Did you?" said Toomey.

"Yes, I really did."

"What time was that?" asked Toomey.

"Ah, you know," she said.

"Should I know?"

"Yes," she said, "of course you should know."

He became grave. He tried to light a match and six matches blew out.

"This is a hell of a ship," said Toomey. "Damn this boat. I never liked the sea, anyway."

"I never have liked it either," said the girl.

He threw the cigarette down and stamped on it.

"I'm trying to think," he said. "Well, when we drove out the other morning—you cared something about me, then."

"Yes," said the girl. "Something." He bit his lip.

"It doesn't matter," said Toomey.

"No," she said, "I don't suppose it matters."

"Not now," Toomey said.

"No, not now," said she.

"You seem to be repeating everything. What's the matter with you this morning, Sally?" he demanded.

"It's the sea," said she. "It always makes me dizzy. It always makes my head go around, and around, and around, and around, and around. You know how it is."

"No," said Toomey. "I don't know anything about it."

He cleared his throat, his collar seemed to pinch him. He stretched his neck a bit, and shrugged his shoulders. That hurt him badly.

"To me," said Toomey, "it seems a little queer—that's all."

"I think it seems queer too," said she.

"There you go again," said Toomey. "Like a—like a—"

"Like a parrot?" she said.

"I wasn't going to say it," said Toomey.

"You've said worse things," said the girl.

"There were times," said Toomey, "when I ventured to act with privilege."

He looked sharply down at her.

"I wish you'd stop it," said Toomey.

"I do, too," said Sally Moore. "I wish I could stop it."

He made a sudden gesture, folded his arms, and hurt

his bandaged shoulder atrociously. He bit his lip almost in two, and set his teeth over groaning sounds.

"Oh, by the way," said Toomey, lightly.

"Oh, yes," said the girl, lightly, "by what way, Toomey?"

He looked at her. Her smile was as naive, as candid, as clear as— He could think of no simile.

"I mean, the other morning in the boat—" said Toomey. "It doesn't amount to anything—"

"I'm sure it doesn't," said the girl.

He ground his teeth.

"I was just going to mention," said Toomey, "that after we left that damned hulk of a ship—"

"It seemed a charming old boat to me," said the girl.

"Oh? Did it? Well, just after we left that rotten old wreck, as I was saying, after most of us had been kicked around a bit, you seemed pretty jolly, just looking into the wind like a dog in an automobile and smiling. Sort of groggy with smiling, if you don't mind my saying so. But of course a girl's smile doesn't mean a thing."

"No, it doesn't mean a thing," said the girl.

"Not a damned thing," said Toomey.

"Not a damned thing," said she.

"But in that particular case," said Toomey, "I don't suppose that you could happen to recall just what degree of emptiness was in your head?"

"I can recall perfectly," she said. "I was thinking of you."

He glared at her.

"I thought so," said Toomey. "It just seemed a little odd to me at the time, was all. Sorry I mentioned it. What were you thinking about me?"

"I wasn't thinking of you by the way; I was thinking of

you all over," said the girl. "I was thinking how you came like a black panther out of the dark and crumpled that brute, and how you smashed the fellow who shone the light on us, and then went ramping through the boat having a fine time of it. I was thinking of that, and—I was really loving you, Toomey, and telling myself that at last I'd found my master."

HE LOOKED HUNGRILY at her.

Then he laughed, harshly. "Ha, ha, ha," said Toomey. "That's a good joke. A master—of you! That's one of the best jokes that I ever heard. Ten thousand wild cats! A master! Ha, ha, ha! So that was the time that you really loved me, eh? The one real time?"

"I didn't say that," she said.

"I personally and distinctly heard the words," said Toomey, coldly.

"That was only part of the real time," said the girl.

"Yes? And what was the whole time?"

"The whole time?" she said. "Well, let me think—I suppose I've loved you better than breath just about ever since I laid eyes on you."

He sat up and stared at the sea.

"Until when?" he said.

"Until now," said she.

"Until I've just made such a horrible ass of myself?" said Toomey.

"You've made one of yourself, but that hasn't stopped me. I just seem to go on and on—like a parrot," said the girl.

He stared at the sea.

"If you're laughing at me," said Toomey. "If you are—"

"I am," said the girl.

"Well, then, laugh and be damned," he said. "Sally, we're going to be married."

"That's a good idea," said Sally.

"You've just been saying that it was a bad idea—the worst in the world," said Toomey.

"You said it. I only agreed," said the girl. "I wouldn't venture to disagree with my husband about any important thing."

"You wouldn't, eh?" said Toomey.

"No, I wouldn't, of course," said the girl.

"Sally," he said, "I don't want to say that you're a conscienceless liar, but you are."

"Yes," said Sally, "I am."

"Quit it, will you?" said Toomey. "And listen to me. I'm going to be jealous, tyrannical, mean, and suspicious."

"So am I—all of those things," said Sally.

"In that case," said Toomey, "we'd better get married."

"There isn't anything else to do about it," said the girl.

They went back to the living room of the suite.

"Hey, back so soon, monsieur?" said the Big Fellow.

"Get up," said Toomey. "We've got to get married, and you're a witness."

"Damn!" said the Big Fellow. "You've won, Sally."

"Won what?" said Toomey.

"The bet," said the Big Fellow. "She bet me that she'd marry you before night. I thought you had too much dignity, I didn't think you could be twisted around her finger like that, I thought you were too much of a man—but—well, let's go and get her married, then."

"Will you go back to one spot," said Toomey, "and tell

me why it was that Crawford was able to make you surrender by sending you two post cards and a poker chip?"

The Big Fellow put down his glass of champagne, turned
gray.

"Never mind," said Toomey.

"I'll tell you," he said, slowly, "I was once in love, like you
and Sally. But she was married to a hound who wouldn't
turn her loose. We tried to persuade him. He hung onto
her not because he wanted her, but to keep me from her.
At last we ran away together. We ran away on a ship whose
picture was sent to me first by Crawford. Second, he sent
me the post card that had the picture of the little hotel
where we stayed for a time in Brittany. And finally we went
to Monte Carlo. We were happy, Toomey. But she was
uneasy. It seemed to her that we were living deep in sin, and
one day she ran into some old friends who saw us together.
Well—it was too much—she went back and locked herself
in her room. She was dead when I found her." He paused.

"I was a man in public life. The story would have ruined
me. I managed to cover it over at the time by spending
money. But that tale would still ruin me in a good many
circles. It looked like—well, like murder. And Crawford
had unearthed the old story. When I saw the poker chip,
I knew that it meant Monte Carlo. I knew that the whole
story was in Crawford's hands. I surrendered!"

He got up, suddenly, and left the room. A long, heavy
silence followed that departure.

Sally went to take off her hat and coat. Toomey followed
her. He took her inside his one sound arm and kissed her.

www.ingramcontent.com/pod-product-compliance
Lightning Source LLC
Chambersburg PA
CBHW031204020726
47499CB00002B/481